N

CCCCXIX
CRUMP FOLK
GOING HOME

By the same Author

THE LONELY PLOUGH

THE OLD ROAD FROM SPAIN

BEAUTIFUL END

THE SPLENDID FAIRING
      (*Femina-Vie Heureuse Prize*)

THE TRUMPET IN THE DUST

THE THINGS WHICH BELONG——

HE-WHO-CAME?

CRUMP FOLK GOING HOME

By

CONSTANCE HOLME

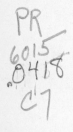

The World's Classics

' Tread softly, because you tread on my dreams '

OXFORD UNIVERSITY PRESS
LONDON : HUMPHREY MILFORD

'*Crump Folk going Home*' was first published in 1913.
It was first included in '*The World's Classics*' in 1934,
and reprinted in the same year, and in 1936.

PRINTED IN GREAT BRITAIN

To
MY FATHER AND MOTHER

PREFACE

THIS was my first published novel, written when not only its author, but the world, was younger in spirit; when motor-cars and aeroplanes were young, too; wireless was still in its infancy; by-pass roads had not so much as been thought of; when even the motor-bus had not yet come to sail its ship of light along the lonely reaches of our dark.

.   .   .   .

It is surprising how easily we are abashed by any evidence of our past youth! Show us a portrait of ourselves, in some incredible garment, and we squirm wretchedly. Show us a letter, written in the fulness of our hearts, and we push it hastily into the fire. Show us a book—!

What is it that makes us shrink from these samples of our past history, which prove us, in many cases, to have been not so much worse than our contemporaries? It is, of course, the trusting silliness of the face under the impossible hat; the trusting egotism of the letter; the unblushing self-revelation of what—fondly imagining it to be perfectly new and original—we dared to call a 'novel'.

Yet, surely, to have lived at all—to have threaded that tangle of terror and ecstasy which we term experience, holding our heads as high as may be until we step, with a gesture, into the grave—is in itself an achievement of which even archangels might be proud? And, to arrive at that grand conclusion, we must have had a beginning; to get out of life, we must first have got into it; to be wise, we must first have been foolish; to be old, we must have been young. . . .

Perhaps every author, looking back on his first novel, feels that it was written by a totally different person in a totally different world? Nobody can possibly be more surprised than he is by the mere fact of its existence. The thing seems just to have happened to him. He is not entirely detached from it, since he admits its claim upon him, regarding it at the same time with a mixture of pride, amusement, and shame. Nevertheless, from his point of view, it remains chiefly an accident; for which, as in the case of other accidents which are laid to his account, he feels bound to offer an apology!

Certainly, the authors of 1913 have more reason than most to believe that they were different creatures in a different universe. The world *was* different, then. . . . It was more leisurely and therefore more peaceful; there was more 'time to stand and stare'. Its rhythms were still set, as it were, to the steady rap of a horse's hoofs rather than to the revolutions of a motor-engine. Things were changing, as they have always changed, but they were doing it tactfully and unobtrusively. People were simpler and less restless; more dependent upon each other for interest and help. Yet, only another year, and the great slide was to begin which was to alter, not only the whole face of the countryside, but the outlook of its inhabitants. Country life was at that stage which, it is said, may be seen in the sinking of a vessel, when the water seems to pause for a second before it swamps the boat.

But, no matter in what age a first novel may

be joyfully perpetrated, it will always have one feature in common with every other. The pathetic paradox will remain that, while it is written, more or less, in the hope that it may be 'read by the world', there is not the faintest conception in the author's mind of what it feels like to be read at all. He does not know what it feels like even to be read by his own village—(though it is a moot point whether this may not be the more terrifying experience of the two). Certainly, he has not the slightest idea that he is summoning torture and trouble with every word he writes. Still less does he know that he is forging a chain which he may never be able to break. Nor is it revealed to him that the royal freedom in which he moves will never be his again as long as he draws breath. There is nothing, therefore, to prevent him from greeting —and writing about—the unknown with a cheer.

And, as we all know, he *does* write about it! ...

This divine exemption from the fear of consequences is not only the best excuse that can be offered for a first novel; it is also its private and personal halo. There is often a happy simplicity about an initial effort—a sort of heavenly idiocy —which is never captured twice. And—granted that any novel, first or last, should ever be written at all—who is to tell us about the young if they may not tell us themselves? The mature cannot tell us, for they have shed the feeling of youth with the lost state of their immaturity. The old cannot tell us, for they see the lovely thing that they once were through the wrong end of a long telescope. Only the young can tell us; and youth, in spite of its apparent candour and volubility, is often secretive and tied of tongue. But, put a pen in its hand, and you may find that you have released, not so much a mere flood of words, as a sort of rainbow on a mountain. Little of what the young author is trying to tell us may either reach us or remain; but he will, at least, give us unconsciously a picture of his inmost self, which we shall never get again.

WESTMORLAND, 1934.

CHAPTER I

THE curse of the old place was upon it—sudden death.

The servants crept quietly, starting when the boards creaked, clutching each other at shadows, and looking for ancestors at every turn. Upstairs, mother and betrothed, doctor and lawyer, convoyed 'Slinkin'' Lyndesay to his latter end. The butler waited at the door, a curious expression on his face, neither of sorrow nor indifference; possibly the look of one assisting at an interesting experiment.

From the library, the only cheerful room at Crump, Christian Lyndesay looked down to the river and over the arch of the crumbling bridge to the bay. A bitter, snarling wind had edged every hill and headland, and the cold tide came up, hungry and gray. He shivered suddenly. It was a thankless night to go out—where Slinkin' Lyndesay was going.

The evening drew on. A flight of rooks came over the park on the fling of the wind, swept against the windows, sank, rose again, and was gone; and the heir wondered, watching them as they swung towards the woods, whether they carried the black soul of Slinkin' Lyndesay with them.

Almost with the thought came the sound of movement overhead, and, shortly after, steps on the shallow stairs. When they reached the hall, he recognised them. Nobody but the lawyer walked with one leg and ran with the other. Then came the doctor, less certain of his dignity than usual;

B

after him, the faint, far-off whispering of silk;
lastly, a light, firm step that told nothing. Christian looked longingly at the French window.

The lawyer's left leg walked in sedately, but
was overrun by the right, which almost rushed
him into Christian's arms. The left backed
promptly, and bumped him into the doctor, but
he was too distracted to apologise. He had a
sheaf of papers in his hand, which he shuffled continually like a pack of cards.

'Your step-brother is dead,' said the doctor,
switching on the light from the door, so that the
oak panelling and the windows went black, and
Christian's fair head stood out sharply like a
young saint's.

He was home barely a couple of hours ago from
a long tour abroad, and both doctor and lawyer
looked at him curiously, standing as he was on the
threshold of a new and unexpected experience.
He had not been of much account hitherto, with
the master of Crump scarcely turned thirty; but
now he was everything. It was astonishing how
simple he looked,—and how little one knew of
him.

'I know,' Christian answered, thinking of the
rooks, and stopped. Not that it mattered, for the
words reached neither of his companions. Looking from one to the other, he beheld the fingering
of a great surprise. The face of the butler returned
to him, and he wondered suddenly what Slinkin'
Lyndesay's death could have had to say to his life.

The silk-whisper along the hall had something
cruel in it, and again he looked at the window.
An old keeper, passing, halted and spoke, and
with a sense of relief he went out quickly into

the bleak night. Doctor and lawyer exchanged glances; the former shrugged his shoulders ever so slightly; then their eyes went back to the door.

Alicia de Lyndesay came in very erect, very composed, her hands and face very still. The day's tragedy had not softened by one whit the set line of her lips. You would never have guessed that she had laid her heart as a broken flower is laid on the breast of the slinkin' hound upstairs.

The lawyer drew forward a chair, and the doctor surreptitiously pushed a footstool, but neither looked at her for more than a second, and they did not look at all at the girl who followed behind.

Deb entered with her head up, white but tranquil, in full command of herself, to all appearance almost unstirred. The lawyer ventured a chair in her direction also, and she took it with a brief word of thanks, folding her hands and looking straight in front of her.

Mrs. Lyndesay touched the bell and ordered tea, and there was a chilling pause, during which the two men stared uneasily at the carpet; while before the mother's hidden gaze was nothing but a slinkin' hound slipping away from her for ever.

'Where is Christian?' she asked, at last, looking round. 'They told me he had arrived.' There was no need in her voice, only desire for information.

'He was here, a moment ago,' the doctor explained hurriedly. 'Somebody called him. I do not know where he went.'

She poured the tea with a steady hand.

'He does not care, of course. His brother was nothing to him, alive. Dead, his memory will be less than nothing. You will go home to-night, Deborah, I suppose?'

The words framed more command than interrogation, but the girl's quiet assent was not in the very least submissively acquiescent. Deb might be poor, might have lost everything she had hoped for in the world, but she was a Lyndesay meeting Lyndesay upon equal terms, and the mistress of Crump knew it.

'Christian will go with you. I will have him sent for,' she went on; and, almost as if he had heard, Christian appeared in the doorway. He shook hands with Deborah silently and rather shyly, for they had met but seldom since they were children; and then, still without speaking, laid a hand on his mother's shoulder, and bent to kiss her. She started violently when he touched her, twisting her head and staring up into the fair, kind face so near her own with an expression that made the onlookers catch their breath; and he withdrew his hand slowly, flushing as he stood away from her.

'Sit down!' she said coldly. 'We can dispense with that sort of thing, you and I. Why were you not here to meet us?'

'Old Brathay called me,' he replied, taking a seat quietly, and handing Deborah a plate which she refused with a gesture. 'One of the puppies is ill. I ought to have been here, of course. I am sorry.'

'I suppose you know your brother is dead?' she went on, in the same lifeless tone. 'You would not have cared to see him, I am aware, and he did not ask for you. But, before he died, he gave us news of importance.'

'Of importance—to me,' Deb put in on her own account, with curious ease. 'We were to have been married, this year, as I believe you know. And now, it seems, he was married already.'

The elder men did look at her, then—at the aloof face, and the straight, slim figure with its loosely-clasped hands; and from her to the rigid mother and Christian's dropped eyes. It was said the Lyndesays always wore a mask.

'That alters things,' Christian observed thoughtfully, with no sign of perturbation in his quiet voice. 'Slinker was always good at surprises. I suppose hounds are probably some other chap's, now?'

'You need not be afraid!' Mrs. Lyndesay broke in sharply. 'He married beneath him—one of those people who do not exist except in the eyes of Government—but at least we are spared—*that!*'

'He married a horse-dealer's daughter,' the lawyer explained hastily and uncomfortably— 'three years ago—a horse-dealer's daughter in Witham. The father has been dead some time, and since she left her husband she has been living with a married sister in Canada. Mr. Lyndesay did not offer us any explanation of his extraordinary—proceedings.'

'I used to know quite a human sort of horse-dealer in Witham,' said Christian. 'Gave me rides when I was a youngster, and told me tales by the hour—an interesting character, in his way. And I remember he had an uncommonly nice daughter——' he checked apologetically—'it's a very wild night.'

Deb laughed queerly, and stood up, and Mrs. Lyndesay rang and ordered the brougham.

The departing guest did not offer her hostess a hand.

'Good-bye,' she said. 'You will be glad to say good-bye. You have never been kind to me, and you will be pleased to be rid of me. We might have been friends, perhaps, for Stanley's sake, but it seems we are not to have the chance. You need not be afraid that I shall ever trouble you again, though I shall not go away, as no doubt you expect. The county must get used to seeing me about, as usual, and in time you will forget that I still live at your gates.'

'Be thankful things are no worse!' Mrs. Lyndesay's voice, grown suddenly strident, arrested her at the door. 'Be thankful you have been spared what you deserve—you who would have married my son for his property and his position, grasping at him with both hands, though caring no more for him than for his shadow on the wall!'

After the shocked hush, lawyer and doctor stood up simultaneously, saying 'Madam!' in the same breath. It was a poor attempt, and she ignored it.

'You never cared! He was Lyndesay of Crump to you—no more. Lyndesay of Crump, with his money and his name and his fine old place. The man was nothing to you—you miserable parasite on a proud old house! You would have married Christian here on the same terms—isn't that true? Answer me! Can you deny it?'

Doctor and lawyer made a desperate bid for the French window, shocked to the depths of their ceremonious souls, but in spite of their haste they could not escape Deb's voice, the voice of a prisoner at the bar.

'It is true!' she heard herself saying, facing the hard eyes of Slinker's mother; and then Christian slid a hand through her arm, and drew her out.

'Old Brathay's in the kitchen with the puppy, worrying the cook out of her wits,' he informed her, as they crossed the hall. 'Let's get down to Kilne as quick as we can. I've always heard that your father was no end of a hand at hounds.'

Footmen hurried them into wraps. An obsequious butler all but lifted them into the carriage. The lamps flashed a moment on the wide hall as the smooth wheels bore them away. Deb cast one glance at the dark pile of the house as they passed; then sat back, silent. Crump blinds had dropped on more than a dead master.

'It's an unforgiving sort of night!' Christian said dreamily from his corner, as they rolled down the last of the avenue, the great trees clashing overhead. 'On nights like this I believe Westmorland breaks her heart for some old sin of long ago. She beats at the heavens, and they are brass. God does not hear. Brathay is like an old hen with hounds, isn't he?'

She sat up, trying to see his face in the pale light over the river.

'You must let me tell you,' she said quickly and tensely. 'I spoke the truth. I did not love your brother. But at least I loved no one else. And he was good to me.'

Christian nodded comprehendingly.

'Slinker had his moments, I suppose,' he said. 'The rest of the time he was—Slinker. I'm glad he was good to you.'

They plunged into the shadow of the bridge, where other maddened giants were at strife. The full tide had swung the river far up its banks, and they could hear the weir above the shout of the wind. Deb leaned back, a growing sense of quiet upon her. Christian's was a presence that asked nothing, took nothing, least of all sought for your miserable, hidden secrets. He accepted you as you were, and, in some utterly unreasoned way, made you feel that he was glad of you. She rested a little in his shadow.

The carriage stopped at the near end of the village, by a creepered house backed by the hill and faced by the river; and Deb, in the road, held out a firm hand.

'You're not coming in,' she said decidedly. 'Brathay knows a hundred times more about hounds than Father. This is good-bye between me and Crump—you don't need telling that. You want to pat me on the head, and I won't have it— not with all the best intentions in the world! So say good-bye quickly, and go, for there's quite sufficient anathema in store for me, without Clark adding that I kept his horses out in the rain.'

He displaced her gently, and opened the gate. Then he took the hand he had ignored.

'Of course I can't come in, if you won't have me,' he said, 'but you shan't always shut me out. Please remember me very kindly to Mr. Lynde- say. And there's no good-bye between Kilne and Crump; you know that as well as I do.'

He dismissed the brougham at the turn to the stables, and walked up the steep incline until the avenue had swallowed him whole. Above him the knit branches rocked and wrestled as the wind tore at their crests. It was pitch-dark under their swaying canopy. Now and then a sweep of rain caught him in the face around some monster trunk. He stood still in the narrow, sheathed road, look- ing up and thinking. How strange it was that

Slinker should be gone, and he himself in his place! It was hard luck on Slinker, he thought, to have been cast out of life so soon and so sharply by the stroke of a whirling slate—to have sped his soul on a tempest-night such as this. Slinker was the sort to have crept out of existence unnoticed, leaving the world uneasily fearful that he might reappear at any moment. The countryside had not christened him 'Slinkin'' Lyndesay for nothing.

Apart, however, from this touch of half-satiric sympathy, he felt little human sorrow for his half-brother. The bond between them had generally been strained to the snapping-point of extreme dislike. He had a hundred times more feeling for his young cousin, Lionel Lyndesay of Arevar, a mile or two over the river, on the far side of Cantacute. Slinker had been unbearable—always. Crump had meant nothing to him but the money it stood for, and the pleasure that ran with the money. He had often gloated over the amount certain fairy woods represented, speculated lightly upon the price of certain farms that he was free to sell. Christian looked through the dark to where Dockerneuk, he knew, lay in the arm of the fell, and thought of the peril that had come so near. It had been within an ace of sale, but it was saved, now. Dixon of Dockerneuk, at least, would be glad that Slinker was dead.

Yet the County—(always with a capital)—had approved of Slinker. Slinker had always made a point of turning up at the right place in the right suit with the right buttonhole. He knew what was due to his position, so Christian had been told—often. Christian himself was supposed to be deficient in this quality—so-called. Christian, home from college, had been the friend of the farmers, made a name in the wrestling-ring, played football and ridden at the shows. 'Lakin'' Lyndesay, they called him—the same clear-witted judges who had framed their delicate sobriquet for his brother. Slinker had merely sat on Grand Stands and distributed prizes, clapped hands and crooked an arm for the principal lady present. No wonder the County had thought a lot of Slinker! He had been so careful about his conduct—in public.

Theirs was a race with a shadow on it, cursed and foredoomed, proud with age and old in pride. Their mother came of the Devonshire branch, and had early married Egbert de Lyndesay of Crump, who had died, two years later, leaving William, his cousin and former heir, as guardian of his six-weeks' child. Within three years William had married the widow, and then Christian was born.

Nominal owner for so long, William never had to face the humiliation of deposition, for he died a few months before Stanley came of age, little thinking that in ten years' time the young man would have followed him to the grave. But now Stanley, too, was gone, and Christian and his mother were left in the old house to find what other mutual ground they might.

She had always hated him, he reflected, almost unemotionally. The situation was too old for new pain. As an affectionate child he had broken his heart over her attitude, but in the end he had come to accept it. Nor had his father shown much feeling towards him, either. Occasionally he had looked at him with whimsical eyes, as if meditating some advance; but his mother's presence had always stultified any growth of happy intimacy. He had been sent to school early, and William Lyndesay, to whom life had given most things at second hand except a bitter sense of humour, had been content to remain outside his child's heart, busying himself with ordering the estate of his supplanter. Yes, they had all worn masks, Christian thought: his father, smilingly impersonal and aloof; his mother, obstinately and apparently unreasonably cruel; he, himself, puzzled and hurt but finally acquiescent; while, as for Slinker—he laughed rather cynically—it would appear that Slinker had worn as many masks as a troupe of mummers!

At last the wind was dropping. He sauntered up to the top of the avenue and out by the top lodge beyond the trees, where a pale moon showed him the land sinking in a vast, watery hollow and then rising again. He thought suddenly of Deb, and wondered how she had ever come to countenance Slinkin' Lyndesay.

Deb was one of the Kilne Lyndesays—a branch more remote from the parent stem than either that in Devonshire or at Arevar, but in many ways closest of all. Kilne Lyndesays had been Crump stewards for centuries, serving the fine estate from father to son with inherited and increasing devotion, which found in Roger, the last of the list, its most perfect expression, and, alas! its culmination, also. For Roger had no son to follow him; only a daughter, to whom the heritage could not pass.

For forty years he had set all his brain, his

energy, and his love to the prospering of Crump, and under his hands it had touched its highest point of fortune. During Stanley's long minority he had nursed the estate like a tender, living thing, backed by William Lyndesay in all he did, and handing it over at last with the mingled anguish of pride and pain which only those know who have given themselves whole-heartedly for what is not their own. He had wished to resign, at the time, but Mrs. Lyndesay had pressed him to remain in charge, pleading Stanley's youth and inexperience, and for two years longer he had stayed at his post. But he took badly to the new position, and the reaction of fulfilled work as well as the languor of old age was upon him, so that the end of the two years found the Crump agency gone from his branch for ever. The wrench had been cruel, at first, but now the peace of evening had reached him, and his mind dwelt chiefly in the past. And at least the old home was left to him. That had been one of Slinker's few gracious acts in his short but singularly ungracious life.

Sometime in his fifty-third year, Roger Lyndesay had withdrawn his attention momentarily from the estate, and married a Morton from Appleby, thrown by fate across his path on a visit; a quiet lady who had drifted gently into Kilne, and almost as imperceptibly out of it to her grave on the high fell-side. So Deb had been a lonely little girl in a lonely house,—a rather fierce, intensely-reserved little girl, pure Lyndesay and no Morton whatever, a strange little girl who loved the woods and the silent places, and rarely made friends with anybody in her own station. She was bred in awe of Crump, and held aloof from the Lyndesay boys in a mood that was half reverence and half resentment, though for Lionel, to whom these sentiments did not apply, she had her moments of kindly condescension. Her education was represented by a series of battles royal with inadequate daily governesses until she was thirteen, when her solitary Morton aunt descended in wrath, and bore her south for five weary and interminable years. She had come back at last, however, polished and finished, a masked Lyndesay as much as any of them.

She had certainly been difficult to know, Christian reflected, looking back upon the four years since her return, and his own college vacations. He had really seen very little of her, considering the tie between the two houses, and their near situation; and for the last eighteen months he had been abroad, glad to escape from the atmosphere of his home, yet tortured always by the Lyndesay longing for his own soil.

He was in Japan when the news of the engagement reached him, and he had written a couple of congratulatory notes, wondered a little, and let the matter pass. It was fairly easy to understand, after all, whatever you might think of Slinker. She was poor, probably ambitious, and Lyndesay of Crump was the Catch of the County (always with capitals). Any girl might have done it, he had thought—in Japan; but to-night he had seen her with new eyes, and he wondered again. She had not looked that sort of girl, he reflected— not in the least the sort of girl to stand Slinker for a second after she had once really known him.

Of course it was easy for him to sneer, to call her

in question. The temptation was not lightly to be despised, a Lyndesay not lightly to be said nay—if only it had been anybody but Slinker! Slinker's face rose before him with its pale-blue gaze, colourless hair and smooth, guileless smile, and he frowned distressfully. Surely she must have shut the eyes of her soul!

He strolled back through the trees in the faint light filtering on to the muddy road at his feet. The striving arms were growing fitfully still; the land seemed to be curling itself into sleep with a tired sigh. He thought fancifully that his very passing had hushed it to rest. It had risen in storm for the flight of Slinker's spirit; for the new master it had sunk into peace. He spread his hands over it in a sort of benediction as he came out in front of the house. He would see that it was cherished.

As he went up the steps, the first stroke of the passing bell came to him across the desolate park and the troubled water, and he stood bareheaded while it told its tale of death, each long pause between the heavy notes fraught full with listening souls that had gone home on the same music. He shivered a little as he turned at last to the empty hall. His mother was upstairs—he did not need to ask where. The land was glad of him, but he wanted a more human touch than that. The place was so lonely, and yet so full of ghosts! Even Slinker would have been better than nothing. But Slinker was dead, and Christian was Lyndesay of Crump. Looking up at the eyeless windows, he wondered how long it would be before he came to lie where Slinker was lying, shot into eternity by the family fate.

CHAPTER II

THE little station looked innocent enough, with its solitary platform and single line, its flower-borders and toy buildings;—innocent and sleepy, awaiting a tardy train; but to Deborah it was a veritable pillory as she stood by herself at its farthest extremity, looking westward to the sea.

Market-day in Witham was drawing its usual votaries in their various degrees, and for all of them Deborah was an object of interest as she turned an obstinate blue-serge shoulder upon whisper and stare alike.

She knew quite well that they were talking about her. Each little knot of folk had something to say on the subject of her late engagement. It had been such an unexpected triumph, followed by an equally unexpected downfall. Both surprises had been so abrupt, so recent, that the district was still gasping. Barely had it learned to look upon Deborah with a new respect when it found her dumped back into her old obscurity; though reflecting, perhaps, a more subtle interest, lent by the atmosphere of scandal surrounding the whole affair.

There had been a Saturday, not so very long ago, when her progress along the platform had been a hateful pageant of success. She scarcely knew which had hurt her most, the ill-concealed surprise or the terrible obsequiousness. Well, to-day, at least, no one troubled her. They left her alone; avoided her eyes; gathered in little groups and talked of her in whispers.

She could guess what they were saying—hear the pity and the blame so subtly intermingled.

Stanley's death alone might have earned her commiseration; his marriage along with it had branded her. It was all so 'queer!' The dead man might have earned the intangible stigma of the foolish word, but the living girl was left to carry it.

Dixon of Dockerneuk drove up slowly, and sauntered on to the platform. There was interest in his reception, also, for it was well known that he had never married because of a certain horse-dealer's daughter in Witham. He looked much the same, thought the curious—the big, slow-moving man with the quiet voice and the cloak of patient and pathetic dignity which is the hall-mark of the true-bred dalesman. He could not have taken it much to heart, after all. It was only when he reached the railing overlooking the sea that he allowed the new hurt look to creep back into his eyes.

He exchanged a brief good-day with Deborah, and the spectators looked curiously at the two who had suffered so similarly under the same up-heaval, whose lives had been altered by the same act of deliberate deceit. Deborah was acutely conscious of the isolation in which they stood, yet she drew a little comfort from the presence of a fellow-sufferer. She made some remark about the crops, and he answered cheerfully; and presently the leisurely train drifted in, almost as if washed up accidentally by the tide. Dixon opened a door, touched his hat, and moved on to another carriage; and her heart warmed to him, recognising his tact.

There were strangers with her, by some happy accident, unaware of her personal tragedy; but in the next carriage, and all up the train, Deborah Lyndesay's affairs had plenty of play.

A silver-haired, dapper little man, being rather sad at heart on the subject, had of course several sharp things to say about it.

'So tiresome!' he observed to the compartment at large. So really *tiresome* of people to do these things! It placed their friends in such an awkward position. Did one bow or did one *not* bow? Was it kinder to pretend that they were not there? Or did one walk up, smiling, and talk about the Insurance Act?

A mackintosh in the corner submitted that there could be no reason why one should not bow —always supposing that one *wished*. Most people, in similar circumstances, removed themselves for a long time, went away and lost themselves for their own sake and everybody else's, till the affair was forgotten. But in this case the lady under discussion seemed to have no self-retiring tendencies—almost appeared, one might say, to be proud of the situation.

Silver-hair seemed a little shocked by this statement. There are canons of good taste even in back-biting.

Hardly *proud*, surely? Of course, it was all distinctly tiresome, but, for his own part, he had gathered from—say, the droop of her left shoulder —that she was rather miserable.

Miserable? Of course she was miserable! This was smartness in blue voile and a cornflower hat, somewhat damaged by a string bag. Hadn't she lost Crump, and gained nothing but the clinging odour of a scandal? Such luck as hers had been quite unlikely to last. And of course she would never have such another chance. Those weeks of triumph would have to last her all the rest of her life.

'So stupid!' Silver-hair murmured worriedly. So upsetting to do these startling things! Of course she was a Lyndesay and a lady, and she played the organ quite nicely, but after all one of the professions would have been more suitable—say, a nice, quiet, country solicitor. It was all very awkward for her friends. And she wasn't even wearing mourning for him! What *he* wanted to know, was—what was one to *do*?

'Give her time,' said Mackintosh in the corner. 'We haven't seen the end of things, yet. She's a pretty girl, and she must have had a way with her, or Stanley would never have looked at her. We all know that!' (Mackintosh's forebears having washed for Crump, she was naturally in a position to speak familiarly.) 'Give her time! There's still a Lyndesay of Crump!'

Cornflower admired her perspicacity with a meaning smile.

'Oh, of course, *that* will be the next thing! She is certain to make the attempt. But Christian will not easily be caught. Christian, I have reason to know, has a fancy in *quite* another direction!'

Cornflower had a daughter of her own, who had had the felicity of being yanked through a hedge by Christian, out basset-hunting. What more was needed?

Silver-hair looked uncomfortable. Cornflower and Mackintosh did not appear to him to be keeping to the rules of the game.

'Of course one did not wish to be *unkind*,' he murmured. But how much nicer it would be for everybody if these things didn't *happen*! One felt one would like to show a little sympathy, only it was so *awkward*! Surely she ought to have known that he was married? It was her duty to know that sort of thing, seeing that she hadn't a mother to make inquiries.

A quiet little girl sitting beside him dropped a library book firmly on his feet, and he picked it up with inward reproach. After all, it wasn't quite the thing to talk scandal in front of anybody so innocent and demure as Verity Cantacute contrived to look, in spite of her twenty-three years. He was fond of Verity, too, and valued her opinion highly in a strictly unconfessed fashion. He knew quite well why she had dropped the book, though he would not have admitted it for worlds.

'Ah!' Cornflower said meaningly. 'A mother's interference is not always particularly welcome! Occasionally, a mother can be counted a positive nuisance; and, in *this* case——'

Verity dropped an umbrella, this time, a sharp-pronged thing that caught Cornflower on the ankle, and hurt her horribly. An umbrella is an excellently-subtle weapon of offence, if you know how to use it artistically. Silver-hair, while applauding mentally, was nevertheless of opinion that Verity had interfered somewhat arbitrarily. After all, Cornflower ought to have known, if anybody did, exactly how much of a nuisance a mother *could* be!

Deborah was just in front of him as they left the station in the swirl of the Saturday stream, and something about her—probably her left shoulder —smote his ridiculously soft heart a second time. He attached himself to her to observe how tiresome it was of the weather to look like drawing to thunder when he had a tennis-party at stake. Deb smiled unwillingly. She had always liked him, but she had her prickles out for the whole world, this morning.

'And the dust!' Silver-hair loved a grievance as cats love cream. Personally, he expected an attack of appendicitis, any day, from swallowing so much ground limestone! Might he carry her basket for her, by any chance?

Deborah gave him a real smile, this time.

'You can just go and talk to somebody else,' she said. 'I'm not going to have any St. Georges convoying *me* up the town. This is my treadmill, and I mean to keep it to myself.' She nodded at Smith's, as they passed. 'You ordered a book there, last week, if you remember. Go in and ask about it.'

She stepped adroitly in front of a passing lorry, and was lost to him, and he drifted meekly into Smith's, wondering vaguely if he could have done anything different. He had meant to be kind, and she had not really been rude—he was not sure that she hadn't meant to be grateful. How tiresome these situations were!

It seemed to Deb that the whole of Westmorland was shopping, that morning, for almost every busy car and sleek carriage held somebody she knew. Slinker had given a reception in her honour, a short time before, and an envious county had shaken her warmly by the hand. To-day, it was remarkable how many motor-folk seemed interested in the fit of their chauffeur's coat, how many traps carried people hunting for something on the floor. Lady Metcalfe, stopping outside the fish-shop as Deb came up, discovered instantaneously that what she really wanted was stockings. The Bracewell girls, hunting hats in Miss Clayton's, remembered in a flurry that they had been instructed to purchase tooth-powder; while the Hon. Mrs. Stalker made no bones about the matter at all, but, having walked straight into Deb's arms, merely remarked to the sky that she desired sausages, and glided over her. Deborah, reflecting, was not sure that hers wasn't the kindest method, after all.

As she came out into the main street, the Crump stanhope passed her, with Christian on the box; but she was very busy doing sums inside her purse, and people who didn't know her thought she must be either blind or stupid to ignore the compliment of so gallant a salute. Apparently she had seen nothing; yet she knew that at Christian's side had sat a dark girl in trim black, and a wave of fierce feeling swept over her—for the woman in question was Slinker's wife.

She was at Crump, now—Deb knew that. Mrs. Lyndesay had sent for her, acknowledged her—more, insisted on keeping her! As Slinker's wife she had taken her place in the county; as Slinker's wife she drove at his brother's side; while the girl he had wooed in such arrant deceit walked stubbornly alone, with a high head and eyes that looked singularly straight in front of her.

When they came back again, Slinker's wife had the reins, and pulled up cleverly in the crowded street close to where Deb's passage was obstructed by a wood-cart. Christian, swinging quickly down, caught her as she looked round for means of escape.

'You cut me!' he said reproachfully, taking her hand in spite of her. 'I don't deserve it, and you know I don't. You might at least have had the decency to stop and ask after the puppy.'

'I'll wire for the latest bulletin,' she responded, moving away instantly in a distinctly uncomplimentary fashion. 'You'll excuse me, won't you? I'm chasing a scrubbing-brush.' But Christian detained her.

'I want you to do something for me,' he said hurriedly,—'oh, please! It's just this'—his voice was uneven and embarrassed—'Nettie—Miss Stone—er—that is—Slinker's wife, you know—wants to know if you'll be kind enough to know her. He—she—I give you my word, she's an awfully good sort—that is to say—you won't regret it!'

Deb stopped short enough now, regarding him incredulously.

'You wish to introduce me to—to that woman?' she asked, her voice very low. 'You ask me to speak to her—in this crowd——?'

Christian cast a glance of easy indifference around him. 'These don't count, dear old things! She's my horse-dealer, as I thought. I've known her all my life. I wish you would—don't you think——?' He saw Deb's face, then, and stopped.

'Oh! How *dare* you?' she exclaimed, her voice shaking with indignation. 'How dare you even think of it? You must know that you insult me by the very suggestion!'

She swept a glance of outrage and pain from Christian's troubled face to the figure on the box; caught the earnest gaze of a pair of bright brown eyes, then plunged into the traffic and was

gone. Christian watched her disappear before
he climbed back miserably, and Slinker's wife
shook the reins lightly, and proceeded down the
full thoroughfare.

'That was a mistake!' she said, nodding cheerfully here and there to a well-known face. 'You
can't have been very tactful, Christian, my child.
But anyway it was a mistake, and I'd no business
to suggest it. Still, we'll do it yet, see if we don't!
Trust Nettie Stone for that!'

She drove on gently, smiling, very sure of herself; but at the corner of Redman Street the horses
swerved without just cause, as if the hand on the
reins had tightened unawares. Dixon of Dockerneuk was standing on the pavement, and he
raised his eyes as she passed above him—Stanley
Lyndesay's widow. She laid her hand on Christian's arm as he stared worriedly at his boots, and
he looked up quickly, wondering at the shake in
her voice.

'Laker dear,' she was saying with a smile, 'I
rather think Slinker was a mistake, too!'

CHAPTER III

THE third thing that Verity dropped, that morning, was three pounds of salmon, right in Deborah's blindly-descending path. She knew Deborah wouldn't step on anything as squishy as
salmon.

'I want to ask your opinion about something,'
she said, leaving the salmon barrier-wise on the
pavement, 'so come along to the café, and be
asked it like a lamb. It's no use pretending that
I've got scarlet fever or a new hat, or anything of

that kind that you simply can't be seen with, because I'm thoroughly bored with my own society, and I mean to have yours.'

'You want to pat me,' Deborah said roughly, looking at her fiercely with reddened eyes, 'and I won't have it! I won't! I won't!'

'How terribly limited you are!' Verity sighed pityingly. 'I want to talk to you solely and entirely about myself. Otherwise, why should I pick you up in the pig-market on a Saturday morning, when you have pointedly cut me three times this week?'

'I shall hold you to that, if I come!' Deborah yielded weakly to the hidden strength in the demure little figure before her. 'And, mind, at the first pat—I go!'

'What did you want to know?' she asked, later, seated at a table in an upstairs room, overlooking the street.

'Know?' Verity, her eyes on the traffic, was a trifle vague until Deborah's stern gaze collected her wits with a jerk. 'Oh, I wondered if by any chance you knew the author of——?'

'I don't!' Deb got to her feet. 'Good-bye!'

Verity pulled her down again.

'No, it wasn't that. It was—let me see——' looking anxiously at the crowd—'oh, I know! Should you think red roses and green tulle——?'

'I shouldn't!' Deb made another effort. 'You're a little wretch, Verity! You might have known I wanted to be left alone.'

Verity clung to her, gazing despairingly at the stairs.

'I've remembered the real reason—honest Injun, I have! I just wanted to know whether the best way to manage a parson is to marry him?'

'Marry him?' Deb sank into her seat. 'Now, Verity, what are you up to? Tell me at once. I won't move till you do!'

'Oh, there's nothing at all to worry about,' Verity replied, pouring out coffee with beautifully-concealed triumph. 'The question hasn't arisen yet, in any way. I put it merely as a business proposition. Something must be done with the new parson at Cantacute, and as I'm much the bravest person in the place—sugar, dear? Here's the cream.'

Deb opened her lips wrathfully, but got no further, for Verity was listening to somebody else, —indeed the whole café was listening,—to an intensely-vitalised young person who roared directions to his chauffeur as he plunged headlong into the building, afterwards tearing up the stairs with the impetuosity of several elephants gone amok. Such was the usual advent of Larruppin' Lyndesay.

Deb knew who was coming before the black bullet head and sturdy shoulders cannoned round the corner into Witham's illustrious mayoress, who had looked in for an innocent glass of milk; and while he was busy picking her up and dusting her down, shooting her to the ground floor and thrusting her into his own car, she called her friend to account.

'Why did you do it?' she asked reproachfully. 'You know I can't meet any of the Lyndesays. And Larrupper will tell the whole town I am here!'

'The new parson——' Verity began innocently, and Deb leaned across the table and shook her. Then she sat down and covered her face with her hands.

'Can't you understand,' she added, very low, 'that it hurts me to meet them, seeing that I can have nothing to do with them any more?'

'Just because one berry had a grub in it, I don't see why you need burn the whole bush!' Verity answered doggedly. 'You've been treated abominably, scandalously! Please credit some of us with sufficient decency to realise *that*. You're behaving as though we were a crowd of savages dancing round you with assegais! And the Arevar Lyndesays had nothing to do with the affair, anyhow. Larrupper's awfully hurt because you've given him the cold shoulder, and I won't have Larrupper ill-treated. It's like being cruel to a— a donkey. And he's quite upset enough as it is over the Mayoress.'

The mayoral catastrophe seemed to have disorganised Larrupper completely, for, upon his volcanic return, he rushed at the nearest table and shook hands with two totally strange girls, before he discovered Verity sitting with shocked eyes fixed on the ceiling.

'Disgraceful!' she observed, looking like a disapproving tombstone. 'I'm not sure that we ought to know you. Sit down and say the first three stanzas of the Catechism, just to let the steam off your voice before you speak to Deborah.'

But Larrupper, crimson with emotion to the thick roots of his inky hair, seized upon Deb's hand without an instant's hesitation.

'Oh, you've been cruel, Debbie dear!' he reproached her. 'I called and called, an' stood outside an' swore an' threw things, an' they gave me the boot every time, an' told me you weren't seein' anybody. We've always been pals, you and I,

ever since we fell into the river together, tryin' to
be trout, an' to shut your door in Larrupper's
pleadin' face is what I'd never expected to get
from you,—hanged if I did!'

'I've finished with the lot of you, Larry,' Deborah said gently. 'I'm going to be a Lyndesay
all by myself for the rest of my existence, so you
can just keep on the other side of the road when
you see me coming, for your poor relation doesn't
intend to know you. It's no use arguing. I mean
what I say.'

Larrupper upset both cream-jugs.

'That's a footlin' way of talkin'!' he said.
'Haven't I adored you always, an' been ready to
lift the roof off the world for you, as you don't need
tellin'? An' just because things have gone to
smoke through that bunglin' bounder of a Slinker——'

'Larrupper!' Verity's little voice was almost
shrill.

'Just because Slinker——' (Larry, when interfered with, always erupted louder than ever)—
'just because Slinker behaved like a—a—a—low-
down, crawlin' scallywag——'

'*Larrupper!*'

'—you think the rest of us are not good enough
to be seen dead with. But we're a fairly decent lot,
for all that; Laker is, anyhow, an' Larrupper's
quite a charmin' imitation; an' if you're goin' to
give us all the go-by on Slinker's account, you're
makin' us responsible for somethin' we didn't
know of, any more than you; an' if that isn't
glarin' injustice, I'd like to hear of a better
sample!'

'I've been hurt,' said Deb, staring at the table,

'so naturally I'm looking round for somebody to get back on. And you happen to be the nearest, that's all.'

'And what about me?' asked Verity. Deb, looking up, caught a look of real pain on the small face. 'If it hadn't been for that three pounds of salmon, you'd have lost the two people who love you best in the world, and serve you jolly well right!'

'Where *is* the salmon?' Deb put in suddenly, her conscience smiting her; and Verity blinked away her tears and laughed.

'Somewhere on the pavement, I suppose. I forgot all about it, to tell the truth. Yours is a very expensive friendship. And, by the way, it was to pay a bet I lost to the parson.'

'What parson?' Larry interjected quickly, with interest.

'The new Cantacuter. (You have to have everything repeated to you, Larry, every time we meet!) I bet him three pounds of salmon that he couldn't get Billy-boy Blackburn to join his Young Men's Soul-Savers or whatever he calls them; and he did, so I have to pay up. It's for their annual bean-feast or something of the kind.'

'He seems an individual with some strength of purpose,' Deborah observed. 'But why were you so anxious to know if the best way——?'

Verity kicked her without remorse.

'He has such dreadfully "Fall in and follow me" views about women,' she went on. 'Expects them to take a back seat when they're not wanted, and run and work like blaz—blacks—when they are—under *him*, of course. Men proudly goose-stepping in front is how he sees life; women trailing meekly behind. That's his line throughout—though I must say he does his best to sweeten the pill with rather painfully-obvious flattery. He comes to see me every other day, to ask me to join things and support things and sing in things and collect for things. He tells me I am so beloved in the village; that I have religious eyes; that my influence for good is—well, little short of the Bishop of London's. And all the time he regards me merely as a tool for his using! I leave Voltaire and Shaw and the Pankhursts about all over the place when he calls, but he doesn't see them—he's too busy collecting me. It's my face and my voice, I suppose, that make him think I'd be a fine tail to his heavenly comet. But I'll teach him, see if I don't!'

'You'd much better leave him alone,' Larrupper remonstrated. 'What's the use of botherin' about him, anyway?'

'Leave him alone?' Verity's eyes flashed. 'Leave my unfortunate village to struggle with him alone? Never! I'm not a suffragette or anything else in the New Woman line, but to have a stranger thinking he's more influence than I in my own place is the very last thing I'll put up with! He may have Billy-boy and the salmon; he may have his own private little gloat; but there'll be something very wrong with the universe if Verity Cantacute doesn't come out top, in the end!'

Deb rose. 'Well, I'm going,' she said. 'I'm very angry with you both, but all the same you've warmed the cockles of my heart. No, Larry, I will *not* be taken home in your car like the remains of the Mayoress. You can come to see me, if you

insist, but I warn you that I shall not be over-polite
to you. Oh, of *course* I love you, you inky-headed
baby! That isn't the point. The point is that
Lyndesays of Crump and Arevar can no longer
be on friendly terms with Lyndesays of Kilne. So
good-bye.'

Larry stood up, looking pathetic.

'An' who's to help me with Verity an' the sky-
pilot? It's always like this. Just as she's thinkin'
she might possibly make up her mind to marry
me, off she goes an' starts a hobby of some kind,
an' I get shoved into the background. Parson-
squashin's all very well, but it takes so much of
her energy, an' she forgets that I'm—well, just
waitin'. And nobody has the faintest influence
with her but you, Debbie darlin', as you know.
Mayn't I really take you home? I've got a
new——'

'Yes, I know,' Deb interrupted ruthlessly. 'A
new carburettor or a gudgeon-pin or a ball-bear-
ing. You always have. Thank you, Larry. I've
given up cars. And I won't, I won't, I *won't* be
patted!'

After she had gone, Verity cried unaffectedly
behind the sheltering screen; while Larry, almost
weeping himself, kicked things miserably and
chopped splinters off the table.

'It's hurt her so dreadfully!' she said, 'every
bit of her; her pride, her affection, *herself*. She'll
never be the same again. And people are saying
such hateful things. I could strangle them—the
—the alligators! Slinker was a rotter, but he was
quite decent to her—she's bound to miss him
a little. And think of all he represented! She
couldn't help but feel that. And now she's no-

thing—nothing—except her name and her pride. What can we do for her? What *can* we? Not that it's any use asking *you*!'

'There's Christian,' said Larrupper, slowly, and Verity looked up with a start. Their eyes met across the table, and Larrupper nodded his black head.

'Laker's a good sort,' he went on, apparently irrelevantly. 'Always goin' about pickin' up the cryin' an' the crocked. It's just meat an' drink an' five rounds of golf to old Laker. There's never any knowin', is there, dear,—I mean, old girl?'

Verity looked at him almost approvingly as she thrust various parcels into his arms, preparatory to rising.

'Larry,' she observed kindly, 'I do believe you're growing a brain!'

CHAPTER IV

LARRUPPIN' LYNDESAY, perturbed by the events of the morning, roared down Hillgate at a pace that sent peaceful marketers flying to the pavement. Dixon of Dockerneuk, coming up leisurely, watched him and smiled—for there was a dog.

The grip of the brakes swung the car close upon Jordan's plate-glass, and several people thought they were killed, but the dog was spared; and Dixon smiled grimly a second time, both at Larry's face and at a certain recollection. When the car pulled up beside him, he could see that the young man's hands were shaking.

The chauffeur, exchanging a friendly wink of much understanding, sprang out and gave him his place beside his master. Dixon mounted after a brief greeting.

'You'll be goin' out, I suppose?' Larrupper said, moving on. 'You'd better let me take you. I'm needin' your moral support badly, Dock, old man. And I got a devil of a fright at that corner—you saw it, I expect? The dog had a silver brush to it. It reminded me——' He glanced sideways at his companion—'Sorry, old chap!'

'Lord, Dock!' he went on, presently, 'if you knew what a time I've had, these last three years, keepin' out of the way of things with a tail at one end and a bark at the other! I dream of them at nights. There's times I think I'll have to quit motorin', an' take to a tricycle. I've been punished, Dock, if it's any comfort to you to know it.'

'Well, well,' Dixon answered thoughtfully and with admirable serenity, seeing that they were full speed on the track of a carrier's cart which was occupying the whole of the road—'if it's learned you to think on a bit before turning a corner, it happen wasn't all wasted. You're one that takes a deal of learning that way, Mr. Lionel!'

Larry chuckled, and then sighed. He did not like to think of that incident of three years ago. He had been fresh home from Eton, a hasty snatch at college and a wild rush round the world, and he had known nothing of Dixon, in those days, or of all the things of the north that Dixon so adequately represented; but in one sharp lesson he had learned much, and at a price.

Dixon, too, went back in mind. It was not his way to dwell overmuch on the past; he took things as they came, ordinarily—one day with another—but he had had other memories stirred, that morning, and he was looking back in spite of himself. As the car whizzed down the white road the two men saw the same scenes re-enacted before them.

. . . .

I

Dixon of Dockerneuk came down the last slope of the fell.

Behind him, the fresh-herded sheep still cried hysterically to one another. In front, he saw the smoke of his farm and the twisted ribbon of the hedged road.

Round his knees flitted a gray and silver thing with adoring eyes hidden by a silken fringe; a silent-footed attendant whose ears lifted at the faintest whisper of command, and who dropped to heel at a raised finger.

Reaching the gate, he paused and looked down at her, and the steady seriousness of his face relaxed a little. Rain, sitting at his feet, flopped a lovely tail and reached out an insinuating tongue, but Dixon's hand stayed at his side. A dalesman does not waste unnecessary caresses upon his dog, any more than upon his other daily companions.

Yet Rain was the pride of his heart. He had bred her himself, trained her himself, as he trained all his dogs, and she knew every shade of his whistle as a child knows the inflections of its mother's voice. The least wave of his hand was enough; two words could give her a complete law of shepherding. The sympathy between them was the most perfect that has ever been known to exist between man and beast—the link between a shepherd and his dog.

He unsnecked the gate, and she danced out, eager for home, waving a silver tail for him to follow, but he paused again, leaning against the stoup. A sound escaped him, so soft that at the bend of the road you would not have heard it, but Rain dropped as if shot, ears cocked, body rigid; and this time Dixon of Dockerneuk smiled ever so slightly.

To-morrow he was to run her at the dog-trials at Arevar, before half the county, and he knew that there was not a dog within a fifty-mile radius that could beat her when handled by himself. Already she was famous; already 'Dixon's Rain' was a familiar phrase in the mouths of shepherds; her judgment, her intelligence, her beauty, were known in every household where a sheep-dog was a matter of serious consideration. She would be eagerly looked for, to-morrow, and he who possessed anything that could beat her would indeed be a proud man by sunset.

With another scarcely-breathed whistle he released her, and turned to hasp the gate and give a final look up the soaring fell, skirted with bracken, crowned by sullen rocks. Rain sprang round—sprang to meet a devil's galloper of satin panels and shining brass, hurled at a criminal speed along the narrow, curving road—sprang and disappeared. She was quite dead when Dixon and the chauffeur drew her out from between the heavy wheels.

A group of those children, who always appear miraculously at every untoward occurrence, thrust frightened faces through a break in the hedge. They knew Dixon and they knew Rain, and if the sky had fallen upon the appalling catastrophe they would hardly have been surprised. They said 'Goy!' at intervals, and held each other's hands, knowing the meaning of the countryman's set face.

Dixon said briefly—'She's done!' through shut teeth; and the chauffeur, rising reluctantly from his knees, dusted his smart livery, and nodded his head, biting his lip. It was not his place to criticise his master for taking other people's risks as cheerfully as he took his own.

A dark young face looked over the side of the car, and eyed the dead dog with a perturbed expression. It was all a beastly bore, but of course he had taken the corner far too fast, and would have to pay for his pleasure. It was a decent-looking dog, too, worse luck! He liked dogs as well as anybody—jolly, wagging things that always met you with a smile. What a fool he had been to peg along at that pace! He might have been sure there would be a dog at the corner. There always was, when *he* was driving.

He fumbled in his pocket, wondering vaguely why nobody said anything except the children in the hedge, who still observed 'Goy!' at intervals. Grange might have helped him out, but Grange was such a fool about animals; you wondered why he had ever taken to machines. Fortunately, the owner did not seem excited about the accident, thought the boy, seeing nothing unusual in the grim face which the northern children read so plainly.

He was a gentleman; and in justice it must be admitted that he offered his apology before he offered his gold; but perhaps his curiously-worded expressions of sorrow conveyed too little to the farmer, just as the gold conveyed too much. Grange made a movement to stop him when he saw the money; he had been bred in the dales. But again it was none of his business, and he shrugged his shoulders and stood aside, awaiting events.

They were not long in arriving. As the careless hand came out, Dixon's brown fist flew up to meet it; the gold clove a glittering path into the ditch, and the stranger subsided into his seat, nursing a damaged wrist.

Then he laughed, and motioned the chauffeur to get in.

'As you please!' he said to the farmer; and— 'Take the wheel!' to his servant; and, as they moved, stopped nursing his wrist to raise his hand to his cap. Dixon stood like a block.

Opposite the children, the motorist checked the car.

'There's somethin' in the ditch, yonder,' he observed, leaning forward, 'that will set you up in bull's-eyes for a month of Sundays!'—and not a child stirred. Behind him, he heard his own laugh echoed sardonically by Dixon—Dixon standing like a block beside his silver-haired darling.

'Grange, you fathead,' said his master thoughtfully, as the chauffeur swung his responsibilities out of sight, 'why, in the name of all that's sportin', didn't you warn me?'

'Sir,' answered the chauffeur, 'I have always understood that you preferred to learn things by experience!'

II

Bowman's Pink trotted nervously in the wake of uncertain footsteps. Life had become a devious and dangerous thing since her master had taken to looking upon the ale when it was yellow; and she followed his erratic curves uneasily if faithfully, since a well-bred dog must always be at its master's heels.

Not that the splendid title fitted her at first glance, as she pattered unhappily along the sticky road. Her slender, pointed limbs were plastered with mud; her black coat with the white star on the chest was rough and matted, and had lost its gloss; the fine, keen little head was shaggy and unkempt. She was underfed; she was uncared-for; and, much worse, she was cowed. A word from her lord set her trembling; a movement flattened her to the earth. Yet she stayed, as many women stay in like case—women whom all the divorce commissions in the world will never reach. And so Bowman and Pink came to the Trials.

They were late. Men whose hour-glass turns with ale usually are late. But Bowman's name was not among the first on the card, and he had not been called, as yet. He pulled himself together as he made his way past the flower-show and the shooting-gallery and the brass band, and Pink drew a little closer, humbly thankful to be free from the perils of the open road. On the left, rows of hard and unattractive benches supported the honourable weight of the flower of the county. On the right, the competitors watched and chatted and compared notes. In front, the long meadow, dotted with flags, sloped upward much as a stage slopes, so that the performance, regularly enacted every ten minutes, was plain to every eye; while near to the Society gathering, just where sunshades and chatter might alarm sheep and distract canine intelligence, was the little pen where the last act of the round was played, the only one in which the owner of the competing dog was allowed to give definite assistance. Society always derived huge enjoyment from this crucial moment. Seventeen-stone Jackson of Dubbs, prancing cautiously around his woolly adversaries, hat in hand, was certainly a sight to be treasured in the memory. The skill of his crawling, quivering lieutenant was apt to be overlooked in the humour of the situation.

Dixon of Dockerneuk sat by himself in a corner of the big field. He had come because he could not stay away, but, now that he was here, the whole business was torture to him. There was scarcely a man on the field but was asking for Rain, and annoying him with well-meant sympathy. Even the ladies had heard of her, fish-hooked each other's hats with their sunshades, and said—'Dear me! How perfectly shocking!' as if their respective cars had never so much as slain a hen. There was an immaculate youth, nursing a bandaged wrist amid a bevy of beauty, who went hot all over at the mention of the dead dog's name.

But Dixon would not be pitied. He shook off sympathy as a man shakes off a troublesome blue-bottle. He was billed to run another dog beside Rain, an excitable beginner that had the root of the matter in him, but at present preferred to regard life in general, and sheep-dog-trials in particular, as a huge joke. Dashing up to his three victims, he greeted them with affectionate exuberance, much as some over-familiar persons fall upon the necks of the dignified poor. Fleeing before his bouncing guidance, they were through the first flags in a rush, merely because that happened to be their line and they could not avoid it; but they ignored the rest, and were down the field and almost upon the laps of the crowd before Dixon's imperious whistle could swing the culprit in front of them.

Lark went back cheerfully enough. A little energy wasted more or less made no difference to him. Another rush brought the resentful trio through the stone gap and between the second flagged limits, but there the happy fluke ended. One sheep broke off from the rest, and for the remainder of his allotted space Lark played catch with it over every square inch of the field. Dixon wrestled with him patiently enough, while Society laughed and clapped, and the roughs in the background scoffed and called for Rain; but Lark, deaf to all admonition, was out to enjoy himself, and came in, when dismissed from the course, with a lolling tongue and a grin that reached from ear to ear. Dixon walked back to his corner without a word, feeling no resentment against the young dog who had made such gorgeous fools of them both. He was only a puppy; he would steady in time; and since Rain was not there— was lying under a new-turfed mound at home —nothing else really mattered.

Bowman's name was called at last by a member of the committee, and he disengaged himself from a group of second-rate acquaintances, and slouched forward. Pink was whining ever so softly to herself as she followed him out into the field, and every nerve in her body tingled with excitement. She had played this game before, and she was wild to get away and begin.

Society laughed again as Bowman's Pink came into view; she looked so small, so hungry, so pathetically incompetent. 'The Pink of Perfection!' observed a scarlet hat, nodding poppies, and was at once fish-hooked in revenge by a Reckitt's Blue sunshade who had been about to make the same witty remark herself.

Bowman gave the welcome signal at last—the least lift of a knotted stick—and Pink was up the long field like a black streak to the far point where three plump, puzzled sheep had been suddenly dumped to await her. She was on them quicker than Lark, but there was no scattering, this time. With one smart, circling movement, she clumped them together and dropped, looking for further orders, a dingy speck on the vivid green.

Bowman had gained sufficient control of himself to appear before the footlights, but, once there, he went to pieces altogether. His fuddled brain could not command the situation; his bleared eye could scarcely mark his little black servant awaiting his will; the hand that waved the stick was as reliable as a weather-cock in a shifting wind. He gave orders, it is true, but they were the wrong ones. Pink, straining ear and glance alike, could make nothing of him. He dropped her when a quick rush was imperative, forced her forward when to move an inch was to court disaster, rounded up at the wrong moment, scattered and separated when close upon the flags. The resulting confusion irritated him; the suppressed mirth of the watchers goaded him to fury. His stick began to wave wildly; he ceased to whistle, and took to shouting, and the tone of his shouting made the bright sunshades quiver.

Pink quivered, too, shamed and insulted, for no really first-class man shouts at a first-class dog; he has no need. She obeyed him, because not to obey would have been as possible to her as to make a live-mutton dinner off the three exasperated creatures whom she was being forced to torture so unnecessarily; but, under the stress of puzzling, contradictory orders, she, too, was beginning to lose her head. The whole fiasco ended in a glorious exit of sheep and sheep-dog over one of the President's newly-laid fences, while the onlookers rocked with laughter, and Bowman, black in the face, was removed peremptorily by the committee.

Pink came back, terrified, puzzled, shamed, but faithful—faithful even beneath the rain of knotted blows, hobnailed kicks and purple objurgations. She cried a little as she pressed her slim little body against the turf and screwed up her frightened eyes, and Dixon from his corner heard her. He stood up suddenly, and thrust himself contemptuously between executioner and victim.

'Hold on a bit, lad,' he said grimly, 'and answer a civil question before you get through with your leatherin'. D'you mind yon clashy winter's night as you nabbed Geordie Garnett's best pup from his shippon?'

Bowman accomplished the almost incredible feat of turning blacker in the face than ever.

'That's a—something—lie!' he stormed thickly.

Dixon stooped and turned up one of Pink's soft ears, showing the letter 'G' within, faint but still discernible.

'I know that breed as a man knows his own barns,' he said slowly. 'Geordie an' I have always been thick as inkle-weavers, you'll think on, and

I'm not like to forget what he had to say, yon night. I'll just step up and have a crack with him. He'll be rarely set up to have litten on his lost pup at last.'

Bowman was understood to remark that, not for all the Dixons gone before to a certain unmentionable locality, should Geordie Garnett lay a finger on what was not, and never had been, his. Dixon eyed him steadily. The fight was healing the hurt places in his soul.

'Look you here,' he said firmly. 'I'll make you a fair offer, and you can take it or leave it, just as suits you! You've shamed the poor brute before the whole countryside. *She* was game for the work, right enough, but you were fair daft. Now, I'll do this for you. Let me take her round just once, just to show Lyndesay and all the lot of them what she can do when she's given half a chance, and, when Geordie Garnett gets her back, I'll never let wit where I clapped eyes on her. Is it a deal?'

Bowman laughed murderously.

'A deal?' said he. 'Ay, a deal, right enough! Take her, my fine lad—take her!'

Dixon bent to obey, but his fingers had barely touched Pink's head before he stepped back with an exclamation, for her teeth had sunk in his wrist. She eyed him sorrowfully, even while the growl rattled in her throat. A well-bred dog could do no less for her master, however unworthy.

Bowman rolled about in drunken glee, urging his opponent to further effort, and Dixon's temper snapped like dry kindling. He took Bowman behind a quiet hedge, and thrashed him into acquiescence. When he reappeared, Pink trotted meekly in his shadow. Together, they sought out the President, who listened a little impatiently to the demand that the dog might be run again.

'What's the good?' he asked, watching his head shepherd making a glorious mull of things at the pen. 'Having been the round once, she is no longer eligible for the prize.'

Dixon growled contempt.

''Tisn't the prize,' he said. 'It's the *dog*. She was run by a man who wasn't fit to run her, a drunken fool who simply threw her away. She comes of the best stock in the county, and she can do better than that, I'll lay my best heifer. She doesn't know me, but I think I can work her. She's been shamed before the whole county. Give her another chance.'

Arevar's eldest son stood up and joined in the conversation. Dixon's eyes met his without the slightest change of expression. The eldest son had a bandaged wrist.

'Let her run, Father,' he said. 'It's not harmin' any one, and everybody should have a second chance in this world, shouldn't they, Mr.—er— Dixon, I think? Let her run.'

Lyndesay shrugged his shoulders, and with difficulty restrained himself from rushing down to assist the head shepherd, who had at last succeeded in penning the whole of two of the sheep and half of the third.

'Very well!' he said. 'Just as you like. She'll do no good, anyway. She's had all the intelligence beaten out of her, poor little brute!'

His son smiled gallantly into Dixon's grim face.

'Everybody should have a second chance,' he said again. 'Everybody—rich or poor, knave or

fool, starvin' sheep-dogs or—motorin' roadhogs.
Let her run!'

There was a space on the yellow programme
hallowed by the name of Rain, but, when Dixon
came out in his order, it was not the silver-haired
beauty but the cowed little tramp that trotted at
his side. Pink had spent a thrilling hour gleaning
new impressions. These included a tentative
grooming with an old stable-brush, a few dry biscuits, a few rough caresses, a few kindly words.
The sympathy and the biscuits had put fresh
heart into her; the grooming had eased her self-
respect. She came out gladly enough to the work
she loved, though her faithful heart still yearned
after the drunken, hobnailed brute slumbering
behind the hedge.

Dixon dropped his hand to the dog's head, and
she cowered to the very ground. He repeated the
experiment until she stood up confidently under
his touch, and the two looked into each other's
eyes. Then he jerked his own head sharply, and
she was gone like the wind up the edge of the
slope, to be checked by a sweet, clear whistle
before she was upon the fresh prey, who raised
innocent eyes, unafraid of the harmless black and
white patch so near. Presently there was another
whistle, a languid wave of a thin ash-plant, and the
quartette was ambling unconcernedly towards
the first of the flags.

Dixon, for all his outward calm, was conscious
of a slight nervousness. He had pledged his word,
so to speak, upon the dog's worth, and would
have staked his last coin, if need be; but every
man handles a dog just a shade differently, and
any sudden lack of sympathy between himself

and his new *protégée* might bring fresh derision upon both. The dog was cowed, too, half-starved, home-sick for her old tyrant; but he knew the stock she came from, and the training that becomes inherited instinct after so many generations, and he counted strongly upon these. Taking a grip of himself, he concentrated all his attention upon the waif in Rain's place, as if she had indeed been Rain herself, charged with all his hopes. And presently his confidence in the power of race changed to exultant wonder, for here was a trained intelligence answering to his will as even Rain had seldom answered. Such tact, such patience, such judgment, such skilled, gentle handling, he had never seen. There was no shouting, now, no furious waving, no volleying of oaths to scorch sensitive feminine ears. The clear whistles hardly clove the air before they were obeyed; the sharp, clipped signal that means 'Drop!'—the long, clear call, lifting at the end, that says 'Come on!'—the shower of quick notes that telegraph 'Round up!' Here were the first-class man and the first-class dog working like a single instrument. The President, his eyes glued to the little tramp, forgot that the head shepherd had never succeeded in penning the second half of the third sheep.

They had passed three of the tests—the top flags, the stone gap, and the oak tree—and were making for the fourth when the first hitch occurred. Dixon, forgetting in his concentration that it was not Rain he was working, after all, employed a special call that he used on the fell to warn his dog of a precipice. It had a curious swerve in the middle, and meant—'Keep together!' and Rain would have had the sheep in a tight bunch right between the flags, but Pink was not fell-trained, and she dropped, puzzled for the first time. Dixon, cursing himself, gave her the signal she knew, but in that fatal pause one curly monster had separated itself from the rest, and taken a bee-line for home. Pink was in front of it in a flash, only to lose the other two, and there followed a pretty piece of handling which agitated the parasols into a perfect frenzy of fish-hooking, but at which Dixon frowned, for the precious minutes were flying.

The sheep were through the final flags at last, however, but their faith in their gentle conductor had been ruined by that sudden separation and breathless chase. They were in the mood to be alarmed by the smallest slip when they approached the narrow door of the uninviting fold. It was then that Dixon made his bold stroke.

Every other shepherd on the field had helped to pen his sheep; it was a recognised fact that even the best of dogs could hardly accomplish the finish unaided, particularly when each of the sheep was as nervous as a cat, and would break on the slightest encouragement. But Dixon had faith in his dog, and he was playing for her reputation. He let her pen them alone.

Slowly, inch by inch, Pink crawled in rear of her charge. Slowly, inch by inch, the frightened heads turned to the pen. Something about it must have suggested safety to the first sheep, for it moved forward, and the second followed. The third, however, lost interest during the pause, and edged to the right, but Pink edged in the same direction. Tossing its head, it swung to the left, but Pink was there, also. This seemed to annoy it, for it skipped round in its own length, and faced the enemy defiantly, but Pink's innocent muzzle was on the ground, her vivid eyes almost shut. The third sheep looked a little ashamed of itself, swung round again and lined up. The first was practically inside.

Dixon of Dockerneuk stood like stone, and Society forgot even to rustle. Pink crept nearer, nearer, and dropped for the last time; and, as she did so, the first sheep, apparently disgusted with the accommodation, swerved like a shying horse in the face of its following, forcing the second sheep into the startled mouth of the third. Even then, Dixon did not stir; but there was no need, for Pink flung herself forward as the Winged Hats flung themselves at the Great Wall, and in another moment three disconsolate noses poked through barren bars, whilst a panting black and white streak stretched across the threshold of their prison.

Dixon whistled ever so softly, but she heard him and came to him gladly. He put out his hand, and she leaped to catch it joyously with her teeth. Through the cheering crowd he sought his way to his corner, but a yesterday's enemy checked him. Larruppin' Lyndesay faced him diffidently but courageously.

'You've given one dog a second chance,' he said. 'Can't you see your way to doin' it for another?'

Dixon honoured him with a long look.

'There's the Ring o' Bells,' he said at last, 'just across the road.'

They went off together.

. . . .

CHAPTER V

SLINKER'S wife drew up with a flourish at Crump
steps, but she relinquished the reins rather wearily. She looked almost tired—Christian thought
—a thing very foreign to her extraordinary vi-
tality. Butler and footman were automatons of
respect as she descended, and she smiled inwardly
as she went in. She knew quite well what they
had said about her when she first came.

Mrs. Lyndesay was standing just inside the hall,
her hard face like ivory against the dark background. There was something inhuman about
her to Christian, coming out of the sunlight into
the frigidity of her presence. During the last
month she seemed to have retired further than
ever into that icy aloofness which wore, for him, at
least, the appearance of hatred. She turned her
eyes away from him sharply as he entered, and he
knew that she had looked instinctively for another
form to fill the door when he crossed the threshold.

Slinker's wife thrust a hand through her arm,
and led her to the tea-table. All through the
meal she talked steadily, while Mrs. Lyndesay
listened with something almost like amusement
in her eyes. Somewhere and somehow, Slinker's
wife had found a chord in that hidden heart
which answered when she struck it.

Christian, ignored, wandered into the garden,
and stood looking across the green of the sunk
lawn and the glory of the flower-beds to the rising
background of woods. There was a stream running flittingly from wood to garden, and he
walked beside it, hearing it but not hearkening,
for he was reviewing his swift and disastrous meet-

ing with Deborah. Emphatically, he had done the wrong thing, and in the most hopelessly-wrong manner. He had hurt her afresh—she, who had already suffered more hurt than one dared think of. After all, what use could Slinker's wife be to her, on any terms? Somehow, the horse-dealer's daughter had inspired him with a confidence in vaguely-miraculous powers. You leaned with a strange trust on Slinker's wife. Something about her made you feel that the world could never be long out of joint, with her capable hands willing and ready to manipulate it. He had known her all his life, or near it, and she was older than he by several years; a million years older in everything else but age.

She joined him, presently, in a white gown, the faint trace of fatigue utterly vanished, and towed him into one of the mossy woodland paths.

'I've finished with those crow's clothes,' she said, slipping her hand through his arm, and looking down at herself approvingly. 'Parker nearly did a faint when he saw me, but who cares? I didn't allow Slinker to be a bore to me when he was alive, and I certainly won't have him a nuisance now he is dead. I'm only his widow by accident, so to speak, and I don't see why I should go about making an object of myself on his account. What's the matter, Youngest One? You seem a bit down in the mouth. Worrying about that turn-up, this morning?'

'Looking back, it seems such a rotten thing to have done!' Christian replied. 'You see, I never gave her time to think, just fell upon her out of the sky and sprang the thing at her. I should have prepared her, broken it gently——'

Slinker's wife laughed humorously.

'I do need some gentle preparation, don't I? Oh, you needn't apologise! And of course public opinion expects us to glare defiance at each other, as if we each had a claw upon Slinker's dead body. It's only natural she should hate me. But that girl's got grit, Laker—the sort of grit you don't meet with, every day in the week. Most females left in a similar lurch would have had nervous prostration and a prolonged visit on the Continent or at the nearest rest-cure. But *she* goes to market slick in the chattering teeth of the whole county—snaps her fingers in their pained faces, and lets them see she isn't ashamed of anything she's done. Why *should* she be ashamed, either, I'd like to know? If Slinker asked her to marry him, she'd every right to say yes.'

Christian shook his head.

'That's what's wrong. And that's what she *is* ashamed of, no matter how splendidly she tries to hide it. She can't really have been able to stand Slinker. No decent girl could. And to marry him for his position—— I say, Nettie dear, I'm horribly sorry!'

Mrs. Slinker smiled with something of an effort.

'Don't judge our rotten sex too hardly, Laker. It isn't always sheer sordidness, even when we do marry for position; there's a glamour it gives the man, no matter what he may be, himself. He's got all his fathers and grandfathers standing bail for him. You kind of catch your breath at all he represents, and shut your eyes to the miserable, moth-eaten bagman you might possibly find him if you weren't blinkered by his grandeur.'

'The glamour couldn't have lasted long; and

after that had vanished, I don't see how she could ever have dreamed of going through with it. A nice girl like that, with nice ideas, and—and—isn't that moss a ripping colour?'

She pressed his arm affectionately.

'It's all right, Youngest One! You can't think of us in the same light; and, after all, why should you? I come of tougher stock, rougher stuff. I knew how to handle a man like Slinker. I could have made something of him—perhaps—something that Heaven wouldn't have been ashamed of—if I'd tried. But I didn't think him worth while, and I don't doubt that the Almighty agrees with me. I didn't even think the estate worth while, with Slinker slung round my neck like an albatross; so I went to Canada to my sister, and thought of him as seldom as possible till I got the news of his death and his charmingly-planned comedy for three. I wonder what he meant by the whole thing?—whether he was waiting for me to hear, and come back? It would have been like Slinker's slinkin' way of doing things. I'd have been bound to come to the church, at any rate; not a step further! I wonder if that's the real solution of the muddle? After all—Slinker cared.'

'Don't!' Christian shuddered. 'Don't you see what a diabolical situation that creates for—for—the other woman?'

She looked at him curiously.

'Yes, I suppose it makes things worse, doesn't it? It wouldn't have been so bad if Slinker had loved her and wanted her too badly to remember that he had some wretched sort of a wife already. Well, we'll leave it at that! What do I care? But you mustn't blame her too much. It's because she's one of your own people that you feel as you do—that she shouldn't have stooped to a man like that for a reason like that. You could forgive a stranger who had done it—a woman who wasn't a Lyndesay born and bred; you could forgive—Nettie Stone, the horse-dealer's daughter!'

He looked at her whimsically, knowing her too well, respecting her too much, to lie to her. He let the statement pass.

'Didn't the place call you more than once?' he asked. 'Didn't all this—the land, the house, the things they stand for—call you ever again after that one moment when you put out your hand and took them?' He looked through the green veil of the wood to the long house lying below them, and over the house to the faint hills. 'Didn't you want it, ache for it, break your heart for it? Oh, Nettie, how did you keep away?'

She shook her head, smiling.

'That isn't in me—how should it be? How should generations of horse-dealing draw any human soul magically to Crump? The house is dumb for me—in spite of the hundred tongues it keeps for you. The land says nothing—no more than it says to every other soul that springs from it and goes back to it. It is our mother—we others. To you, it is your child.'

'But, if you don't feel, how do you *know*?' he asked, laying a hand for a moment on an ancient trunk. 'And you *do* know!'

'Intuition, I suppose. Besides, the thing radiates from you. One has only to watch your eyes—listen to your voice. It must mean more to you than to us whose forefathers owned no more than the six feet of earth doled them for a grave. You don't get a soul for soil out of that! No. Just once the whole thing caught me—the glamour of Lyndesay of Crump; but never again. I never felt it again.'

'What kept you—came in between? Why did you never want to take your place?'

Slinker's wife looked up and up to where the quiet smoke of Dockerneuk chimneys curled in the pure air.

'Because I had once seen something better,' she said, 'and, after I had done the irrevocable thing, the remembrance of that better thing came back to me. I saw quite plainly what a good man was worth, and the worth of a good man's love—just everything that Slinker couldn't mean to me, in spite of Crump. I might have taken it before, and come out all right in the end. But after that I couldn't have taken it and saved my soul alive.'

'What stopped you, Nettie dear?'

'A little thing—a very little thing. Just the sound of a two-horse grass-cutter on a summer morning. It was miles away from here, in another part of England, in an hotel in some beastly little town; but soon after dawn I woke as if some one had whispered, and, far away, ever so far, I heard the whirr and the click and the call to the horses. And the smell of the hay—that came too; and all it stood for—all it stood for! I couldn't stop, after that. I told Slinker I was going, and I went; and I never had anything to do with him afterwards. I knew then what I wanted—what I had wanted without knowing; and though I couldn't have it, I could at least refuse anything less. Crump was less, Lyndesay of Crump was less—and Nettie

Stone the most wretched, ashamed reptile that ever crawled the earth!'

Christian kissed her hand.

'Thank you for marrying Slinker,' he said. 'You belong to me, now, and I shall not be so lonely any more. Thank you for marrying Slinker.'

CHAPTER VI

DEB found her father in his usual place by the window, looking out over the road and the rush-edged river, and up the slope of the park to the plantation outlined against the sky. The *Estates Gazette* was in his hand, but he was not reading; he was looking out at the land he loved. He was always looking out.

He turned as she entered, and she tried to smile, for in the transparent old face was a content that she had sorely missed during the last, long, trying weeks. The trouble was dying, now, and the spell which had made his chief happiness in life had hold of him once more.

He had never questioned the wisdom of his girl's engagement; and, to the amazement of the unthinking neighbourhood, he had followed Stanley respectfully to the grave, showing no outward resentment against his daughter's dead lover. Many people thought it strange and almost inhuman, but Deb understood. What he honoured was not the body of a wild young blackguard, but the representative of the race which he and his forefathers had served. He would have done the same had Slinker wrecked them both, body and soul.

He asked her the state of the market while she

ate her late lunch, and drifted on to inquiries about the folk she had met in the town. She mentioned several of his old cronies—*that* ground was safe enough—commenting on their health, business and conversation. Then at last came the question she dreaded.

'Anybody in from Crump?'

He had not meant to ask it, but you cannot put a question every Saturday for years without becoming more or less its slave. His thin hand clasped and unclasped nervously on his knee, but, when once the sentence was spoken, he stood by it.

'Christian was in,' she replied, fixing an intent gaze on the mustard. 'He was driving;—yes—the stanhope.' (Cars were nothing accounted of in the old man's conservative eyes.) She tried to stop the next words, but they came in spite of her. 'Stanley's wife was with him.'

The stately old man crimsoned to his snowy hair.

'She is still there, then—that person—old Steenie Stone's daughter? I heard she was stopping, but I did not believe it. I could not!'

'Mrs. Lyndesay would not let her go. They say she has taken a fancy to her. A somewhat embarrassing attention, I should think!' Deb smiled faintly, paused, and began again. 'She—Stanley's wife—wanted to know me.'

'To know you? *You!*' The old man was trembling, now. He struck his ebony stick sharply on the floor. 'She presumed to demand an introduction? You did not grant it, of course?'

Deb shook her head, anathematising herself for opening the subject. 'No, I did not.' Rising, she laid a hand on his shoulder, and turned him to the window. 'The Highland cattle are coming down to drink. Do you remember where we got them?' (The old steward 'we' still clung to the lips of both.) 'Dixon says the hay crop is going to be first-rate, this year. When will you have the paddock cut?'

But for once the enthralling topic of the hay did not serve to turn his attention.

'You've been crying!' he observed, looking up at her. 'Did any one dare—was anybody rude to you in Witham?'

She slid down on her knees by the sill, and laid her chin on her arms.

'Not rude, Dad. Not exactly what you might call rude. Some of them weren't precisely on the same planet—that was all! And others came too near, which was worse; good little Verity, for instance, and dear, blundering Larrupper.'

'Lionel, do you mean?' he asked quickly. 'Then the Lyndesays stood by you? The Lyndesays sought you out?'

'Oh, dear, yes!' She laughed rather shakily. 'The difficulty was to get away from them! I had to dive into a cheese-shop to escape Christian, and Larry wanted to bring me home in the car.'

'Then the rest don't count!' the old man answered, unconsciously echoing Christian's words of that morning. That had been his attitude all through life. God made the Lyndesays, and the rest—didn't count. His face cleared, and his eyes went back more restfully to the window.

'I wish I hadn't gone!' Deb said brokenly. 'I thought I was brave enough, but I found I wasn't, after all. I've always been able to rely upon myself before, but to-day I went all to pieces. I wish I hadn't gone. They all think I should have left the district, I know. They think it would have shown nice feeling and good taste! But I'll not go—they shan't make me. I'd hear the very 'bus-boy jeering as he drove me to the station; and I'd come back and fight the lot of them! They shan't hound me away from you and the old place, shall they, Dad?'

He laid his hand for a moment on her hair, but he did not turn his eyes from the window.

'The Lyndesays stood by you,' he said again, as if no other argument were needed; and again he added—'the rest do not count.'

Deb was silent, watching the long-horned cattle paddling blissfully deep in the cool water. What was the use of trying to explain that it was Lyndesay kindness that made the real difficulty? At least she would receive no unwelcome patronage from the mistress of Crump, she reflected ironically, and fell to wondering how Stanley's wife had besieged that fortress so successfully. Presently she began to talk about the hay once more, and this time her father entered into the subject with zest. From that, they came back to the cattle again, over which he shook his head in unwilling admiration. He was a shorthorn man himself—was still one of the finest shorthorn judges in the country—and the picturesque, rough-coated beasts looked out of place to him on Crump land. Deb had the history of half the famous shorthorn herds in the kingdom before she finally escaped to her own room. That looked over the park, too. Father and daughter lived half their lives with their faces turned to Crump.

At least he was happy again, she thought, with a sigh of relief. He would settle down, now, and under Christian's rule nothing should happen on the estate to spoil the old man's last days. For him, at all events, there was peace ahead.

Under the big beech on the old bridge, a man and a girl sat on the low wall, looking down to the bend of the river, bringing back to the watcher in the creepered house the night when on that very spot Stanley had asked her to be his wife. Shutting her eyes, she felt again the warm darkness of the leafy arch, heard the hurry of the water under her feet, and Stanley himself as no more than a voice in the dusk. Something that was not Stanley at all had cried to her from without, and to that, and that only, had she yielded. Stanley was only its mouthpiece. Could he come back this very night, free to claim her given word, she knew that she would yield again.

CHAPTER VII

'WHY not cut it down?' Mrs. Slinker asked, from the deep window-seat in the hall. She had been riding, and had come straight to her favourite post, from which she could see the old pele tower of Dockerneuk through the cloud of wood.

'Why not cut it down?' she said again, and she lifted a gauntlet and shook it vindictively at some unconscious object without. 'Horrid, grewly old thing, standing there gloating over the misfortunes of the house! It shouldn't stop another day if I had the ordering of things. Why don't you get rid of it?'

Christian, standing behind her, shrugged his

shoulders as she glared at the huge cedar, centuries old, standing alone in its patch of emerald lawn, as if the hand of a witch had ringed a curse round it.

'Swank, I suppose!' he said, smiling. 'I can't think of any other particular reason. Only I can't fancy myself setting out, on my own responsibility, to grub up the family fate. Perhaps, if I spoke the truth, I should say I was afraid! I hardly know.'

She turned and looked up at him.

'You don't honestly believe that because, hundreds of years ago, one of your ancestors hanged another on that horrid old object, no Lyndesay of Crump will be allowed to die a natural death as long as the tree stands in its place? Laker, you're a cuckoo!'

'I don't doubt it! Nevertheless, the fact remains that very few Crump owners have died peacefully of old age. We go out fighting, hunting, shooting—moving, anyhow—always rebelling, never acquiescing; and generally in pretty good time. We do not die as most other men die.'

'*That's* swank, if you like!' she answered him teasingly, and he coloured hotly, biting his lip. 'No! Don't curl up. There never was anybody less snobbish than you, Christian. But you've got the family-feel very strong. It showed in Slinker, too, at times, though you never believed it was there. *He* said things like that, occasionally—generally when he had had too much to drink.'

His face clouded a little, and she turned squarely upon him.

'Look here, Laker, you've got to learn to bear it! I'm not your sort, and I never shall be; and if

I'm to go on living here for the present, as you say you wish, you must get accustomed to my way of talking, and the things I may shoot out at any moment, even if they do drive the footmen into hysterics, and old Parker into dropping the beef. If I'm to stop, I'll not be glossed and veneered and shoved into a glass case. I'm not a Lyndesay, in spite of Slinker. I'm Nettie Stone, the horse-dealer's daughter; and if I can't use my native unparliamentary language under your venerable roof, I must go and use it out in Canada or some other place where ears are less tender and the air is free!'

'I beg your pardon!' he replied, very gently, and with a ceremonious but perfectly sincere inclination, and this time it was she whose colour rose.

'Oh, you—you aristocrat!' she said under her breath, with a little laugh; and he parted suddenly with his new-born dignity, and flung himself boyishly beside her.

'Heavens, Nettie, how serious we're getting! And all because of a silly old tree-thing! Let's skip back a page. Tell me some more of your impressions of our cranky old family.'

'Well, I can't help thinking it's just idiotic,' she went on, 'to sit round watching that old trunk flapping a curse at you without so much as trying to answer it back. You can't *really* like the idea that you may find yourself shoved into eternity at any minute in the twenty-four hours. Anybody with half a yard of backbone would have gone out and talked to the gloating old ghoul with a bill-hook, centuries since, before it got into its stride.'

'I suppose the real reason is that it is part of ourselves, by now,' he answered thoughtfully. 'It

may have been superstition, in the first place;
cussed pride, later on; but for myself it is just
simply that I would sooner put a bullet through
my skull than give orders for the tree to be destroyed. It's a link between owner and owner—
myself and all the other freaks gone before—(that
must be how I look at it unconsciously)—and to
break that link would mean annihilation of spirit
more terrible than any possible annihilation of
body. I've got all the other fellows looking on
and lending a hand, you see. If the tree went,
I should be left standing alone.'

Again she looked at him curiously, as at something not wholly within her comprehension.

'It sounds all right when you put it like that, of
course. Very majestic and Back to the Flood and
all that kind of thing, don't you know?—though
it isn't exactly comfortable to think of the family
spooks perching like a lot of lost roosters on that
slimy cedar. But I should have thought you
would be glad to be free of them. Thank the
powers *I've* no family ghosts to be pulling my back
hair when I'm out to enjoy myself! I've been
standing alone ever since I wore openwork socks,
and I feel fit enough to go on standing till the
Judgment! But, from what I've seen of life,
Christian, there comes a time to every man when
he's got to learn to stand alone; and it strikes me
very forcibly, Laker, my lad, that you'll have to
take your turn along with the rest!'

She laid her hand on Christian's for a second,
with the freedom of good comradeship, but, as her
eyes dropped to the square strength of her fingers,
foiled by the slender strength of his, she drew it
back and pulled on her gloves sharply, conscious

again of the intangible barrier that had arisen momentarily when he asked her pardon. 'I'm just talking through my hat!' she added, with an angry little stamp, while he watched her in amused bewilderment, having no clue to her change of mood. 'Well, go on dying as often and as suddenly as you please—you and your bunch of devil's firewood! And now I'm going out to talk on my own level—to the stable-boy!'

After she had gone, a message came to Christian from his mother, and he climbed the stairs to Slinker's own room, which still was as he had left it, and was likely to remain so as long as Alicia Lyndesay reigned at Crump. Slinker had disdained the library and the other rooms on the ground floor used by his conservative ancestors, and had fitted himself a den overlooking the stable-yard. 'Too many eyes looking on,' he had said of the family portraits, and graced his walls with others, obviously minus family, and chiefly remarkable for teeth. 'No rotten old views for me!' he had observed likewise, and had blocked sky and air daily with a cloud of expensive smoke.

The room was full of sporting implements of the newest type and the highest finish; beautiful, untried things stuck in corners or against a wall to drag out a useless existence; for Slinker had been no sportsman. He liked the look of the things well enough—the old blood spoke sufficiently for that —but he rarely handled even a gun, though in shooting-kit he was a most convincing spectacle; so much so, indeed, that few had ever grasped his real form as a shot, except a nervous keeper or two with eyes down their backs, or some badly-frightened dog.

From over the mantelpiece Slinker himself greeted his entrance, slim, sleek, irritatingly guileless in expression. To the casual eye there had been sufficient resemblance between the half-brothers to arouse a sense of impotent wrath in Christian's very dissimilar soul. Both were fair and blue-eyed, gentle-voiced and quiet in movement; points, however, which really served to mark an amazing difference to one intimate with both. Christian's athletic grace had been in Slinker chiefly the artistic wisdom of an over-patronised tailor. Christian's gentleness was fear to hurt; Slinker's, mere backstairs policy. Christian's charming serenity was the outward expression of his inward self; Slinker's guilelessness veiled deceit as deep as the sea.

Eluding the eyes of the portrait with difficulty, Christian experienced an actual shock as he met those of Deborah from the opposite wall, grave and rather haughty, as if disturbed by the picture-postcard society around her. Moved by a sudden unaccountable impulse, he placed himself before the photograph, so that Slinker's travelling gaze could no longer reach it.

His mother was seated at the desk in the recess by the fireplace, surrounded on all sides by Stanley's papers. Judging from her face, she was not finding this voyage of discovery any too plain sailing.

Without speaking, she motioned him to a chair, and, avoiding Slinker's ostentatious saddle-bags, he dropped obediently into the Windsor which the dead master had kept for his tenants.

'It is time things were settled,' she said at last, turning just sufficiently in his direction to indicate that she was addressing him and not Flossie Featherfin cake-walking in the alcove. 'I suppose you know that Stanley had engaged a new agent? We cannot keep the man waiting any longer. No doubt you are willing to confirm the appointment?'

'I wanted to ask you about that,' Christian put in. 'I had a letter from him, this morning. He seems all right, of course—good testimonials and all that kind of thing—but I should prefer a personal interview before settling anything definite.'

'How anxious you are to assert your new authority!' she sneered, and waited while he winced. 'Stanley's judgment after years of experience is of course not to be weighed against that of an untried youngster fresh to his responsibilities! Probably you would prefer one of the country yokels with whom you are on such intimate terms, to an educated gentleman, trained in his profession. But there is the estate to be considered before your own personal tastes—you must please make an effort to remember that.'

'Of course the estate comes before everything,' Christian answered quietly. 'Why will you never believe that I care for the old place?'

'It is certainly difficult to realise,' she retorted coldly, 'seeing that you have never shown any sense of your position! *That* must be changed, at least. Now that you are Lyndesay of Crump, you must break finally with the individuals who have hitherto made demands upon your time and pocket—all those persons whose chief object in life seems to consist in going about hitting somebody or something with something else.'

'Do you mean that the games must go to the

wall?' Christian asked wistfully. 'Is it really necessary? They keep one fit, you know—and—and—it seems rotten to be throwing flowers at oneself, but I'm considered pretty useful——' He broke off under her mocking eyes, his enthusiasm dropping dead.

'All that is over!' she said very distinctly. 'Lyndesay of Crump cannot go out into an open field to make sport for spectators. There is absolutely no second word on the matter. All that is over.'

He sat silent, wondering vaguely why he did not rebel; conscious of something beyond and stronger than his mother forcing him into acquiescence. He felt suddenly very desolate. He had loved that part, at least, of the old life, and he was not ready for the new.

'I never approved, as you know,' Mrs. Lyndesay went on. 'But, while Stanley lived, it was not of paramount importance. I never thought Stanley would go—so soon.' She looked up at the portrait, setting her lips, and Christian ran a gentle finger down the smooth cane of a rod. It had been hard on Slinker, poor chap, in all conscience: yet Slinker had never loved a swinging game as he loved it, nor ached to get at grips with an adversary in fair and amicable fight. At that moment he would have been almost content to change with him.

'You must get to know the county,' his mother was saying. 'You have been very much of a boor, refusing invitations when you were at home, and going your own way entirely. Lyndesays of Crump have always led, have always been expected to lead, and you must take your place. You must get to know people.'

'Some of them are such slackers!' Christian answered sadly. 'I'm afraid I like people who do things for themselves instead of those who run a reputation upon others who did things for them. But I'll get to work on the county points at once, if you like. And I'll'—he rose abruptly, and turned his head away—'I'll give up the games.'

He could feel the leather sphere under his arm, the rush of wind past his ears, the thud of his feet on the firm ground, the final pitch into glory on the far side of the line. That was gone for good. Again he crossed the ring with outstretched hand, sank his chin on his opponent's shoulder, braced his muscles and suppled his wrists ere he felt for the final hold. That, too, was gone. Breathing deep, he came back to the foreign atmosphere of Slinker's den, and found himself looking once more into Deb's eyes. With a kind of mechanical deftness he lifted the picture from its ambiguous position, and slipped it into his pocket, turning towards the door.

'And you will confirm that appointment?' his mother asked again, without looking round; an interesting document in Slinker's theatrical collection having sprung upon her.

'Very well. I will write at once. No doubt it will be all right. And if there's nothing fur-ther——?'

In the library he drew out the photograph and looked curiously at the gravely-aloof face.

'Why did I save you, I wonder?' he asked both of it and of himself. 'Because you wanted to come away so very badly, I suppose. Yet you went of your own free will. Why, oh, why did you go? Couldn't you *feel* that it was all wrong? I'm not blaming you, of course—and yet I *am* blaming you—I *am*! Almost anybody else might have done it, but not you. You shouldn't have taken the risk.'

He dropped it into a drawer, and turned the key.

CHAPTER VIII

BLACK coat-tails came whisking up Heron drive on a bicycle, and Verity tore to the drawing-room to set about her usual preparations.

From some obscure corner a dusty *Doll's House* was dragged into the light of day; *Ann Veronica* scuttled into position beside the latest problem novel, *Woman Enthroned*; Zola and Oscar Wilde shared the shelter of the same chrysanthemum; while from the silver table Mrs. Pankhurst addressed the world at large.

The hall-door opened, and Verity, scattering a few Mormon tracts at random over the sofa, flung herself at the piano and dashed into the new war-song—'Way for the Women!' just as the Vicar was announced; only to be conscious, as she rose to greet him, of the utter futility of her dramatic efforts.

'The man sees nothing but the inside of his own head!' she told herself, as she welcomed him prettily, and watched him settle himself among the Mormons. 'It's a real waste of time trying to be artistic with him, and I think I'd better take Larry's advice and give it up.'

'I'll tell my mother,' she added aloud, moving to the door. Mrs. Cantacute was a widow and an invalid, which was considered by some to be Verity's sole excuse.

The young parson, however, sprang to his feet, putting out a protesting hand, his dark eyes very bright and eager.

'No, no, please don't!—that is, not just yet. There is something I want to say to you alone, Miss Cantacute, if you will be kind enough to spare me a few minutes.'

'Of course!' Verity shifted Ibsen from his chair, and sat down with him in her lap, the title invitingly uppermost; and Mr. Grant looked at the little figure in blue with its shining head and downcast eyes, and thought of Raphael and Correggio and Fra Angelico and ladders of angels and Rebekah at the Well.

'I want to ask you a favour,' he began, picking up a Mormon, and crackling it nervously without looking at it. 'You'll think I'm very interfering, I expect, and perhaps very impertinent, but I don't doubt that you will see my point of view in the end. One has only to look at you, Miss Cantacute, to know that you are incapable of any but the very highest and noblest instincts concerning any subject of spiritual importance.'

Verity looked up deprecatingly without saying anything; then refixed her gaze on the buckle of her left shoe. The Mormon crackled harder than ever.

'I hear that you are arranging an elaborate Pierrot entertainment,' he went on, 'the work for which is to occupy a large portion of the winter. I don't want to discount your kindness, Miss Cantacute, in organising displays of this sort for the amusement of an isolated little village, but I do ask you to consider one particular point. As you know, I found, when I came, that many of the

usual church efforts for promoting spiritual
growth had fallen into neglect. There was no
mission-work, for instance, no special service for
men, no Girls' Friendly or Temperance League;
there were no sewing-parties, night-classes, or lectures. I have worked hard to alter that state of
things, and at last I earnestly believe I am beginning to succeed. Most of the young men and
women of the parish are at present pleasantly and
profitably employed during each evening of the
week, striving to become worthy helpers in the
great Cause. Now you, Miss Cantacute, propose
to distract their minds by musical and dramatic
rehearsals held almost daily; and I ask you, very
humbly, and with real anxiety, whether you
think yourself justified in interfering thus arbitrarily with the work of the Church? I love my task,
as you scarcely need telling, but at the same
time it has its disagreeable side. I have had my
battle to fight, like every one else, and it has not
been a small one, by any means—far from it! But
at least I was beginning to trust it was won. Now
—I don't know. I don't know!'

He rose sharply, and began to pace up and
down the room, his hands behind him, passing
Ann and Oscar without so much as a glance.
Verity still said nothing.

'I had heard so much about you before I came,
Miss Cantacute. I was told how clever you were,
how charming, how heart to heart with the villagers, how affectionately regarded on all sides!
I had it said to me that, with Verity Cantacute
under my banner, I need never know an hour's
uneasiness. I have tried very hard to enlist you;
you will admit that. I have asked you to work for

me—the very highest compliment in the world! I have offered you posts second only in importance to my own. I have done all in my power to demonstrate to you that, after myself, I regard you as the greatest influence in the parish. And yet, despite all this, you have met me, time after time, with rebuff on rebuff, refusal on refusal—rejection, discouragement, almost contempt!'

He looked again at his silent hostess—at the prayerful hands, lightly clasped, the Madonna-like parting of the hair, the subdued, gentle bend of the neck, and his hopes rose. Surely, surely she was touched! He sat down thoughtlessly upon *Woman Enthroned*, and leaned anxiously towards her.

'Can't I persuade you to give up this entertainment, my friend? I don't say that it is wrong in itself—I am not as ridiculously narrow and one-sided as that—but I do say that it comes at a very critical moment in the spiritual life of the parish —at a time when even an innocent amusement may be grasped by the devil as a weapon of offence. My boys and girls will come to you in preference to me—it is only natural. Music and laughter will of course appeal to them more than lantern-slides on Church History—singing and dancing please them better than lectures upon How to Keep Bees. There will be big gaps in my hitherto well-filled rows of faces—faces which send me to bed happy every night of the week. They will be with you, Miss Cantacute, enjoying themselves and learning to be very clever; but will they be learning to be—good?'

Verity was white to the lips as she pushed her chair back from him a fraction, so that the *Doll's*

House slid heavily to the floor; but she smiled at him quite sweetly.

'There's Billy-boy Blackburn to be considered,' she said very gently. 'I *did* pay the bet, you know, so we're quits again and can start afresh. And I want Billy-boy back.'

He stared at her, puzzled, worried, helpless before the workings of this strange little brain.

'I don't think I quite understand,' he said at last. 'You can't mean, I suppose, that you want Billy as one of your Pierrots? Such a thing is absolutely out of the question!'

'But why?' Verity opened innocent eyes of wide surprise. 'Billy-boy sings like an angel, and he has a perfect ear. As for dancing, you should just try reversing with him—oh, of course you can't—but I give you my word that he's positively divine.'

' "Divine" is certainly the very last term I should think of applying to him!' Grant snapped hastily, forgetting for the moment that he was a parson, and remembering only that he was a man. 'If you insist upon having this performance, I must request that he shall not be included. You cannot have him to practise in your drawing-room. You cannot appear with him on a public platform. I—I shall speak to your mother about it, and in the meantime I absolutely forbid it!'

Verity laughed tunefully, and he was filled with a sudden and rabid desire to shake her.

'Oh, I shouldn't worry about it, if I were you!' she said kindly. 'I was brought up with Billy-boy Blackburn, after a manner of speaking, and I know how to manage him beautifully. He'll be a lamb, you'll see, and dance like a duck. I'm dreadfully sorry, but I feel bound to go on with the entertainment, now it's started. Church History is a little—well—a little *historical*, isn't it?' She smiled angelically. 'And, you know, I *did* pay the salmon on the nail!'

He got up for the last time, also very white, and desperately hurt.

'You are exceedingly foolish!' he said, struggling to speak quietly. 'Foolish and headstrong and very unfair.' He turned rather blindly in the direction of the door. 'And very unkind!' he added, groping among the Mormons for his hat; and Verity bit her lip. It was only to his official side that she mentally put up her fists. When he was boyish and puzzled she wanted to promise everything and give him an orange. But to yield now meant defeat for all time, and that simply couldn't be thought of, so she hardened her heart and refused to let Israel go. The next moment she congratulated herself, for he wrecked his cause at the very door.

'You will be sorry if you do this thing!' he said, losing his tact utterly before her steadier nerve. 'You can't really care about a foolish concert, and who knows what souls may through it be laid to your account? Give it up and come to my help with the Girls' Friendly. I'm badly off for subordinates in several cases, just now. And if you really want to do something artistic, you might teach the Sunday School a little fairy play. Think it over!'

Verity laughed again, but openly, this time, gaily and whole-heartedly. The dear thing was so deliciously funny!

'Billy-boy Blackburn is too old for Sunday

School,' she said pleasantly, 'and I can hardly picture him as a fairy, can you? After all, Billy is the point, you know. Don't you think we might as well be frank and admit it? And I *do* play fair, whatever you say. You mustn't forget that I paid the salmon!'

CHAPTER IX

IN the middle of the long, steep hill up which the village of Crump climbed, Augustus sat firmly on the best green velvet footstool out of his mother's parlour. He was not a model son. Though still in petticoats, and the owner of soft brown eyes and a head of girlish silken hair, his extraordinary determination rendered him far from easy to live with. To desire was to have—with Augustus. He had never any doubts as to the attainment of his end.

His mother, the wife of a prosperous cattle-dealer, came to the door of the low, pink-washed house, and demanded the footstool in peremptory terms; but Augustus merely turned his back upon her, and she retired discomfited, not daring to resort to physical suasion. For Augustus had a voice, and she feared it.

Larruppin' Lyndesay came rocketing over the hill with his cap pulled over his eyes, sitting apparently on the back of his neck. Augustus surveyed his approaching end with the utmost serenity, and stirred not an inch. He was so small that Larrupper nearly missed seeing him altogether, and only managed to stop, his heart in his mouth, when a stout Dunlop tyre was grazing the minute figure with its sash round its knees.

Rising in his seat, he peered over the screen at the lord of the street.

'Treasonable offence, obstructin' the King's Highway!' he informed him severely. ''Tisn't playin' the game, hidin' behind a pebble like that—'tisn't really! Don't mind if I ask you to move, do you, old chap?'

But Augustus, thrusting his thumb into his mouth, merely turned upon him a large gaze of such supercilious condescension that he withdrew his demand on the spot, reversed the car meekly and took a standing jump at the kerb of the green, landing with a rattle that seemed to loosen every bolt. A second rush wedged him neatly between the ancient posts of the churchyard gate, where he was discovered by Deb, coming out of the church, followed by a hounddog of sorts, full of smiles. She stared at him in amazement.

'What in the name of goodness are you doing, Larry?' she demanded unkindly. 'Bringing the car to be christened? I do wish you'd behave decently in *my* village, whatever you do in your own or in Verity's. Take the horrid thing away at once!'

Larrupper, with a final effort, wrenched his new mudguards into freedom, and pushed back his cap, panting.

'I'm hanged if I can understand why life should be so disappointin'!' he grumbled, turning pathetic eyes upon her stern countenance. 'I had to climb up here to avoid slaughterin' somebody's baby, an' then you come along an' pitch into me for jackin' up my own mudguards! By the way, what are you doin' with one of Christian's chickens?'

Deb looked down at the smiling pup at her feet, flapping a curving tail lustily against her skirt.

'It fell upon me, an hour ago,' she explained worriedly, 'and I'm afraid it thinks it has acquired me. We've been playing hide and seek all over the village, and it always wins. I've had an awfully expensive time with it, too. It sampled all the cheeses in Turner's, and ran a cat to earth in an open box of biscuits. I thought I'd escaped it when I rushed in to try the new organ-stop, till I suddenly saw its nose sticking out from under the altar! Do please haul it into the car and run it up to the kennels.'

'Right you are! Sling it over.' Larrupper stretched out an inviting hand, and the puppy backed promptly. 'Come on up—up, my beauty! Here, boy—here! Good dog—good old dog—nice little dog—hang the brute, I'm afraid it isn't havin' any!'

Deb stooped for the hound, but it flopped round to the back of her, and it was only after a wild, teetotum chase that she succeeded in grabbing it. Breathless and dishevelled, she pushed her limp prey into the car, and stood back; whereupon it eluded Larry's grasp with an eel-like wriggle, and instantly fell out again.

'You'll have to come, too,' Larrupper said, alternately shrieking with laughter and trumpeting every hunting call he could think of, but Deb shook an obstinate head.

'No. I'm not coming in that direction at all. It's got to go in the car whether it likes it or not. You can hold it all right if you *try*. And I'm sure there must be something wrong with you, Larry, when so young a dog hates you horribly at first sight!'

Five times she bundled it into the motorist's arms, and five times it escaped him with ease, rushing back to the girl with ecstatic recognition; but the sixth time Larry grabbed hard and drove away like the wind; and a cruelty inspector rushed his bicycle in front of him, and demanded his name and address.

'Shameful, sir! Something shameful!' he stormed, snatching out a notebook, and propping his machine against Larry's new paint. 'Dog was hanging head downwards out of the car—a sight I'd never thought to see in a civilised land—on my word, sir, never! Valuable dog, too, I should say, knowing a bit about dogs and given that way myself, and likely to suffer for it all its days if not put out of its misery at once and shot!'

Larrupper signalled wildly for help, and Deb came up running, weak with hysterical laughter, to be fallen upon rapturously by the quite-un-harmed devil in the machine.

'Tell the man it's Christian's——' Larry began desperately, horribly alarmed by the party in uniform, but the last unfortunate word merely drove the enemy into further frenzied scrapings of paint.

'Christian is just what it *ain't*, sir—anything *but*! —More like them there savage caballyairos, over in Spain! Oh, the dog's the lady's, you say, sir, is it? Makes it all the worse then, being two of you. Your name and address as well, miss, *if* you please!'

It took some time to convince him of the purity of their intentions, and when he finally let them go, it was only on conditions.

'You'll kindly take the dog along yourself,

miss,' he announced firmly, still eyeing Larrupper with distinct distrust. 'Oh, I've no doubt the gentleman *meant* well and all that kind of thing, but to go 'anging an 'armless dog out by the 'eels isn't exactly nice behaviour to *my* way of thinking. So you go along with him, miss, and then I'll be satisfied.'

'But I can't—shan't—won't—don't——!' Deb protested weakly, but he waved her objections to the winds.

'Don't let us have any more arguments, miss,' he entreated plaintively. ''Tisn't a very pleasant subject, now is it, when all 's said and done? Not one as you might *dwell* on. You get in, and I'll hand you the dog.'

They drove away thoroughly chastened, even the puppy having been quiescent in the inspector's grasp, and poor Larry slammed on top speed, seething with exasperation.

'I might have known any sort of a dog-thing would bring me bad luck!' he groaned dismally. 'This'll be fine hearin' for old Dock, won't it? It's sure to be rampin' all over the village before we're well up at the kennels. Why on earth couldn't you come at the beginnin', Debbie dear, an' save us makin' a cinematograph of ourselves?'

'I told you I didn't mean to know you,' she answered firmly, 'and I'm not coming up to the kennels in spite of the inspector, so you can just stop and let me out at Kilne as you pass. Don't you think if you put the puppy under your arm—so—and covered it up with the rug—so—?' She prepared for active experiment, but Larry edged away with a jump, nearly pulling the car into a passing butcher.

'Lord, no, Deb! Keep away. I won't have it! An' you're not even to think of gettin' out. What's the bettin' old Fuss-pot isn't trackin' us for all he's worth? You've got to deliver your own goods, so don't be makin' any more bones about it. I don't know what I've done that you can't bear ridin' with me,' he added, very hurt. 'We've had some rippin' spins together, you an' I, an' now you won't even let me take you the length of the park!'

'How's Verity?' she asked, to change the subject, and Larrupper groaned again.

'It's simply heart-rendin'! Whenever I drop in, she's up to her eyes in music and ankle-deep in patterns of clothin'. She's havin' some sort of a sing-song, you know, an' she's trainin' crowds of the awfullest people you ever saw in your life to sing an' dance an' sit up an' beg. She's never any time for me, nowadays, an' I feel like drownin' myself, Debbie dear. If I fall in, of a mornin', she's always busy makin' blots with tails to them, an' if I stop long enough, I have to listen while she sings the blots to see if they're in the right place. In the afternoon she's dancin' out of a book with a chair or a table or Larry Lyndesay, or any other sort of a block that happens to be standin' about doin' nothin'; an' in the evenin' every blessed squawker in the place is there, makin' night hideous, so I never get any notice worth mentionin'. It's sickenin', I can tell you!'

'You're not half firm enough with her, Larry, and you're a donkey to stand the way she treats you. Why don't you pack her in your pocket and carry her off to the nearest registry-office, without asking her anything about it?'

But Larry shook his head.

'I'm not wantin' her on those terms,' he said. 'I've got a little pride still stickin', for all I'm her ladyship's football, an' when she comes to me it'll have to be jumpin' an' willin', an' not by the hair of her head.'

'Then you'll never get her,' Deb replied, lifting the puppy in her arms as the kennels hove in sight. 'Verity's the sort that has to be captured, and if you don't sail in and do it, you may go on playing round till Doomsday. You *must* put your foot down, Larry!'

'No!' Larry set his mouth. 'No. She's just a little bit above herself an' ready to ride the world, at present, but it won't go on for always. Some day, she'll find that life isn't all beer an' skittles an' top o' the mornin', an' when she scrambles out of the ditch she'll be glad to see me sittin' in the hedge. Till then I can wait—though I'm not sayin' but the hedge is a bit thorny!' He heaved a sigh. 'Hi! Hold on! Where are you goin'?' for Deb had slipped off the car as they neared the gate.

'There isn't any need to drive in,' she said, avoiding the puppy's wild and wet farewells. 'I'll shoot the thing inside—it will wander up all right —and then perhaps you will be kind enough to run me back home.'

Larrupper agreed; but, the next instant, catching sight of two figures above in the field, and with a dim remembrance of a café conversation floating through his mind, made his first effort at diplomacy.

'Oh, but I'm forgettin' I've to see old Brathay!' he announced, bending to gaze at a perfectly satisfactory lubricator. 'If you don't mind, I'll just drive right up an' give him a hail. I want to ask him about some—you know—what-d'you-call-em—what's-its-names!'

Deb hesitated, looking at him suspiciously.

'Oh, of course—if you *want* to go——!' she began reluctantly, a little puzzled. 'But I can see hounds are all out, and you know Brathay always has a fit if there's a motor within a mile of the pack. *I* know! I'll wait here with the car while you run up to the kennels; and you can take the puppy with you.'

'Not much!' Larry refused flatly. 'I wouldn't touch the thing with a ten-foot pole. I'm simply a yawnin' death-trap for dogs—it would never reach its cubby-hole alive. An' if you think I'm goin' to leave you waitin' in the mud like a beastly chauffeur—how do, Laker, old man! Where have you been puttin' yourself all the week?'

'Rather neat groupin'!' he congratulated himself, leaning anxiously over a sound and blameless wheel, while Deb swung round with the puppy in her arms, to meet Christian's pleasant smile and a grave bow from the stranger beside him.

'One of the puppies'—she explained hurriedly and incoherently, put out by the sudden encounter, though unaware of Larrupper's machinations. Wandering about the village—cheese—had Brathay missed it? Yes, it looked a good one—and such jolly things they were, too, weren't they?—oh, only too glad, of *course*—*any*body would—and it was more than time that she was getting back.

'But I want to show you our improvements,' Christian protested, taking the hound from her, and introducing his companion. 'Mr. Callander —Miss Lyndesay—my cousin, Larrup—I say,

Lionel, what on earth *do* you call yourself? Mr. Callander's frightfully pleased with the kennels. I do want you to look round and give everything your blessing—please!'

'Tell your father what's doin', an' all that kind of thing,' Larry supplemented, with amazing readiness, and again clapped himself on the back, for she yielded at once. She never denied her father information concerning the least detail of the estate.

She walked up the field between the two men, puzzling out a means of escape, and listening vaguely to Christian's thanks for her salving of the puppy, while Larry followed with the car, hooting furiously at inquisitive noses and waving sterns. Her last visit to the kennels had been made with her father and Stanley—the conversation including 'points' on the one side, and 'The Merry Widow' on the other. She had wondered why hounds had met Stanley with distant recognition while greeting her father with effusive joy; and she had wondered, moreover—but what was the use of wondering, *now*?

'I'm hunting them myself, this season,' Christian was saying. 'I used to hunt them for Sl——' he cast a glance at his agent—'for Stanley, you remember, when I was at home. Sl—Stanley—wasn't keen on the sport—left it to Brathay, as a rule. It's good exercise, if you care about that kind of thing, and now that I've given up the games——'

Larrupper let out a yell that brought the old keeper racing down the hill with his heart in his mouth.

'Give up the games? You're rottin', Laker!

Give up the wrestlin' and the jumpin' an' the footer an' the—Brathay, my good idiot, the whole blessed lot are as safe as houses, as you could see for yourself if you were any use at countin'!'

'I do mean it,' Christian replied, looking at the ground. 'I've—there's a lot to see to, now, you know, and games are rather a waste of time—I suppose.'

'Footlin' piffle! You don't mean to be gluin' yourself to the place all your life, do you? Your agent will keep it runnin' all right if he's a decent chap; an' you *are* a decent chap, aren't you, Mr. — afraid-your-name's-gone-missin'? *Slinker* had time for playin' round a bit, we all know *that*! *Slinker* had his little hobbies——'

'Your engine has stopped, Lionel.'

'Who's mindin'? Crump'll jog along in the same old cart-track without you everlastin'ly shovin' behind; and, hang it all, man, you'll be wantin' a bit of amusement *some*time! What's worryin' you *now*, Brathay dear? I wish you'd run away an' play!'

'Can't count more than fifteen couple, sir. Rest must be somewheres about, and hounds is that curious—likely they're some of them underneath.'

'An' likely they're roostin' inside the bonnet as well, you—you old Buff Orpin'ton! Now look here, Brathay. I'm doin' no harm on your rubbishin' premises, an' I won't be hustled off for all the over-fed, under-run hounds in creation!'

'You make hounds that nervous, sir! They're very easy upset.'

'You're dreamin', Brathay! Why, the darlin's simply dote on engines. I've never been out with them yet but they've gone steamin' full lick for the line whenever a train came along. Laker, tell him I won't be bullied!'

'Do you good!' Christian smiled, nodding to the old keeper; and the sounds of violent altercation followed him as he led the way to the kennels. Brathay and Larrupper were joyful enemies of long standing.

'I remember, now!' Callander said suddenly, as they reached the door. 'I saw a picture of you somewhere in wrestling-kit—one of the papers, I forget which—and your nickname—"Lakin"' Lyndesay, isn't it? I thought I knew your face.'

'That's it.' Christian looked uncomfortable. 'Some bounder caught me with a camera, I suppose. It's a good game——' He broke off abruptly. 'You remember old Rosebud, of course, Deborah?'

He spoke the name stiffly but with determination, definitely sealing their distant relationship and their slight but ancient acquaintance. 'The Lyndesays stood by you!' she found herself quoting inwardly, as she caressed the old hound, and took the puppies in her arms, while Christian pointed out the alterations in the buildings. Callander, who had an artist's eye, looked with interest from the quiet young master to the bright face of the kneeling girl lifted above the soft heads of white and tan. He remembered Christian well enough, now—had heard of him at Grasmere, at Olympia, at the Highland Games. It was a curious record for a son of so proud and ancient a family, but perhaps it was better than the one left by his brother. Already his ears were filled with the gossip running rife in the countryside; and, watching the clear eyes and the brave bearing of the heroine of the drama, he wondered greatly where the truth of the matter lay. Not in the mere sordid love of riches, surely, nor in the foolish, flattered vanity of youth? Behind, he felt, was something deeper, out of reach.

There was no sign of Larrupper when they came out, and Brathay, with a grim face, his fingers shut upon a lordly tip, explained that he had evicted him without ceremony; whilst Larry, who had instructed him thereto, chuckled with Machiavellian glee as he raced homeward.

'I will walk back with you, if I may,' Christian said, opening the little gate of the stile. 'Shall we go by the park?' And when Deb hesitated— 'Why, surely you don't prefer the road, do you?' he added, in surprise.

She did not answer—she could not tell him she had never set foot in the park since the day of Stanley's death—and, while she stood silent, Callander bade them good-bye and struck off towards the marsh. Christian kept his hand on the gate.

'There will be frost, to-night,' he said, looking over the land. 'The deer will be making for the buckhouse. The beeches are stripping fast, and the river is like glass. Do you really prefer the road?'

Did she? She walked beside him over the springy turf, while the red ball of the sun dipped towards the bay, wondering why every channel of love should be always first and foremost a channel of pain. The quiet of the old woods etched black against the yellow sky caught her by the throat. The silver river smote her like a sword. The homing rooks called the heart out of her. And the land—the green, good homeland around and beneath her—ah! *did* she prefer the road?

'How quiet the hills are!' Christian broke silence, half-way across the park. 'Have you ever noticed how the first frost stills them like the touch of a cold finger? In summer they are almost restless, but as the winter strengthens they gradually fall asleep. I like them best asleep.'

She made no reply, and he felt rebuffed. Perhaps she did not care for that sort of thing. Perhaps, as his mother had said, it was the house that called her, the position and pride of place—he thought suddenly of her pictured eyes in Slinker's room, and put the charge from him self-reproachfully; then remembered that she had seemed to prefer the road, and was chilled anew.

Down in a hollow, a couple of panting, writhing forms thrust apple-red cheeks over each other's shoulder, and he checked at once, forgetting the girl in his sudden interest.

'The Younger Generation!' he laughed, watching the herculean if highly unscientific efforts of the children, and, drawn gradually nearer in spite of himself, began to issue instructions.

'Your hold is too high, Jimmy. Get your feet more apart—you, whatever your name is. Now! right foot—lift—strike inside—got him!'

He came back to Deb apologetically, after superintending the traditional handshake of etiquette.

'I'm ever so sorry to have kept you standing about, waiting! You must think I'm horribly rude, and of course you're wanting to get home. I've always been crazy about the sport—I suppose because it's our own. It's a fine thing for a county to have its own game, to feel that it's bred in the very bone of you, and that it calls you as it calls no one else on earth. It marks a county's character, too, keeps it individual and strong. And I couldn't let them go on making a muddle of it, could I? You see, it's at the start that things matter. Catch them early—that's the way to get style. Later on, when a man's set——' He looked at her averted head. 'But of course all this can't possibly interest you.'

'Can you tell me the time?' she asked, without turning. (Would they never cross the park?) And then, almost as if the words had been dragged out of her—'It's a fine sport,' she added, and again Christian wondered, not knowing that his speech had put the final touch to the fierce passion of heritage which was tearing her asunder as she walked dumbly at his side.

On the bridge he stopped again, to look through the frost-mist on the river to Crump, bare and lone against its black shield of woods and the cold sky overhead; but Deborah hurried on, and, as she turned the corner, saw him still gazing. She had another picture of the bridge, now, for all time—one that had Christian's face clear-cut by the frosty light against the darkening slope of the hill.

He caught her up before she reached the house.

'You're the only Lyndesay I ever knew who didn't stop on that bridge!' he said reproachfully. 'Nearly everybody stops on bridges, haven't you noticed it? It must be because they feel a little bit nearer Heaven. But you didn't stop, and I'm afraid you preferred the road!'

She looked up at him, conscious that he guessed at the existence of her mask, yet ready to fight for it at all costs.

'Perhaps I did!' she answered casually, and stood aside to let her father greet him in the porch.

Christian sat for long in the little, lamp-lit parlour overlooking the river, while the old man told him tales of farm and field with the easy memory and sure knowledge of one who carries recollection in his heart. Deborah came down at last to find them standing at the window, the fair head close to the white one, and Roger Lyndesay's hand marking the curve of the hill under the sharp light of the risen moon.

'Cappelside?' the old man was saying. 'I could find my way to Cappelside in a blinding blizzard! 'Twas there I courted my wife, as my father before me. Lyndesay stewards love all Crump better than their own souls, but they love Cappelside best. They will be found there, sure enough, when the earth gives up its dead!'

'How you feel about the old place!' Christian exclaimed. 'It's home to me, of course, but, if love alone were a claim, you'd have a better right to it than I. Yes, and by right of work, too, your own and your fathers', Crump should be yours, Mr. Lyndesay!'

'Crump *is* mine!' Roger Lyndesay returned, with curious emphasis and conviction. 'Do you think either deed or descent could give it me as the long years of labour and knowledge have done? You are master, and I am only servant and lover, but I own it, in my heart. Crump *is* mine!'

Christian's voice was very gentle as he bade the

old man good-night. 'I will try to hold it worthily for you,' he said; then smiled whimsically at Deb. 'But *you* preferred the road!'

CHAPTER X

SLINKER's wife was restless on Christmas Eve. At dinner, she talked in feverish snatches, and ate nothing; and, when the dismal meal was over at last, she wandered nervously from room to room, lifting blind after blind to look at the white waste of the park. Christian followed her like a puzzled dog, oppressed once more by the mighty loneliness which had lifted a little since her coming, until she turned on him brusquely with a little jump.

'For goodness' sake, Laker, don't go trailing after me like a broken bootlace! I'm a bundle of nerves, to-night, and not fit to speak to; its the snow, I suppose.' She shivered, looking almost fearfully at the inky spectres of the avenue flung upon the sinister white of the hill. 'How near it is! Somehow it makes me feel as if I couldn't breathe. Life can make you feel like that, too; as if you'd fastened yourself into your coffin, and couldn't get out.

'And couldn't—*couldn't* get out!' she repeated, beating her hands on the frosty pane; and the next instant had opened the hall-door and was half-way down the steps before he realised that she had gone. Springing after her, he caught her arm and drew her back forcibly into the warmth.

'What's the matter with you, to-night, Nettie? You're not a bit like yourself! This isn't the weather for moonlight walks, and I can't have you catching your death of cold while you're in my charge. Come and sit by the fire, and let us talk.'

He struck the log with his foot, sending up a shower of sparks, but she drew away from him, and back again to the door. He looked at her in surprise. He had never seen her like this—her eyes wide, every nerve tensely strung.

'I'm going out!' she said quickly. 'Don't try to stop me. I'm not ragging, Youngest One—I *must* go! Yes, fetch me something to put on, like an old dear, only be quick about it.'

He brought a coat and a scarf and wrapped her in them, and gave her his hand down the slippery steps; but when he would have come further she checked him imperatively.

'I'm going alone,' she said, pushing him gently from her, 'so scoot back at once, Laker child! I'm not going far, and I'm going alone. I shan't take any harm, so don't get excited, and if you dare to sit and freeze on the steps, I'll leave Crump to-morrow! I can't stop in the house, to-night, and that's all there is about it. It's full of Slinker from garret to cellar, and I just can't bear it. Couldn't you feel him at dinner—that awful ghost-walk of a dinner? I wondered how you could sit in your chair and swallow your port! He was there, all the time—just shrieking to come back! Oh, Christian!—suppose he should?'

He took her hand again, looking at her with concern.

'Why, Nettie, there's certainly something very wrong with you! Come back into the house and sing something, and let's be happy. There is nothing to be afraid of. How could there be any thing to be afraid of on Chistmas Eve?'

She clung to his fingers, staring up at the house.

'I should hear Slinker singing along with me. He had a voice, you remember—a queer sort of voice like an owl squawking in the night! Christian—suppose that window opened up there, and Slinker's face looked out—Slinker's face—Christian——!'

He gave her a peremptory little shake.

'Stop that at once—do you hear? And you're just coming back with me, this instant, so you can make up your mind to do as you're told for once, instead of twisting the whole world round your little finger!'

She shook her head, pulling herself together with a trembling sigh and a smile.

'No, I'm going on. It's all right, Youngest One. I'm quite sane, and perfectly fit to be loose. Go in and wait for me in the hall, and brew me some nice warm gruel to drink when Christmas comes in. I'm going to the place where I'm safest in the whole world. Oh, if I'd only guessed it, long ago!'

He watched her disappear up the avenue, a dark speck on the purity of the white track, walking firmly and with purpose, and then he returned reluctantly to thaw himself, keeping an eye on the half-open door the while. No sound came to him from any part of the house but the creak of the stairs and the running talk of the fire. In the oak chair with a high back he looked very young and very lonely—the new master sharing his shadowed home with his ghosts.

Slinker's wife walked fast—fast, like a woman going to meet her lover—and her heart beat and the colour burned in her cheek. She clasped her hands tight in the wide sleeves of Christian's coat, and her breath came unevenly on the frosty air. Leaving the arch of the avenue for the full moonlight, she saw beneath her a wide sheet of bright ice, and, to the right, the long, low buildings of Dockerneuk Farm. She stopped, then, as if a hand had barred her way, trembling violently and leaning against the stoup of the gate.

Work was long done, at the farm. The clash of milk-pails was still, long before. The cattle had had their extra Christmas feed, and the men had gone home. The blinds were drawn. The kitchen had red blinds through which lamp and fire glowed warm. From the parlour a piano tinkled a Christmas hymn.

Slinker's wife, leaning against the stoup, needed no open doors for her sad eyes. She knew so well the wide kitchen with its open range and oak settle, the spotless stone of the floor, the shining pans, the queer things that hung from the oak rafters, hams and Christmas puddings and great, dry bunches of sage. She knew the parlour, too, with its yellow-keyed, silk-faced piano, its pot dogs, wool mats and vases of honesty; but it was to the kitchen that the passionate eyes of her mind strayed and stayed. For Dixon would be in the kitchen.

She saw him as she had seen him often in the old days, when the tie of a distant relationship through her mother had brought her to Dockerneuk for many a long week; saw him in his deep wooden chair by the steel fender, his dog's head against his knee, as they listened together to the little hymn played by his sister's child. The door would be open between the rooms, she knew. Dixon loved both children and music.

He would be sitting very still in his big chair, with that curious, almost fateful stillness of the men bred in the dales. His tall, slow-moving figure would be bent a little, his square, quiet hand laid along the smooth wood of the chair-arm, his tranquil face turned towards the fire.

It would be such a good fire, too—Slinker's wife, through Christian's warm coat, felt the cold strike her like a knife—a great, roaring, glowing, gladsome fire, filling full the big mouth of the chimney, and flinging splashes of brightness over the half-shadowed room. There would be holly, too, perhaps, and a bunch of mistletoe over the outer door. Dixon had once wanted to kiss her under a bunch of mistletoe. He had held her hands and looked at her with grave eyes, but he would not kiss her in jest. Slinker's wife, laying her head against the icy stone, knew that the mistletoe might have saved her. But Dixon had not known that you may win or lose the whole world with a kiss; or perhaps he had known it too well, and would not dare the risk.

The piano stopped suddenly, and the parlour went dark, so that she knew the door into the kitchen had shut. The child was going to bed. Dixon would stoop his tall head to bid her good-night, and presently her feet would patter on the polished, carpetless stair. His old mother would be waiting to settle her warm and safe for the night, and to steal in later with sweeties for her little stocking. Soon he would go upstairs himself, and the lights in Dockerneuk would slide out silently; and, when the moon sank, the dark would swallow it up as if it had never been. Slinker's wife hid her face against the stoup and cried aloud, and one of the fine-eared dogs in the stable heard her, and barked quick and deep. The kitchen door opened instantly in response, and Dixon came out into the porch.

He did not need his dog's repeated signal, for he could see her figure plainly enough under the moon, but some instinct kept him from speaking until he was near enough to discern her face. She stayed quiet, leaning against the stone, and they looked into each other's eyes.

'It's sharp, to-night,' he said gravely, and saluted her with a raised finger. The tiny action put the whole world between them. 'Were you wanting anything of me, Mrs. Lyndesay of Crump?'

She shook her head. 'Nothing. I—it's Christmas Eve. I just—walked up.' She gathered her courage, and looked up at him again. 'Can I come in?' she begged. 'I want to come in—oh, please—let me come in!'

But Dixon shook his head.

'Crump's your place. You chose Crump. You'd a right to choose for yourself—I'm not denying that. But it's done, and you must bide by it. You've finished with Dockerneuk for ever.'

'No, no! Oh, no, no——!' she stammered, suddenly broken-hearted like a child wrenched from a happiness just within its grasp. She put out her hands, the quick tears running down her face. 'Anthony—I've come back. Why did you ever let me go? Anthony, take me in!'

And again he shook his head.

'You chose Crump!' he repeated doggedly. 'All the wishing in the world won't change it. You're Crump, now, and Crump you must bide till you die.' He moved forward. 'They'll be missing you at the Hall. I'll set you back.'

But she caught his arm, brave through her confidence in the man's fine nature and his faithful love.

'Ah, don't turn me away! It's my home, for all you may say—mine as well as yours. I belong to you and to Dockerneuk, though I never knew it until it was too late. You'll take me back, Anthony—you'll take me back?'

He gathered her cold hands into his warm ones.

'I've thought the world of you always,' he said. 'Your place was ready for you ever after I had once set eyes on you. I could scarce bring myself to bolt the door of a night because it seemed to shut you out, and yet the house had you in every corner. I used to sit, of an evening, and think I heard you laugh—you were so close. And in the morning, when I came in from the shippons, I'd look to see your face at the window. But, when you married Lyndesay, you shut the door yourself, and I never saw your shadow in the old place again. You went into a different world, and I couldn't follow you. You're Crump, now, and you'll never be Dockerneuk no more. You've learned quality's ways such as I never learned— fine talk and fine manners, dinners, carriages and footmen. What-like would farm-life seem to you, *now*? You've had a gentleman to your husband— a liar and a wastrel, happen, but a Lyndesay and quality for all that. Dixon of Dockerneuk's not quality, and you'd remember it—ay, and I'd know you remembered! It would be hell for both of us. If once you're quit of your own folk, there's never any getting back in this world, for it's you that changes, no matter how you may think things look the same. There's no help—no way out. You left me and Dockerneuk behind you, and all the longing in the world won't ever bring you home.'

She tightened her clasp on his, and spoke steadily for the first time.

'There's no change can harm love,' she said. 'I didn't know, when I married Stanley, but I knew, soon after. I knew that you were the best thing in my life—ah, no!—that you were the whole of it! I married Stanley for Crump, right enough, but when once I saw clear, I never raised a finger to take it. I knew where my real place should have been, by then, and I wouldn't come. I came when he was dead, because, when once I was free, I couldn't stop away from you and never see you; just as I'll stay, Anthony, till you take me in, if I've to come begging like a tramp every night to ask it!'

'I can't believe it!' Dixon's voice was harsh and troubled. 'It's not likely you'll ever stoop to me, now. Think what folk'll say—Dockerneuk after Crump! You've got to make me sure it's right before I'll take the risk for you. I'll not snatch at what I want, and be hated for it all my days. I couldn't bide that—to see you eating out your heart for things I couldn't give you. You're Mrs. Lyndesay's darling, nowadays, they say. She'll find another Lyndesay for you, likely, or some other of the quality.' The first touch of bitterness crept into his voice. 'I can't think you'd ever be happy with me. 'Tisn't in reason. You've got to prove it.'

'How can I prove it better than by being here

to-night?' she asked piteously. 'Did you ever know Nettie Stone go on her knees before?'

'It's not enough,' he answered, loosing her hands; and a cloud went over the moon. 'It's not enough! To-night's to-night, but there's half a lifetime to think other in. Only prove it, and you'll find every stone of Dockerneuk calling for you; but till then we must go our different ways, and bide it as we may.'

They descended the avenue in silence, to meet Christian speeding anxiously up it. His face lightened when he saw Dixon, though he made no comment; only gave him a Christmas greeting, and pressed Crump hospitality upon him. But Dixon refused obstinately.

'Thank you kindly, sir, but I'd best be getting back. I left the door open, and my old mother'll likely get feared. *He* never asked me, Mr. Christian, and he's been dead such a short while. I can't rightly feel that he isn't still there.'

'You've infected him, Nettie!' Christian said, as lightly as he could, when Dixon had vanished among the trees. 'You've told him all the things you thought you saw, and all the other things you thought you felt.'

'I told him nothing,' she answered bitterly, 'but I'm not surprised. He felt the chain at my heel. If you put your life into the hands of a man like Slinker, you'll never quite escape him after, alive or dead!'

In the hall, she slipped out of his coat, and he brought her a steaming glass; and, as she took it from him, over the snow-smooth park the bells began to ring. Christian opened the door, and let the joy of them flood the sombre hall. The

clock struck in the dimness under the stair, and
at the foot of the steps the fiddler broke into his
thin, wailing hymn, and the shouter cried them
their Christmas mirth. Mrs. Slinker laid her hand
lightly on Christian's shoulder, and kissed him.

'A Merry Christmas to you, Laker, my dear!'
she said, with a thrill in her voice and a kindly
look. 'Here's luck to Lakin' Lyndesay!' and she
lifted her glass and drank. Then she raised it
again, turning south to Dockerneuk. 'And here's
the right home to every soul, and to all the lost
dogs a-seeking!'

CHAPTER XI

DEB turned from earnest contemplation of a
window of tinned fruits to find the Hon. Mrs.
Stalker's carriage at the grocer's steps; that august
personage herself enthroned therein, wearing a
fur garment of such dimensions as to send all the
Crump cats scuttling for shelter to the nearest
drain. The coachman touched his hat, but the
great lady appeared to find the street perfectly
empty, though Deb stared defiantly, her back to
the tinned fruits. Silver-hair Savaury of Tasser,
marking the situation from the Post Office,
hurried to her relief.

He bestowed a sweeping bow upon furred grandeur as he passed, and the Honourable smiled and
put out a hand, for Savaury of Tasser was 'quite
all right', and not to be ignored by anybody; but
Savaury merely waved a lavender glove gracefully in her face, and, throwing her an airy 'Re-
joiced to see you, dear lady! So sorry—important
business,' pulled up in front of Deb. 'Can you

come to dinner?' he added loudly, with his back to greatness, and all Crump heard him.

A faint giggle came from somewhere behind the Honourable's tiger-skin, but Deb was too much upset to catch it. She looked at her knight with more doubt than gratitude in her eyes.

'Thanks very much—I don't think I can——' she hesitated, praying for escape, and Savaury snorted and waved his glove again.

'Oh, of course you can come! I insist. You can tell me about the new stop on the organ. I can't manage it—so tiresome! And Petronilla thinks she's got mumps or appendicitis or something. It will do her good to have a dinner-party. When? Oh, let me see! Hardly to-morrow, of course—no! Shall we say Wednesday?—yes! Now don't be tiresome and send us back word. May I walk with you as far as the park? Oh, you're not going that way? I'm sorry.' The Honourable was about to descend personally upon the shop, and he raised his voice as Deb fled. 'Petronilla sent you a message, by the way. Wants you to go with her to the Cantacute concert—Verity's performance, you know. And don't forget about Wednesday!'

A second chuckle came from the victoria, and he looked round quickly. Slinker's wife, glowing like a rose in her dark furs, leaned towards him.

'Won't you ask me, too?' she begged prettily. 'Don't pretend you don't know me just because we haven't been introduced. My grandfather was your grandfather's stable-boy at Tasser, so that's quite a bond, isn't it, and ought to make us friends on the spot! Do ask me to dinner, there's a dear thing. I want to meet that nice girl ever so badly.'

'But—but—my dear lady——!' Savaury stammered helplessly, clutching at his hat, and dropping the lavender glove to a slushy bed.

'I'm not a lady. I'm old Steenie Stone's daughter. But I'm an imitation Lyndesay, nowadays, for my sins, so you can ask me to dinner quite comfortably, without upsetting your ancestors.'

'Of course—of course!' Savaury managed a gallant smile. 'But I was not aware that you were—going out—and—there's Miss Lyndesay!' he bungled desperately, hoping fervently that the men-servants were not listening.

'Oh—etiquette!' Slinker's wife flapped her big muff contemptuously. 'It's a bit late to start being conventional about this affair, isn't it— Stanley's general behaviour, I mean, and mine?' He cocked a nervous ear, and she shrugged her shoulders. 'Oh, it's all right! They know a good deal more about it than you do. I belong to them, you see, so I don't value their opinion like you aristocrats!'

She smiled at him enchantingly, and he responded involuntarily, though inwardly sadly pained.

'As for Miss Lyndesay, she'll get used to me. People do, you know. Mrs. Stalker's taking me back with her to tea, so I *am* going out, you see. And I'm just dying to know that girl, so you'll ask me, won't you?'

'Certainly—only too delighted—honoured— enraptured!' Savaury murmured, as fascinated as any rabbit by a boa-constrictor. 'But you must admit it will be a little bit *awkward*.'

'Oh, well, I'll bring Christian along, as well,' she said kindly; 'and then, if things are going wrong, you can shove him in between. Christian's a beautiful buffer. Don't you fret. We'll worry through, somehow, and come up smiling. Wednesday? All right. You're a duck!

'I eat quite decently, at table!' she called after him, as he turned rather blindly up the street, 'and I don't need introducing to a finger-glass. And—oh, yes!—I always take a fork to sweets. Thought I'd better tell you—save you worrying, don't you know!' and he could hear that she was still laughing as he stumbled, gasping, into the saddler's, and gave a lengthy order for tea-cakes.

'So tiresome!' he condoled with himself, peering round the doorpost to make sure that the coast was clear before emerging. 'Really a most distressing occurrence, not to say calamitous. And yet, without doubt, a decidedly pleasant woman! But, goodness gracious, how am I to tell Petronilla!'

Petronilla took it very well on the whole, being a woman of character, whose quietly-regal demeanour was equal to most situations; but it was a distinctly nervous host and hostess that awaited their guests on Wednesday evening in the long, low-ceiled room, where the lamplight caught the flowers in the old punch-bowls, and the firelight rippled along the shining surface of chintz and deep-tinted china, and warmed the mellow delicacy of the miniatures on the walls.

'If only she would come *first*—Deborah, I mean!' Savoury agitated, all black and white and pink and silver, waving eyeglasses distractedly on the hearth-rug. 'Then I could take her aside and just *explain* to her, while you kept the others away till she settled down. I wish you'd have let me tell her beforehand, just to get her broken *in*; and then—well, then——'

'*Then* she wouldn't have come!' Petronilla finished serenely.

'Well, no, I don't suppose she would. But you must admit it's simply *horrid*, not to say *painful*! Suppose she won't bow, or goes out and walks home in the mud? And I ordered such an extremely nice dinner!'

'She won't do that. Deborah is too well-bred to make her hosts uncomfortable. What *I'm* wondering is how the High Sheriff will take the horse-dealer's daughter. He's a Radical, you know. And I'd quite forgotten that Crump used to owe Whyterigg a grudge—oh, dear! Still, it's a very long time ago, and one can't ask just *any*body to meet Mr. Lyndesay, even if it *is* only Christian. But a horse-dealer's daughter! Perhaps she'll get on with the parson.'

'Don't you pin your faith to the parson!' (Savaury seemed to have followed this curious speech with perfect ease). 'Mrs. Stanley isn't the parson-sort, from what *I* saw of her. Oh, I don't mind *anything* if only Deborah doesn't try to shoot her! I hope to goodness she'll come first!'

But Deborah did not come first. She came last, hoping to escape the painful minutes before dinner, so that the stage was fully set by the time she entered the warm, delicately-tinted room. The High Sheriff was discussing the exact date of the carved fireplace with his hostess, dropping an occasional lofty remark to Christian, while Slinker's wife, her dark head framed by an alcove panelled in yellow satin brocade, and crowned by the blue and gold of old Worcester on a white shelf, dragged the Arevar parson across Canada with a celerity which left him gasping. The High Sheriff's sister and the parson's sister sat together on the broad chintz sofa, listening politely to the Crump doctor, who was saying nothing. They had been born to sit on sofas out of the limelight.

Deb took in the group at a glance, and for a moment she stood still in the middle of the room, lifting her head with the startled grace of Christian's fallow deer; every line of her rigid with reproach in her white gown, as she cast a steady look of condemnation at the conscience-stricken Savaury, who prepared for any catastrophe in that fateful second.

But Petronilla saved the situation. Leaving the High Sheriff with a weighty sentence hanging in the balance, she moved placidly forward, took the girl's hand and kissed her; then flung her into Mrs. Slinker's arms before she had time to retreat.

Slinker's wife made no attempt to hold her; merely gave her a courteous bow and smile, and continued to expand the parson's mind, at the same time manœuvring Christian skilfully and unobtrusively forward. Deborah found herself inquiring after the runaway puppy in perfectly normal tones, though the miniatures swam round her, and a helpless fury possessed her galloping heart. It was not until she met the disapproving gaze of the High Sheriff's sister that she became fighting-cool. The High Sheriff's sister had cut her in Witham. To-night Deborah Lyndesay cut the High Sheriff's sister.

Yet the dinner passed smoothly, for all the high tension and the warring sympathies. It was a frantic situation, as everybody realised, but convention has its own transforming magic. Savaury, in after years, when the terror of it had left him, was known to say that it was the most successful dinner he had ever given. Perhaps everybody made a special effort, even the sofa-people. Perhaps the spice of danger in the air lent the touch of excitement necessary to brilliance. Perhaps both accounted for it—or neither. Perhaps just the wizardry of Mrs. Slinker, with her heart knocking for admittance at Dockerneuk gates. Savaury was at her feet before he had swallowed his first fish-bone. The High Sheriff's head had turned in her direction by the time the entrée was served. And when dessert had been reached without fiasco, she had the whole table listening to her.

Christian looked at her with affectionate admiration; then back to Deborah at his side, remembering with some bewilderment their unrewarding stroll across the park, and her steadily-averted head. To-night she had plenty to say; to-night he saw the curve of her mouth and the even flash of her teeth, the satisfaction of a clear skin and the clean line of a cheek that has centuries of straight breeding behind it. Glancing from that revealing profile to her hands, so strangely like his own, for the first time he realised their kinship with a thrill of pleasure and pride. As for her, she had long ceased to look at him; for, where a man matters, a woman looks at him once for all time. She knew by heart his easy grace, the light on his hair and the charm of his quiet eyes.

They were in full tide of a discussion on wire-fencing—amazingly and volubly interested—when Slinker's wife leaned forward and addressed Deborah deliberately across the table. She wore

black, to-night, as a concession to poor Savaury
and his ancestors, and her vivid face rose from a
cloud of soft drapery which spelt Crump's widow
as little as it spelt horse-dealer's daughter.

'I want you to tell me, please,' she said, 'the way
to the wishing-well in the Pixies' Wood. Christian says he has forgotten it, and Mrs. Lyndesay
says she never knew it. But of course your father's
daughter will know it. You *can* tell me, can't
you?'

'Why, yes!' Deborah answered, without stopping to think. (How could she resist such a question? Oh, weirdly-wise Mrs. Slinker!) 'The path
is lost, now, but I knew it well, in my childhood,
and I couldn't forget it if I tried. Old 'Buck'
Lyndesay fought a right of way over it, you know,
and though he lost, he shut it in the teeth of the
law and everybody else, and by degrees people
gave up going, when they got tired of pulling
down the wall in protest. Some say that the well
is lost altogether, but that isn't true.'

'And how does one start to find it?'

'Oh, it's easy enough, at first. You take the
bridle path through the Home Plantation, and
break out along the common to the foot of the
Pixies' steps. You must shut your eyes when you
climb the steps, or the pixies will turn you blind;
and always, always you must pluck the gorse that
grows at the top, and think of the one that you
love best, or you may leave your heart behind
you! Then you see the great pine from which a
Lyndesay flew the flag that threw his father's
yacht on Aill Sands; and, after that, a long,
feathery line of firs like fairy fingers beckoning
from a moss-green velvet sleeve. And on the left,

where the wood sinks and the bracken grows to
your waist, the well lies in a limestone cup——'

She broke off, meeting the wonder in Christian's eyes, and knowing herself hopelessly betrayed; and Slinker's wife, too wise to press the
situation further, smiled her thanks, and turned
a polite ear to the High Sheriff, who, either because of his position or his politics, thought himself justified in addressing her across the parson's
sister and the dumb doctor.

'Suppose we find it together?' he suggested,
kindly. 'Christian has asked me over to lunch,
next week, I believe, and I—I collect wells. I'm
sure we could find it together!'

Rishwald was forty and still unmarried, hand-
some, if pompous, rich and immensely run after,
so that the table gasped at his amazing condescension, whilst Petronilla offered up spiritual
sacrifice to every fetich she possessed; but Slinker's wife merely shook her head, smiling.

'It is only safe to visit a wishing-well with one
of three people,' she said gently; 'yourself, another
woman, or—the Right Man.' And in the clear
well of wine in her hand she saw Dixon of Dockerneuk's face.

'So you didn't *really* prefer the road!' Christian
murmured in Deborah's ear, and became ac-
quainted a second time with the back of her
head.

'Yes, I did!' she returned obstinately. 'Shall
I tell you what I wished for when I last visited the
fairy well? A motor-car!'

'That's a lie!' Christian said in his gentle voice,
and the farthest person from him was the only
other that heard him—the High Sheriff's sister—

and she had her own reason. Even sofa-people may have longings eating the heart out of them.

'I'll prove it to you!' he added quickly. 'I've had an offer for that wood, just this last week. There's some especially fine timber, they say, and I could do with the cash to spend on the farms. The wood will be just as fine again in another hundred years or so. So I'll write to-morrow, closing with the offer——'

Although he was prepared in a measure, he started before the Deborah that faced round on him with blazing eyes and trembling hands.

'You dare!' she cried, under her breath, but as fiercely as if she had shrieked. 'You dare! You just *dare* to touch a root of those trees——!' She saw the trap, then, and stopped, but she was still trembling when he rose, laughing, to make way for her, as Petronilla left the table.

'I was right!' he whispered exultantly. 'I was right, and you are a wicked deceiver. You *didn't* prefer the road!'

Later, they played Pope Joan in the hall, with a wonderful old gilded bowl and mother-of-pearl counters; Rishwald planting himself firmly beside Mrs. Slinker, and magnanimously paying her double when she won, though she was both a luckier and a better player than he. There was no mistaking his complete captivation, and Nettie, as he slid the counters tenderly towards her, thought of Dixon's words. She had got into a different world; she would marry into that world a second time; there was no going back for those who once stepped out.

Savaury, who detested cards, played soft nothings on a dim piano, and, at the end of the first game, moved by some unaccountable impulse, invited the horse-dealer's daughter to sing. Nettie got up at once, glad to escape further mother-of-pearl attentions, and went across to him. She sang 'Veils'.

> I drew betwixt us blue mist of the main,
> The gray mist of an English winter's rain,
> The black mist of intolerable pain:
> Yet, if I draw even Death between us twain,
> Through its white mist I still shall see you plain.

'A silly little song!' Savaury snorted, by way of gratitude. 'A tiresome, silly little song—quite too absurd! For goodness' sake sing something else!' and sang the silly little song in his sentimental little heart for the rest of the night.

Mrs. Slinker laughed. A song, like any other work of art, can only give you what you bring to it, and Savaury had never needed to shroud his soul from Petronilla—Petronilla and her Pope Joan bowl, framed in her old-world hall.

'Sing again!' Savaury commanded; and she sang—

> All in the April evening,[1]
> April airs were abroad;
> The sheep with their little lambs
> Passed me by on the road.
>
> The sheep with their little lambs
> Passed me by on the road;
> All in the April evening
> I thought on the Lamb of God.
>
> The lambs were weary, and crying
> With a weak, human cry.
> I thought on the Lamb of God
> Going meekly to die.
>
> Up in the blue, blue mountains
> Dewy pastures are sweet:

[1] Katharine Tynan.

Rest for the little bodies,
Rest for the little feet.

But for the Lamb of God,
Up on the hill-top green,
Only a Cross of shame,
Two stark crosses between.

All in the April evening,
April airs were abroad;
I saw the sheep with their lambs,
And thought on the Lamb of God.

April was in the room when she ended—April,
full of the passionate hope and the heart-break
that make each spring an agony of resurrection.
She heard the lambs cry as they turned in at the
gate of Dockerneuk fold. She heard Dixon's call
to his dog and the quick reply. The soft spring air
wrapped her round; the quiet night came up; the
hills sank. And still the lambs called and cried.

Christian heard the blackbird that sings every
evening on Crump lawn all through the spring.
Just at dusk it starts, sweet as a harp-string, and
you dare not shut your ears though it tear the very
heart out of you. All you have lost it tells you, and
all you have hoped for and may never find.

And Deborah thought of young grass springing on the land—of the smell of the brown earth
turned by the plough, of the rooks swaggering
bravely in the furrows behind the horses, fearing
the servitors of their spring-feast no more than
a human the fingers round a sacramental cup.
And, later, when the plough was idle, and the
ploughman gone home, they, too, would turn
home to Crump. . . .

Out on the drive, Rishwald's chauffeur started
his engine with the hardihood of despair, and
Mrs. Slinker's spell was broken. The great person

bade everybody else a hurried adieu in order to spare her a long moment of farewell.

'Then I may come, next week?' he inquired eagerly. 'You will be there, of course, won't you? Promise you will!' and went off with a mother-of-pearl fish tightly clasped in his hand; Petronilla beholding the departure of her cherished heirloom with well-bred serenity. It was not until he was four miles away that he remembered it, together with the facts that his new adoration was old Steenie Stone's daughter and barely a ten months' widow—and didn't care.

Deb's hired brougham was waiting, too, but there was no sign of the Crump car, and Christian, remembering that it had been running badly all day, was for setting out in search. Mrs. Slinker demanded goloshes, declaring that she would walk home, whereupon Savaury at once offered his own carriage; but Deb, thinking of his warm horses and autocrat of a coachman, was suddenly stricken in conscience.

'Won't you come with me?' she asked, rather shyly, looking full at Mrs. Slinker for the first time. 'I can just as easily go round by Crump, you know, and you really must not think of walking. We may meet the car on the road.'

So thus the incredible thing happened—Slinker's wife and Deborah Lyndesay driving through Crump lanes in peace and amity, with a very much astonished Christian sitting opposite. His trust had not been misplaced—Nettie Stone *was* omnipotent, after all! Again he gave her full meed of admiration; and then again felt the thrill of claiming pride towards his shadowy kinswoman in the other corner.

'Aren't they old dears?' Mrs. Slinker laughed affectionately, as they left Tasser behind them. 'Petronilla and Co., I mean. Not that they are *really* old, of course, but you feel they must have been rooted there for centuries. They just *fit*, don't they? You want to thank them for being so beautifully in the picture, and you hope they'll go on Pope-Joaning for at least another hundred years.'

'Wait till you see Whyterigg!' Christian said, his voice faintly quizzical as he mentioned Rishwald's place. 'It's a lot older than Tasser, and has a priest's room and a ghost, and suits of armour running up against you in every passage. You've been there many a time, Deborah, of course?'

'Not I!' Deb answered. 'Never once. Wild horses wouldn't drag Father into Whyterigg! You'll remember it was Crump property, once upon a time, and the Rishwalds got it by some rather curious hanky-panky. Crump and Whyterigg have never been friendly, you know,' she added, and both her hearers felt themselves, suddenly, to be outsiders.

'Of course. I'd forgotten for the moment,' Christian replied, almost apologetically. 'I'm not half as well up in the family history as I ought to be. You know much more about Crump than I do.'

'It was my great—three times great—grandfather that was done over Whyterigg—we were stewards of Crump, even then. *You* might forget that sort of thing, but *we* couldn't. We were responsible, you see.'

'Kleptomania seems to run in the family!' Mrs. Slinker said quaintly, and they all laughed, thinking of Petronilla's fish. 'I suppose he'll have to come to lunch, Christian, but you'd better keep an eye on the spoons!'

In the lane above the park, they met an apologetic chauffeur, waving a spanner. The car had struck work by the top lodge, and Christian got out to assist.

'I'm glad the silly old thing stuck!' Mrs. Slinker observed, as they drove on, leaving him to follow. 'Fate doesn't mean you to pass me by on the other side—*that's* clear, anyhow. You can't ever really hate me again, now you have done me a kindness!

'You won't speak, I know,' she went on impatiently, turning on her silent companion. 'Your class never does! But I'm not afraid of speaking, and I'm just sick and tired of the whole position. It's been a wretched muddle from beginning to end. I invited myself to that tea-fight, to-night, as you may or may not know. It isn't exactly a habit of mine—going where I'm not wanted—but I'd have done more than that for the chance of straightening things out with you. You mustn't treat me as though I'd deliberately harmed you. It hurts; and it isn't fair. I've got my own punishment to grin and bide, as it is. Anyhow, life's hard enough without going round collecting enemies for amusement. Won't you try to tolerate me? Can't you be kind to me, as though Stanley had never existed?'

' "Kindness" would be an insult, surely!' Deb said slowly. 'I don't hate you, of course. I'm not as absurd as that. And you were the more wronged of the two. But it is an impossible situation. We can never be friends.'

' "Never" is a long word!' Nettie said stoutly. 'I deserved what I got, if it comes to that. I should have stayed with my husband, instead of leaving him free to run after other more attractive people. But I had to be quit of him—I can't pretend anything else. It's no use blinking facts, my dear—neither you nor I had any business with Slinker at all, and we were rightly served. Vanity was the pebble I tripped on—I won't ask what was yours. Anyway, there's no sense in not making the best of things, and I want to be friends with you—I do! I'm not going back to Canada if I can help it,' she added, smiling wistfully in the dark, 'so you'll have to learn to make the best of me. Oh, you *will*!' she finished passionately, and fell silent; but when she offered her hand, at Crump steps, it was not refused.

The car had caught them up, and Christian, jumping out, was at the carriage-door when they stopped. He wished to come on to Kilne, but Deborah would not hear of it, and, as she drove away, took with her that glimpse of him standing on the steps, smiling; and, though she did not know it, a new spell wove a shuttle through the old. Crump had her now for all eternity.

CHAPTER XII

EVEN at the gates of Heron, Grant sighed, for sounds of song came roystering down the drive to meet him. A tambourine rattled bravely, a piano banged, and that last instrument of depravity— the bones—chattered cheerily in his ears. Verity's Pierrots were getting into their stride. The concert was beginning to loom definitely on the horizon, and their repute had gone forth on all sides. It behoved them to strain every nerve.

In the hall he found Larruppin' Lyndesay sitting on a hard, polished chair, hugging a large pile of music, and gloomily studying the pattern of the parquet floor. He raised his head to nod funereally, and to point to a second hard, polished chair beside him.

'It's no use your tryin' to see her,' he observed cheeringly. 'If you walk inside, she'll only get the plumber or the fish-man to throw you out again, an' there's no sense in takin' risks. I'm just let in to deal the music, an' then I have to git. If you've come inspectin', I can give you my word that everythin's O.K. and as strict as Leviticus. Think it sounds a bit rowdy from outside? Oh, well, that's *music*, old man,—there's no helpin' *that*! Music is a great and glorious gift of God—Martin Luther or some other Johnny said so, so you can't be disapprovin'. *In*side, it's as flat as a funeral an' as dull as a donkey-race. It's somethin' distressin' to see them strainin' themselves an' gettin' thin, tryin' to be humorous. Verity's nothin' but skin an' bone. As for Larry Lyndesay, I haven't had a decent dinner this week, aeroplanin' over to practices!'

From the drawing-room came the final crashing chords of 'Boiling the Old Black Pan', and then a lugubrious bass began to sing 'Queen Amang the Heather'.

'Just listen to 'em!' Larry groaned miserably. 'Harry Lauder in white piqué! 'Tisn't self-respectin'! I'm thinkin' of writin' to him about it. An' now Verity's gettin' her hair up again. There she goes! If you feel like sailin' in after *that*, you must be a double-barrelled Balaclava bronchobuster!'

Verity's voice had broken clear and command-ing across the lumberings of the embryo Harry Lauder.

'Begin again, please, right at the beginning, and get the thing *along*! It's as heavy as a stale loaf, at present; more like an elephant trying to dance than anything else. This is how you sing it, if you care to know.' (Faithful if uncomplimen-tary imitation.) 'A great deal more dash about it, please,—a *great* deal more dash! And just have a look at the notes, will you? You don't seem even to have *seen* those dotted quavers!'

'It hurts to hear her conversin' like that!' Lar-rupper threw at the silent parson by the drawing-room door. 'She looks such a kind, soft little thing, doesn't she? She's no business to be roarin' like a drill-sergeant fifty inches round the chest. She's jolly clever, of course, an' she knows what she's doin', but it kind of makes me squirm when she slogs at the grocer or starts bullyin' the big fish-an'-chips.'

'It hurts me, too,' Grant said in a low voice, without turning.

'Yes, but it hurts me all over,' Larry mourned, his black eyes pools of misery,—'inside an' out-side, my head an' my heart an' my charmin' dis-position. It only hurts *you* in your parson-part, old man!'

Grant turned half an eye upon him, but made no effort to contradict him. 'Are you engaged to her?' he asked, suddenly, apparently of nothing but the grain of the drawing-room door, and the white china finger-plate.

'Oh, yes, I'm engaged to her all right!' Larry pronounced firmly, plunging into search after a missing copy, so that he did not see the other's back stiffen. 'I should have thought you would have known that without tellin'. I'm always gettin' congratulatin' letters. The only worryin' thing about it is that *she* isn't engaged to *me*!'

Grant gave a short laugh which might have meant either amusement or relief.

'Do you think if I were to knock——?' he began, summoning his determination, but was cut short by a fresh star within, swimming soothingly into his ken with—'Honey, there'll be dancin' in the sky!'

There was no peremptory checking, this time, no request for 'dash', no insulting recommendations as to quavers. The accompaniment murmured tenderly beneath the pure, easy tenor, and the parson jumped round with an unspoken question on his lips, to which Larry nodded a solemn assent.

'That's so,—but it's no use disturbin' yourself, old man. It's Billy-boy Blackburn, right enough, and can't he just sing, bless his dear, innocent little heart! Sounds like somethin' in a surplice with wings, doesn't he? An' now he's dancin',— you can hear the old Nanki-Poo joinin' in!'

'I'm going to speak to Miss Cantacute!' Grant announced sternly, but Larry sprang up and grabbed him.

'Not on your life!' he said anxiously. 'I'm Verity's watch-dog, an' it's my job to see you don't go bargin' in to worry her. What's the use of excitin' yourself, anyhow? Tisn't what *I* was brought up to, either, if it comes to that, but perhaps we're a bit old-fashioned, an' ought to keep movin'. He *can* dance, too, dear old thing! He won't smash anythin'. An' Verity likes it.'

'She's no business to like it!' Grant snapped angrily, opening the door in spite of him. 'Blackburn's a wastrel,—a real outsider—and Miss Cantacute ought not to have anything to do with him. She's too young and—and too pretty!' he finished defiantly. 'And if you're engaged to her, as you seem to think other people think you think you are, you shouldn't have allowed it!'

Larruppin' Lyndesay crimsoned indignantly.

'D'you think I'd have him on the same planet as my girl if I could help it?' he asked hotly. 'Don't I know Billy-boy Blackburn's winnin' character as well as you an' everybody else in the parish? But if you imagine it's any use sayin' "no" when Verity says "yes", you're labourin' under a very highly-coloured delusion! You'll get no good by breakin' in an' makin' yourself disliked, young feller-me-lad, and—oh, very well, go to blazes! *I* don't care!'

Verity did not see the black figure at first as she bent earnestly over the keys, looking up now and then to smile approval at the performer, and joining heartily in the refrain.

> So the minutes slip away:
> We get older, every day:
> Soon we'll be too old to play.
> (Honey, there'll be dancin' in the sky!)
> 'Nother night we'll both be dead:
> 'Nother couple dance instead:
> Honey! Lift your pretty head—
> Honey, there'll be dancin' in the sky!

Billy-boy sank panting into a chair, and it was not until Verity had finished applauding that she had time to perceive the intruder. The perfection of Billy-boy's 'turn' must have softened her heart, for she rose with a smile and offered Grant a welcoming hand.

'I'm afraid you find us rather busy to-night. Are you wanting anything important? If not, won't you sit down and listen to a few of our items? You may be able to make some suggestions.'

Grange, Larrupper's chauffeur, offered the vicar his seat, which the latter took, after a moment's hesitation, and sat in silence while Larrupper himself, looking rather sheepish, doled out a fresh batch of copies. He hated the job frankly. Larruppin' Lyndesay hadn't an ounce of either self-consciousness or pride, but he did feel a bit of an ass distributing 'My sweet sweeting' and more of that stuff to his own chauffeur. He had a strong suspicion that Grange thought him an ass, likewise, for all that he looked like a bit of the furniture. Besides, Grange could sing, and Larry couldn't. Perhaps that was the rub.

It was certainly a very select troupe. Grant, looking round upon the prim party of twenty, had to admit that;—decidedly O.K., as Larry had put it. Billy-boy was its only blot, thought the parson, and instantly his artistic sense (sternly repressed) responded that, on the contrary, he was its only saving grace. For, when Billy-boy sang, the chorus were magnetised into rhythm, attack, spontaneity, and life; but, when Billy was silent, they were merely so many stuffed dolls, hanging heavily upon Verity's little fingers. The audience, considering the big, black-bearded smith, with his gentle voice, step as light as a cat's, and character,—well, not worth mentioning,—pondered sadly upon the pitfalls of the artistic temperament. Not one of those present but despised the man, shrugged a meaning shoulder when speaking of him, or shook a condemning head; yet with one consent they bowed to the artist in him, and paid it tribute by giving him of their best. No wonder Verity had counted him as her leaven of magic in her barrel of commonplace material! Yet he chafed to see the man under her roof, sharing her society; for in his thoughts Verity floated always as the whole host of heaven float in the top half of an old Italian canvas.

Many of his church-workers were present, and both his artistic and his official sense pronounced violently that they were thoroughly out of the picture. The girls were stiff; the men desperately polite. Grange, in spite of his voice, looked as though he might touch his hat, at any moment. 'My sweet sweeting' left them all unstirred; all except Billy-boy Blackburn, on whose lips the old English words took on instant meaning and colour.

Grant, falling greatly, allowed himself to delay his special mission until Billy had contributed his second solo; and again he marvelled, for it was merely a simple lullaby, sung simply as only an artist could sing it. His own mother had sung it often; yet he found himself unable to resent either interpretation or interpreter. Art was the subtlest lure of the devil, he concluded, sitting with closed eyes, the parson struggling with the man. He had long ago decided that St. Paul's thorn in the flesh must have been the curse of the artistic temperament.

When the cradle-song finished, he rose nervously, his thin hand grasping the back of the chair before him, his bright eyes fixed on Verity's face.

'You will think I am always a spoil-sport, Miss Cantacute, and I can assure you I feel one, entering with an ulterior motive upon this pleasant entertainment, but I have to remind my friend Blackburn of a promise. He undertook some work for me, this winter, a position in the service of my Master and his, which, lowly as it might seem in your eyes, has a very great importance in mine. He has neglected this undertaking for your rehearsals, Miss Cantacute, and those who had grown to look for him and depend on him are now left a little sadder, perhaps, than if he had never been. I went to see him about it, naturally, and he told me that he was not in the least tired of his work, but that Miss Verity wanted him, and therefore he couldn't come. You did tell me that, Blackburn, didn't you?—just that—that Miss Verity wanted you, and therefore you couldn't come?'

Billy-boy, his blue eyes very solemn in his dark face, responded 'Yes, sir', respectfully, touching an overhanging forelock, and Verity smiled at him. She could afford to smile.

'I'm very sorry, Mr. Grant,' she said frankly, with the honest sympathy born of success. 'Of course I didn't know Billy was doing anything special, but in any case I don't see that we could have managed without him. He makes all the difference, doesn't he?' she added to the choir, who replied affirmatively in various shades of tone, being divided between their dislike of the man and the consciousness of their own superior merit under the guidance of his genius.

'It is too bad, certainly, to leave you in the lurch,' Verity went on, with maddening kindness, 'but you see I want Billy simply frightfully myself. I'd give him up if I could, but it's out of the question. I'm really awfully sorry, but I don't see how I can help you, except, perhaps, by finding you somebody else.'

Undoubtedly she enjoyed that last knife-edged sentence. It is difficult not to be a snob when flanked by twenty staunch flatterers of lower degree.

Grant looked at her sadly and a little whimsically.

'Thank you, I think I know by now the extent of parish service available,' he answered, with a faint smile. 'We are almost on the verge of the press-gang, as it is! But you see, this happens to be Blackburn's job, and nobody else's. I'm not in the pulpit, but you don't need to be told that we all have our own job somewhere in the world, and this was Billy's. I shall be unhappy every day until I see him back in it.'

'Was it very important?' Verity asked, touched in spite of herself by his earnestness. 'Really important?'

'As Christ counts importance, Miss Cantacute!'

'Then, if Billy will go, you may have him.'

Grant took an impulsive step forward, and there was an instant murmur from the troupe. Faced with the possible loss of their star, there was no shadow of doubt as to his value. One or two of the men started a protest, but Verity ignored them, fixing her eyes upon the subject of dispute.

'You have my permission to leave us, Billy, if you think it best. I don't like to feel that I've stood in the way of your duty. Will you go?

You know I wouldn't keep you against your will,
I'll try to do without you, if I must.'

Billy touched the overhanging lock again,

'Thank you, miss, but I think I'll stop.'

'You mean that, Blackburn? You won't think
it over, and change your mind?' Grant leaned
towards him eagerly. 'Miss Cantacute is kind
enough to say you may come. I fully appreciate
the sacrifice, I assure you, but I feel it my duty
to accept it. Won't you come back, my friend?
Won't you?' But Billy shook a firm refusal,

'Not till this here's over and by with, sir, I'm
sorry, but Miss Verity comes first, of course. I've
always done for Miss Verity. She's top-dog in
Cantacute, and always has been; and, if Miss
Verity wants me,—well, sir, to put it plainly, I'm
just there an' nowhere else!'

There was a pause, while Grant's hands
clenched and unclenched on the chair, his sor-
rowful mind reckoning up his defeat; and then
Billy said again—'Miss Verity's always been top-
dog in Cantacute!' and a sharp echo of assent
ran round the choir. Afterwards, they would remember that they had followed Billy-boy's lead,
and be annoyed about it,—also that they had
shown him his importance far too obviously,—
but at the moment there were no side-issues; the
point at stake loomed too large. That murmur of
assent showed Grant where he stood as nothing
else could have done,—showed him his opponent's
strength and his own helplessness, the single-
handedness of his own fight, and the long power
of her prestige.

Verity's gaze was on the floor, and her attitude
told nothing, yet he knew as if he had heard it just

what pæan of triumph was swelling her conquering soul, with the inspiring word 'salmon' as its passionate *motif*. She had smitten him to the dust, although in a thoroughly ladylike manner. She had humiliated him in the eyes of his own parish without apparently raising a finger. She had won her victory and proved her power by snatching back his hard-saved lamb to wander once more in the wilderness.

He said nothing further,—just let his eyes travel round the group, not reproachfully but rather wistfully, as if wondering by what reason one man should be ready to die for a cause, while another simply yawned in its face; and looked for one long, final moment at the bent head of his conqueror,—and in that one moment thought, curiously enough, not of his own shame and her treacherous subtlety, but of the way the light played on the fine gold of her hair.

'I knew you'd make a bally ass of yourself!' Larry remarked comfortingly, outside. 'I knew you'd absolutely no earthly of any kind. Why couldn't you take a sportsman's advice? You've gone an' upset Verity all for nothin', an' that means a devil of a time for Larry Lyndesay. She'll be as snarky as anythin', after this, I can tell you. She doesn't *really* like playin' Alexander all round the place. No nice woman does; only the hat-pin kind. I can't think why parsons are always bargin' in an' settin' people by the ears!

'All the same, I was admirin' you no end!' he added confidentially, on the steps. 'Grange was admirin' you, too,—my shover, you know. I could see him sketchin' you on the back of that "Sweetin'" thing. I'll bag it, afterwards, and send it round. You might call it "Beardin' the Begum". An' don't you get worried about Verity an' Billy-boy. She'll probably post him along to-morrow, done up in a neat parcel. All Verity requires is a little cultivatin',—just cultivatin'. Haven't you noticed that most of the parishes round here are engineered by women? You can't get your Salic business runnin' all in a minute, you know,—not in Cantacute, anyhow. Just you take my tip, old man, an' you'll not regret it. Try a little cultiva-tin'!'

Larry's worldly diplomacy rang in poor Grant's ears all the way home. Would he really be justi-fied in 'cultivatin'' his proud little lady? Didn't it mean the sacrifice of his most rooted beliefs, the upheaval of the foundations upon which his very life was set? As representative of his Church, he was her spiritual superior; for all that, as man, he longed to kiss her feet. To yield to her banner would be rank treachery, and all the more be-cause beneath it stood no foe but the dear form of Verity Cantacute. All night he thought and fought and prayed, and all night he sang without ceasing to her bent head—

> So the minutes slip away:
> We get older, every day:
> Soon we'll be too old to play.
> (Honey, there'll be dancin' in the sky!)
> 'Nother night we'll both be dead:
> 'Nother couple dance instead:
> Honey! Lift your pretty head—
> Honey, there'll be dancin' in the sky!

Was she right, after all?—argued Billy-boy's song. Soon they would all be in the dark, and the more fools they who had missed the sunshine and the mirth! Perhaps he was hard, his creed damnably drear. Yet he had been happy in it until he had heard Verity piping on the green. Had he been harsh to her, the pretty, piping thing? Had he hurt her for the sake of a soul that perhaps none could save?

Oh, Honey! Lift your pretty head!

CHAPTER XIII

A SLOW but sure affection was coming into being between the old Crump agent and the new. As a rule, this particular sympathy is far to seek, for the young man is nervous of the elder's criticism, the old man impatient of the younger's methods, while both are held apart by the jealous love that always clings to land; but Roger Lyndesay had retired too long to be irritated by trifles, and, moreover, the mismanagement of a decidedly indifferent successor had broken him very completely to patience. Callander was to be hailed with delight after Slinker's other selection, whose sole recommendation had been a genius for extracting rents, and who had finished an altogether doubtful career in the river, when fishing. The new man, quiet and unassuming, slow to push himself among strangers, found life a little solitary in his house across the park, and by degrees he came to spend many an hour at Kilne, though he had a habit of slipping in unobtrusively, and he never seemed to say very much. It was old Roger who talked, and Callander who listened and learned—many things.

Deb was happier since his coming, for he had brought a new interest into her father's day, and she would sit sewing by the fire, listening to the pair of them as they traced dates, conned agreements and settled valuations. Roger had many a tale to tell, too; of floods on the marsh, of the Great Cattle Plague, of the dobbies that haunt the lanes, of Royal Shows, shoots and rent-dinners. Callander would try to cap them sometimes with tales of his own; but his Shropshire experiences had no atmosphere in the heart of Westmorland, and he was content to steep himself in the glamour of the new life with which he felt so mysteriously satisfied.

He said less even to Deb than to her father. It is difficult to keep up a society conversation along with a discussion upon swedes and the merits of ground limestone, or the vexed question of small holdings. Yet, though he scarcely seemed conscious of her presence, he had a disconcerting habit of turning round on her with a question in cases of difficulty, and she was always too much taken aback to conceal what knowledge she possessed. She might wear a mask with Christian, more or less successfully, but Callander's curt directness got behind it every time.

One afternoon, he persuaded them to drive with him to a farm on the marsh, and it did her good to be welcomed in the old way, and to spend an hour chatting with the farmer's wife while the men went round the buildings. It was a quiet day in February, and the sands were a dim brown beneath the mountains' dim blue. Only the new-turned earth struck a rich, deep note against the faint tones surrounding. They drove home in silence, drawing in the magic that encircles a certain northern marsh.

But at the gate of Kilne their peace was rudely

broken, for the Crump victoria came up, carrying Mrs. Lyndesay, pale and stiffly erect, and as the old agent stepped from the dog-cart and stood aside, hat in hand, she passed him without the slightest sign of recognition.

It was like a blow in the face to the proud old man. Still bareheaded, he stood gazing after the retreating carriage as in a dream, and when Deb laid her fingers on his arm he pushed them off with a shaking hand.

'And that's what I've earned from Crump!' he cried at last, hoarse and trembling. 'I was William Lyndesay's right hand for twenty years, and now his widow cuts me at my door! It's time I was under Crump sod when Crump no longer knows me!'

Then he turned to his daughter in a sudden access of blind helplessness, the tears running down his face.

'She *did* know me, didn't she, Deb? She couldn't mistake Roger Lyndesay at the very gate of Kilne? She must have known me,—she couldn't have taken me for somebody else?'

'It's getting dark so fast, Dad,' Deb said quietly, but cut to the heart and bitterly blaming herself for his pain; for was not this moment of humiliation the direct result of that in which she had engaged herself to Stanley, not a hundred yards from where they stood? 'It's so easy to look at people without seeing them, if you happen to be thinking of something else. And there isn't any reason why she should cut you. She knows what she owes you too well for that. Don't be upset. It was only an accident, Dad, I'm sure!'

But it was not an accident, and she knew it, and

Roger knew it, too. He took her arm, and let her lead him into the house, walking like an old, old man who had had a heavy fall; and, after a moment's hesitation, Callander whistled up the Kilne man to his horse, and followed them in.

He stood just inside the parlour door in the dusk, watching Deb as she leaned comfortingly over the distressed old figure in the armchair, and listening to that note in her voice which was never struck for any one but her father.

'It isn't true that you're forgotten at Crump! Why, it's only a few days since Christian spent the whole evening with you! He sent you the new photograph of the house on your birthday,— don't you remember?—and the old servants gave you the walking-stick of Crump oak with the inscription. Don't fret, dear. There isn't any need, —really there isn't!'

But all Roger could say was—'Crump passed me by! Crump passed me by!' beating his old hands against the chair, and catching his breath like a struck child. Deb looked round despairingly, and saw Callander, big and burly, outlined against the shadowy wall. He was scribbling something on a folded note. Then he stepped forward.

'There's a special meet at Crump, to-morrow,' he said casually, 'to finish the season; the first since the hard weather. Mr. Lyndesay's hunting, himself. He sent you this notice by me, sir, and hoped you'd come along. It should be a fine day, I fancy, by the sun.'

He laid the twisted paper on the table, and the old man's eyes fixed pathetically upon it.

'Read it, Deb!' he told her, quietening a little,

his face clearing, and, after one quick look at Callander, she took it up and opened it. It was merely the ordinary notice that Christian was in the habit of sending to keen followers of the hunt, together with an invitation to lunch, but there was a Lyndesay signature at the foot of it, and that was enough for old Roger. He sat with the paper in his hand, his fine dignity gradually reasserting itself, while Callander went on talking in his usual unemotional manner.

'Hounds are in fine condition, this season, and they've done pretty well, too, so old Brathay tells me. He was fit to tear his hair during the hard spell, and if it freezes at midnight he'll be nearly out of his mind!'

'It will not freeze,' the old agent put in, with weather-wise certainty. 'The wind's too low, and there is too much water in the land. It was kind of Christian to send me word. I have business to-morrow morning, or I might at least have attended the meet; but Deborah will go, of course, in any case.'

Deb started violently.

'I'm afraid it isn't possible—I shall be busy—' she began, in protest, taken aback utterly, but he stopped her with a courteous gesture.

'One of us must go,' he said decidedly. 'We cannot both refuse, and, as I shall not be at liberty, it will have to be you, my dear. You have no appointment on your own account, I suppose?'

Deb shook her head, at a loss for excuse, realising that her engagement and its consequences had faded from his mind, leaving nothing clear and certain but Christian's courtesy.

'Then that settles it!' he said, rising and laying the paper on the table. 'You will be able to give me an account of the day's sport. The meet is at ten, I believe.' And, drawing himself slowly to his great height, he walked shakily but with restored serenity from the room.

When he had gone, Deborah picked up the note once more, and turned it over. Christian had never sent them a hunt-notice, and she knew well enough what delicacy of feeling had prompted the omission. She did not need the scribbled 'R. Lyndesay, Esq.' in Callander's hand to tell her that the note was Callander's and not theirs.

'I doubt I've only made things worse!' he said apologetically, joining her by the fire. 'But it satisfied him for the time being, and that was the chief thing, wasn't it? He'll have forgotten all about it by to-morrow, and you needn't go.'

'I'll have to go,' Deb said wearily, dropping the note into the fire. (There must be no risk over that 'R. Lyndesay'.) 'He might forget anything else in the world, but not a thing like that. It doesn't matter. You were very kind and quick, and it comforted him. Anything was better than seeing him cry!' He caught the gleam of tears in her own eyes as she leaned against the mantelpiece in the firelight. 'You couldn't possibly know what you were letting me in for, and, after all, it only serves me right.' She laughed shortly, drawn out of her reserve by the intimacy of the dusk. 'I've made a nice mess of things for him,— poor old Dad! This will happen again, of course; and you won't be there another time to label Christian's notes!'

He was silent, wondering how far it was safe to follow her lead. By now, most of the local gossip had come round to him—(he was that silent type of man with whom people are apt to let their tongues run loose)—and he knew what was said of the girl who had engaged herself to Slinkin' Lyndesay, merely to be mistress of Crump. Instinctively he felt that there was something in the background, some powerful motive in the strong, self-contained nature that never gave a hint or made appeal for pity. He had had a gentle mother, and clinging, backboneless sisters, now married; and the stubborn, still strength of this young creature standing alone roused in him a sudden impulse of chivalrous admiration. He would back her if he could, but it behoved him to walk warily, for she would be helped by nobody, and she would reveal nothing.

'Then you will go?' he repeated, at last, returning to the point on which he had fallen silent, sure of that ground, at least.

'Oh, yes, I shall go!' she threw at him recklessly. 'It's a special meet, so half the neighbourhood will be there, and they will have such a painful time, poor things, pretending not to know me! Will Mrs. Lyndesay have me turned off the drive, do you think? At least I can take refuge in the middle of the pack! *They*'ll be glad enough to welcome me, and old Brathay will see me through.'

Her voice was terribly bitter, and Callander stirred uncomfortably, thankful for the deepening twilight.

'But you will go with me, won't you?' he asked, rather awkwardly. 'I shall be there, of course, and I had hoped for the pleasure of escorting you. I had meant to ask you, in any case. We could wait for hounds at the top lodge,' he added innocently, and was taken aback when she faced round on him like a young tigress.

'If I go, I go alone!' she told him, passionately. 'Straight across the park and into the thick of the crowd! You mean well, I know, but do you think I'll crawl to Crump steps at the back of a stranger? The invitation was yours, remember, —not mine; so I must go unasked, since my father wishes it. I can take my place with the rag, tag, and bobtail. At least I have a standing invitation from the dead!' She dropped her head on her arms. 'If only Stanley were here!' she added bitterly. 'You'd none of you dare to be "kind" to me, *then*,—you wretched Samaritans!'

'And what about Mrs. Stanley?' poor Callander asked, in his matter-of-fact way, and Deb's sense of humour stirred, and she laughed.

'How beautifully sane you are! I've made a fool of myself, I suppose, but I'm glad it's to you and nobody else. You won't give me away. I'm going alone, as I said, but you can come and unhook me if you see me sticking in a hedge.

'Though it would be wiser if you didn't,' she added, with a fresh touch of bitterness. 'I'm meat enough for the gossip-cats, as it is. You should see them crowd to their doors and put out their ear-trumpets when Christian stops me in the street! But Father will want to know every yard of the run when we get back, so perhaps you had better keep near me, and then I can tell you things.'

'You know Crump like a book!' he said,

smiling, and cursed himself, for she was back into her shell at once.

'Oh, indeed I don't!' she replied curtly. 'I've just picked up things through listening to Father, that's all. They're in the air—there's no getting away from them, as you can see for yourself. It's like having a chemist for a father, and learning all about pills. And it's equally boring!' she added defiantly.

'That isn't Roger Lyndesay's child speaking!' he answered bluntly, preparing to take his leave. 'Crump names are music on your tongue,—one's only got to hark. Some day you'll show me your real self. I can guess at it already, but some day I'll see it whole!

'And some day I'll know why you would have married Stanley!' he added to himself, as he went away.

CHAPTER XIV

DEB opened her window to the soft, damp breath of a real hunting morning. The trees on the hillside showed weirdly through the gray mist. The river below looked like a tarnished ribbon run through an ancient cobweb veil. When the sun broke, it would be smooth silver, and the tree-trunks would be black, and the wet slope of the hill green as an emerald sheath.

From the kennels she could hear the eager hounds, already scenting the day's sport, and smiled to find she could still distinguish between them—from the deep-throated note of old Conquest to Chanter's steady baritone and the hysterical tremolo of young Mornington. The quiet air thrilled with the promise of vivid life soon to be unleashed upon its quest of death.

As she had prophesied, the meet was still uppermost in her father's mind, and he looked approval when she entered the room in her short skirt and nailed boots. He had a stout ashplant in his hand, which he pushed across the table as she sat down to breakfast.

'It's the stick I used to take hunting in William Lyndesay's time,' he told her. 'I kept it for rough work, and I haven't seen it for at least ten years. You may not believe it, but it fell upon me out of a corner as I came downstairs!'

'It must have heard hounds and got hankering!' Deb laughed, picking it up and running her finger appreciatively down the good grain. 'The wind's that way, you know. Poor old thing! It shall have its day out all right. It shan't be left at home to hanker in the dark. It has good taste in weather, too,' she added gaily, 'for it's going to be a grand day.'

'Yes—perfect!' Roger's eyes went round to the window, to see the first pale gold of the sun climbing the shoulder of the hill. 'I feel very much inclined to postpone my appointment, and come with you to the meet, after all.'

'It wouldn't be very wise, would it?' Deb asked hurriedly, keeping her eyes on her plate, for she knew he was only waiting for the slightest sign of encouragement, having evidently forgotten the episode of the night before. 'It will be very damp under-foot, I'm afraid, and you haven't worn your biggest big boots for some time. I'm not quite certain where they are, to tell the truth!

And, if we make for Monteagle, as we're nearly sure to, it will be pretty bad going, you know.'

Roger Lyndesay nodded, disappointed but acquiescent.

'I thought I might just have walked up to the house,' he said wistfully, and again Deb longed passionately for a resuscitated Slinker, at whatever cost to herself—'but I should only want to follow, when once I was among hounds, and I don't feel equal to that. I've done that Monteagle run in all weathers; ay, and seen the hare swim the river with hounds no more than a yard behind! It's hard to keep indoors when their music's in the air.'

'I'll tell you everything when I come back, Dad. We'll follow every ring, and cover every yard, and struggle together through every spiky fence. You'll feel as though you'd tramped every inch, you'll see, instead of sitting quietly in your own arm-chair. And you'll be able to correct Mr. Callander about all sorts of things when he comes for his next lesson in Crump geography. Nothing is so upsetting to your sense of locality as running rings round the same hill and crossing the river every ten minutes.

'And even if we were both dumb, the ashplant would have plenty to say, anyhow!' she added lightly, flourishing it as she went out. 'It feels as though it were ready to walk out on its own. I could almost swear it was alive!'

She walked quickly across the park, a straight, slim figure in her dark jersey and close cap, and waved her hand to her father standing at his window on the other side of the fast-running water. Not until she was half-way to Crump did she realise that she had crossed the old bridge without a second's hesitation, and with never a whisper of Slinker's in her ear.

Sportsmen were approaching from all directions, cycles, traps and cars hurrying up and converging at Crump front; small boys playing truant, with shining eyes and sticks much taller than themselves; all classes and kinds and species, from the High Sheriff to half the loafing element of the village, who were only equal to an hour's good work under pressure, but could pant after hounds all day on a crust of bread and the dregs of a split soda.

The keenest spirit of this last contingent caught Deb up on the narrow track. They had hunted together in the old days, and he was confident of her smiling greeting as he touched the remains of a cap. He had the plans for the day by heart, as well as any amount of private and possibly valuable information, gleaned from keeper, farmer and beck-watcher; and he remained beside her, pouring out eager opinions as to their chance of sport, and the best means of obtaining it.

Hounds were at Crump door, by now. They could see old Brathay sunk in a climbing sea of black and white and tan, and at the reiterated throaty chorus they quickened their steps instinctively and at the same moment. Deb, looking at the ragged figure beside her, half-starved, consumptive, little more than a log, any other day, but alive to his finger-tips on this, wondered what could be the real nature of the spell that summoned them both alike. Not merely the lust of death, surely, for hares were scarce and exceedingly cunning, and a kill was rarely in the day's programme; moreover, she loved every animal, and the little man at her side owned a miserable mongrel who was always fed, even if his master went hungry. Something higher must lie at the back of that eager response to pack-music and winded horn—something born of the smell of the good earth and the soft, spring morning, the clean air and the quick movement—some great wine of joy that Nature keeps for those who have the soil and the chase in their blood. Deborah Lyndesay and the loafer had this heritage in common, and the godlike, unforgettable days it gives. They came to the steps of Crump sporting equals.

Hounds were grouped a little to the right, round Brathay and the young whip, and Deb paused to say good-day and to pick out her favourites, while her ragged escort stood on anxious guard as wheels rolled perilously near.

Close to the house, the crowd was thickening, and among the group on the steps she could discern Nettie, lending an inattentive ear to Rishwald, while her eyes strayed eagerly over the press in front. They sought for Dixon of Dockerneuk, in vain.

Savaury of Tasser had come in a brougham and a button-hole, and was fearfully bored. He kept pulling out his watch and remarking that the best of the day was going, and was positively rude to Mrs. Lyndesay about the hall-clock.

'We must wait for Larrupper,' Christian said soothingly, looking very young and fair in the rough green of the hunt. 'He's late, of course, but then he always is, and we can't leave him to follow, because he'll make such a howling nuisance of himself all over the county, asking his way.'

His eye fell suddenly on Deb, and he made his way to her at once, nodding brightly on all sides. The Bracewell girls, who had turned well-cut backs upon Deborah, while endeavouring to collect the wordless doctor for a subscription dance, had the same trap set for the Master, but he evaded it smilingly and passed on. The Honourable tapped him on the shoulder from her majestic landaulette, and inquired if he intended standing for the County Council, but again he escaped; and, after skirting several other dangerous dowagers, and a farmer or two bent on shippon repairs, arrived at last at his destination.

'I'm ever so glad you've turned out!' he said eagerly, acknowledging her attendant's anxious salute with a kindly nod. 'Callander told me there was just a chance you might. I've often wondered if you would care about it, but I knew you'd be there, if you did. Lyndesays don't need invitations from Lyndesays, do they?' he added, smiling, veiling the reason he could not speak.

'Father wanted me to come——' she began, and coloured sharply, for the sympathy in his eyes told her that he was in full possession of the facts.

'I wish he could have honoured us on his own account,' he answered, stooping to respond to the earnest pleading of a sleek head at his knee. 'I'm coming in, to-night, if I may? I want some advice. And look here, you'll stop out to lunch, of course? We're making straight along the river to Monteagle, and probably round by Bytham to

Halfrebeck. It's a grand day, and we should have some sport.'

Here Swainson broke in breathlessly with information, and Christian listened attentively, putting in a word from time to time. Then he turned to Deborah again.

'You haven't seen Larry anywhere about, have you? He'll look after you, of course—and Callander. And Nettie wants to know whether *you*'ll look after *her*, though I expect Rishwald will take that as his prerogative. I wonder if he's returned that fish-thing of Savaury's, yet!' Their eyes met, and they laughed. Then he lowered his voice. 'May I see you home when we draw off?'

'Certainly not!' Deb answered quickly, turning hastily to look for signs of Larrupper. 'You're wasting too much time on me, as it is—Mrs. Stalker thinks so, at least. And the Master's place is with hounds until they're safely back in kennels —surely you ought to know that!'

'Yes, but Brathay can take them all right, and he simply loves walking them along the road, with all the kiddies in the place admiring behind. And you know I want to see your father.'

'Then you can come after tea, when I shall be busy writing to registry-offices,' she told him unkindly. 'And if you intend to hunt, to-day, you'd better get started, especially as I can see a streak of mud in the distance that is probably Larry.'

It was. He came racing through the crowd just as Christian snatched the last word of the conversation. 'I'm coming!' he insisted, in a tone she had not heard from him before, and gave her no chance of reply, turning away to drag his tardy cousin out of the splashed car.

'No end sorry, Laker—shouldn't have waited —sprintin' like the deuce!' he gasped, throwing off his leather coat, and beckoning to a groom in the stable-yard. 'Grange goin' huntin', too, old man,' he explained kindly. 'Awful sport, Grange. S'pose your chap can shove the beastly thing in somewhere?'

Without waiting for an answer, he fell upon Deborah, and with his arm through hers marched her off at the tail of the pack in full view of all present, as Christian started up the avenue.

'I'm badly in want of soothin', Debbie dear,' he announced plaintively, bending his black bullet head to her cool cheek. 'I ran over for Verity— she's always been a nailer at huntin', you know— but there was no gettin' her off the spot, she was so busy slavin' for that evenin' shout of hers. She was sittin' round sortin' hanks an' hanks of white piqué an' a stack of black, fluffy bobs; and all the time I was persuadin' her to come huntin' she was fixin' a skirt-thing on me, an' tryin' the bobs up an' down it, to see where they looked best. It was no use tellin' her what a rippin' day it was, an' plenty of scent, an' real interestin' news like that. All she said was—"Yes, dear, just an inch or two to the right"—an'—"Yes, dear, five, I think, instead of six"—all that sort of irritatin' piffle. So at last I got rattled an' cleared out to go huntin' without her, but old Grange grabbed me half-way down the drive an' said I'd forgotten to leave the skirt-thing behind; an' just as I was rushin' back, blushin', two of the squawkers arrived for a mornin' sing-song, an' giggled fit to kill themselves. Of course I pretended I was used to goin' about like that, but I felt dancin' mad, I can tell you, and I want soothin' very badly, Debbie dear, so you can just start in an' do it!'

'Oh, Larry, I *wish* you'd come in the skirt!' Deb laughed blissfully. 'What a dear old crack-pot you are! I'm sure Verity must be frantically busy; these things take no end of trouble and arranging. I'm going over, to-morrow, to give her a hand. The concert will soon be over, now, so try not to worry her until she's recovered.'

'Worry her?' Larry exploded, dreadfully in-jured. '*Worry* her? Why, I'm her right-hand man and the L.N.W.R. and the Army and Navy Stores combined! I spend my days shootin' into Witham after music, an' droppin' notes on the squawkers, an' judgin' patterns an' huntin' up words that look a bit rocky in the programme. D'you suppose I find it amusin' playin' errand-boy and encyclopædia, an' all the rest of the tommy-rot?'

'Why, yes, you simply love it!' Deb said firmly. 'You like being ordered about by Verity and told to do things, because it saves you the trouble of thinking. You care for each other all right, but you don't take the matter seriously enough—either of you; that's what's wrong, Larry dear. Some day you'll have a big row over something that goes deep, and you'll not be able to get back. You should stop away from her, and refuse to be played with any longer. She'd soon find that she couldn't do without you.'

'How can you turn your head one way an' your heart another?' Larry asked reproachfully. 'Or keep away from the fire when you're freezin', or lock up the ginger-beer when you're thirsty? You're not a bit soothin', dear old thing! An' I don't see that I'll ever quarrel with Verity, in spite of your interestin' prophecy. She's not playin' Queensberry, I'll admit, but she's as straight as a regiment, for all that, an' she'll never do anythin' that I'd be ashamed to own up to in my little girl!'

Deb's maternal heart warmed towards Verity's black donkey.

'You're just the very nicest person that ever was, Larry!' she exclaimed affectionately. 'And Verity knows it as well as I do. You're both dears. But oh, *do* be careful not to crock up things by accident!'

As they quitted the road for the river-bank, Mrs. Slinker lined up with them in thankful haste, leaving Rishwald to propel the Honourable through the narrow stile. Larry knew her, of course—he knew everybody—(especially the members of that interesting force, the county police)—and greeted her with a pumping handshake.

'I hope you're soothin'?' he inquired pathetically. 'I've had a nasty jar, an' Miss Lyndesay's out of practice, this mornin'.'

'I should have thought the morning itself would have been sufficiently soothing,' Mrs. Slinker replied, looking at the quiet, brown-hedged land with the river curving from field to field between the white gleam of snowdrops, and the faint sun gilding the green in patches. Christian was in front with hounds bunched close at his heels, walking easily yet with that covering swing that must be followed to prove its pace. The whips were a yard or two behind, keeping a stern watch on any sudden desire after a stray rabbit. Then came the field at a respectful distance; here and there a red jersey or a blue wing standing out on the soft background. Horses came to the fences and lifted surprised heads. Cattle lowered theirs anxiously, and followed awhile in mild curiosity; while the sheep, in meadow after meadow, within sight or out of it, huddled together, facing outward, with the unerring prescience that warns them of anything canine close at hand.

Nettie, looking nervously behind her, saw Rishwald shuffle the Honourable on to the doctor, and, with a wild signal of distress to her companions, slid through a hedge before their astonished eyes. Scouting by means of a gate, they discovered her on the far side, sitting in a bramble.

'I hadn't any conversation left about tea-caddies,' she informed Deborah, when Larry had extricated her. 'And I was quite right about kleptomania being in the family. He's always talking about "collecting" things. It's the modern form, you know. I kept a strict look-out when he lunched at Crump, but he didn't actually make off with anything except a few match-boxes and a handkerchief of Christian's; though, as we haven't been through the inventory, yet, there's no knowing what may have happened to the drawing-room silver!'

Hounds found in the marshy bottom by Guard Hill, and were over the ditch and half-way across the big meadow before the field had got into its stride. Deb found Callander beside her as she measured her distance for the slippery jump into the thorny arms of the well-laid fence in front.

'Well, was it very bad?' he asked bluntly, when

he had engineered her through the prickins, and they were racing side by side over the short grass. 'I didn't see you hanging out any signals of distress, so I kept away. And I rather think myself that you're enjoying it!'

She laughed, turning a glowing face towards him.

'Swainson took me under his protection,' she said breathlessly, as they climbed the hill. 'It's an honour, though it may not exactly jump to the eye! And the people who cut me are wallowing in that last ditch, which is distinctly cheering. No, it wasn't so bad, except when Larry marched me out at the head of the procession. And of course I'm enjoying it!' she added, as they stopped at a closed gate. 'It's good for the soul to run up and down the earth in the spring of the year, and come home covered with mud and scratches and full of fresh air. It's a pity one can't always do it.'

'You're stopping in too much,' Callander growled, arguing with a Westmorland method of securing gates that had not as yet come under his notice. 'You stick in that pretty little house of yours and mope. You should get out, and stop out. Things are right enough, out of doors. Do *you* know how the confounded thing works?'

Deb solved the problem for him, and they hurried on, for hounds had vanished round a plantation.

'Life sounds so simple with you men of the land!' she said, smiling. 'Your recording Angel doesn't need to use shorthand! And of course you're right. It's a true gospel, at least, for us who "belong".'

He glanced at her sideways—that 'belong' had been a revelation—but she was watching eagerly for the reappearance of the first smooth head, and was evidently unconscious of her last words. She did indeed 'belong', he thought, looking at the alert figure, the lightly ruffled hair and sparkling face. She was part and parcel of the picture rolling away beneath them—plough and meadow, hedge, river, plantation, and snug-laid farm, backed beyond and beyond by mountain and sea. She had been made of the warm, living earth, the crisp wind, the soft, gray-blue sky. Given every tie that binds humanity to the soil, she 'belonged' to the land by heritage, by affinity and by love.

Nettie and Larrupper were at their heels by the time they reached the top gate of all, which Larry fastened with great deliberation in the face of a panting horde behind, while his companion stamped with impatience and entreated him to come on, for hounds were still in full cry below.

'Etiquette of huntin'!' Larry reproved her gravely, fumbling with the chain, and placidly ignoring the shrieks in rear, faint but pursuing. 'Looks a bit wantin' in feelin', perhaps, but it's etiquette, all the same. Leave a gate ajar, an' you'll have all the field scuttlin' through without so much as givin' it a hitch. That's how a huntin' crowd gets itself disliked. An' you needn't get worryin' about hounds, I assure you. They're certain to lose her in the long covert. They always do.'

They did; and there followed a long check, during which Rishwald resumed his private chase with a discourse upon snuff-boxes, much to

Larry's disgust, as he was finding Mrs. Slinker distinctly 'soothin',' he informed Deborah, aside.

'Of course I'm not sayin' she's in the same street with you, Debbie dear!' he added apologetically, 'but she's so sportin'—you *do* think she's sportin', don't you? An' she's simply burstin' with good sense, almost as bad as old Grange. She makes you feel the world's so clinkin' all right, doesn't she? I expect that's why Slinker took a fancy to her. Slinker was always pessimistin' about things. Lyndesays are generally grousin' an' wantin' a leg-up.'

'Yes, we're a depressing crowd,' Deb answered cheerfully. 'We want a desperate amount of encouragement. And you needn't apologise, Larry. I admire Mrs. Stanley myself.'

They moved along by Quinfell and into Winderwath, and there they chopped a hare in the first five minutes. Mrs. Slinker instantly disappeared round the nearest corner, her fingers in her ears, but Deb stood rigidly where she was, though Callander saw the hand on the ashplant quiver when the quarry screamed.

'Mrs. Stanley said we were all brutes, both hounds and men,' he observed. 'Is that your opinion, Miss Lyndesay?'

'I suppose so,' Deb said slowly. 'I'd choose a sharp death in the open, myself, rather than lingering misery in a sick-room. But a hare is so soft and so—afraid——' She stopped, shutting her lips determinedly. This man was getting to know too much.

Larry came up with a long face and an air of having been warned off the premises.

'Mrs. Stanley's been callin' me names!' he

informed them, desperately wounded. 'Says
I thoroughly enjoyed seein' the poor brute
chopped! It's very disheartenin'. I'm afraid
she's not as sportin' as I thought. I offered to
borrow a herrin' an' let hounds have a shot at
collarin' me, just to see how it felt, but she thought
I was simply foolin'. Rishwald's car's followin',
an' he's goin' to take her home—just at lunch-time,
too! Laker will be ravin'. It's very upsettin'.'

The lunch-cart was in the lane close by, with
the butler already at work; the field standing
about in groups or scattered haphazard on wall
or bank. Christian seized Deborah as she looked
longingly towards the near plantation.

'You're coming to lunch!' he said firmly, pilot-
ing her to a spread rug. 'I'll not have you sneak-
ing away and eating biscuits in the hedge, or
pretending you're not hungry. Callander, keep
an eye on her while I go and forage!'

'Did you know that you were a favourite of
Parker's?' he added, when he returned. 'He was
quite snubby to me on your account, over the
sandwiches. "Miss Lyndesay, sir, doesn't eat
potted rabbit!" he informed me, coldly. How
on earth do they know these things, the dear old
Marconis?'

The next moment he was beside Rishwald's
car, looking up at Nettie with his face full of
concern.

'You're not really going, are you? Won't you
stop for lunch, first? Oh, very well—you'll be in
time at Crump, if you fly; and take Rishwald in
with you, will you? I say, dear, you're not ill, or
anything else? Didn't like the worry—was that
it? I suppose we're a lot of ravening savages, but

that's hunting, you know—the sport of gentle-men, they call it! I'm frightfully sorry if you're upset!'

'I must be getting old,' Mrs. Slinker answered, smiling with rather an effort. 'It hurts me to see things harried out of life. I just hate making a fuss, so let me slip away quietly, Youngest One, there's a lamb. I reckon this sort of game's got to be in your blood. I liked the running and the scrambling all right—but oh, Laker, why didn't you warn me that a driven hare screams like a frightened child!'

Rishwald thought himself in clover all the way to Crump, and covered four miles with descrip-tions of a pet jug, to which he referred familiarly as 'my little Toby'; but he was a little downcast when they stopped to find that she had under-stood him to be talking about a dog.

The field fell off sadly in the afternoon, Honour-ables and other notabilities vanishing like clouds upon the horizon, and sport improved—perhaps accordingly. Grange had gone back with the Crump cart, and, later, spent a trying hour chasing his master up inaccessible lanes. Larry had a dealing practice at five. He was on the point of offering Deborah a lift back to Kilne, when café diplomacy suddenly prompted other-wise, and he faded silently through a hedge into Grange's thankful embrace, feeling very mean and destitute of manners.

Deb, however, did not notice his departure, for she herself had designs upon a hedge in a totally opposite direction; the situation having suddenly taken on a very awkward complexion. The last halt had been called near the Bracewells' house, and the girls were inviting the tail of the field in to tea. The dumb doctor, whose patients had finally decided to die without him, was swallowed up in an instant; and even wary Callander was collared before he realised that Deb was not of the party. She was well across the next field, keeping close in the shadow of the fence, when Christian dropped beside her.

CHAPTER XV

'I suppose you were flattering yourself you'd lost me,' he observed, falling into step, 'but I took care to notice when you scurried away. It's no use trying to disguise yourself in the hedge—the flowers aren't out yet!' he added quaintly, clinching the compliment with a whimsical smile. 'Are you sure you're not too tired to walk? It's been a long day, you know. I had the cart sent back, in case you preferred to drive—Clark's with it in the lane by the Bracewells'. I told him to wait about for another ten minutes.'

'I'd rather walk, thanks,' Deb replied. 'There's a short cut out of Halfrebeck over Linacre. It's not very far, really, and very straight. Why didn't you go in to tea?'

'Because I'm coming to tea with you,' he said easily. 'I want to sit on your big fender-stool with my feet on the fire-irons, and drink tea out of a brown tea-pot. The Lyndesays always have brown tea-pots. It's a rule of the house. The Bracewells have a silver Queen Anne with a crest grown in Edward VII, and you sit on mock Chippendale or imitation Adam, and scrape their elegant legs with your muddy boots.'

This was not like Christian, and she wondered greatly what had occurred after her abrupt departure. She could not guess that, when he joined her over the hedge, he had been hot with resentment at the treatment she had received.

'Oh, yes, we've got the brown tea-pot,' she responded curtly. 'Father wouldn't dream of countenancing any other. It's very silly, of course —no, it isn't! Father's quite right. He's always right. Except when he goes hunting by proxy!' she added rather wearily, for the excitement of the day was passing, and the strain beginning to tell.

'I'm awfully sorry about last night!' Christian said hurriedly. 'Callander told me everything. You don't mind, do you? I'm afraid my mother must have meant it, though I'd give anything to prove I was wrong. It was a cruel thing to do— nothing can excuse or condone it, but we've got to remember that she is still breaking her heart over Stanley and—and all that happened. She has nothing against Mr. Lyndesay, of course.'

'She has—me!' Deb answered bitterly. 'Oh, it's I who have been to blame, all through, I suppose! I earned him that blow in the face. I ought to be shot. Yet I'd do it again!' she added obstinately, setting her teeth. 'You none of you understand, except perhaps Mr. Callander, but I don't care. I'd do it again!'

They had paused at a gate on the last slope dividing them from the road below, where the dead beech-leaves stood out in bright strips on the black hedges. The land was darkening fast against the evening sky. The earth-line opposite, rising again gently, was fringed with a border of feathery brown fingers etched against the opal. The fresh morning breeze had dropped. The long, straight road was empty except for a plough-boy whistling piercingly sweet. In the uppermost bough of a thin young pine, straight as a lance of God, a thrush flung them its largesse of golden song. And always the rooks went home, flying high with the promise of good weather.

'We must put things right, somehow,' Christian said with determination. 'We can't allow him to be hurt again. But I haven't much influence with my mother, you know. She was wrapped up entirely in Stanley—she had nothing left for me. And yet they were unhappy together —we were all unhappy. It seems a bit hard that we Lyndesays should never be allowed the every-day home contentment of other folk.'

'There is more than one curse on Crump!' Deb said, frowning. 'We are dreamers of dreams, all the lot of us—even Larry—and we carry sorrow in our hands like a guarded gem. Your mother, too, although she seems so cold. And my father is the King-Dreamer of us all. I sometimes think he is the Dream of Crump itself.'

Christian nodded assent. 'But Slinker—Slinker had no dream,' he said slowly.

'I'm not so sure about that! It was a long way off, perhaps, but he would have come to it in the end. He would have sold Dockerneuk without compunction, but he left us Kilne. I once saw him half kill a keeper for starving the deer, though he kicked his own spaniel, the moment after. The herd is so old, you know. He used to take off his hat to it, laughing. And you remember that he wouldn't allow the Antiquarian Society to search the Pixies' Parlour? It wasn't just disobliging-ness, as you all thought. He didn't want strange hands digging up his ancestors' soil, though he stripped the woods to pay his betting-book. There were other things, too——' She stopped, frowning again. 'What does it matter? He's dead—poor Stanley! But Father's alive, and I've got to keep him happy, and you must help me.'

'There is a way,' Christian said hesitatingly, 'though perhaps you may think I have no right to suggest it. We're good friends, aren't we? And I believe we feel the same about things, though it isn't often you show me the real Deborah. We can take care of your father between us, if you'll give me the right to take care of you, too. You would have married Slinker. Can't you make up your mind to marry *me*?'

She stepped back, staring at him, the colour leaving her face, but the surprise was too great to allow any room for self-consciousness. In all her thoughts of Christian, friendly and even tender as they had often been, such a possibility had never entered her mind. Their intercourse had struck the note of comradeship—no more. Even the tie of their distant relationship had taken them no further. Accustomed as she was, by now, to his cheerful, impartial friendliness and apparently unthinking serenity, she had never even vaguely pictured him as being in love with her. Nor had she thought of loving him. He was something aloof and apart, an integral but indefinite part of her dream.

'You cannot be speaking seriously!' she said at

last, keeping her voice even with difficulty. 'How could it possibly happen? You know nothing about me, to begin with—and Stanley hasn't been dead a year. Mrs. Lyndesay wouldn't consent, in any circumstances. And the other people——'

'Need we take the other people into consideration? As for my mother—she may rule me in other things, but at least I will choose my own wife!'

He lifted his head, and for the first time she guessed that he, too, had his share in the strain of iron running through the Lyndesay blood, in spite of the drifting acquiescence with which he seemed to accept life. This was the Christian who, as Nettie had prophesied, would some day learn to stand alone. 'As for Slinker'—his voice quickened—'why should Slinker come between us? God knows we owe him nothing, either you or I!'

He took her hand as they stood by the gate in the growing dusk, two lonely young souls caught in the endless maze of temperament and heritage.

'It all sounds so cold-blooded, doesn't it, dear? It's new and strange, at present, but you'll think it over, won't you? I'm giving you what Crump owes you, that's all. And I'd be good to you, you know that. I've not made much of my life, yet, but you can help me to it, if you will. I've never wanted any woman before, but you leave a blank even when you pass me in the street. Perhaps you think I haven't known you long enough to care, but I do. I want you for my own sake—not for Crump or your father or any other reason—only for Christian, Debbie dear!'

She listened to the kind voice speaking Larry's cousinly endearment, yielding to the clasp of the kind hand, but she did not look at the earnest young face. This was not love—yet—whatever it might become. He was reaching out to her, half from quixotic chivalry, half from an impulse born of affinity and race, but not with the overmastering desire to which alone a true woman lays down her arms. If she took him, she would take him as she had taken Slinker, notwithstanding the deep tenderness in her heart towards him. He was too good for that; a thousand times too good; and yet —and yet—! She looked up at the tired rooks, slowly forging dimly through the dusk. A few more miles, and they would be nested safe behind the Hall, in their haven of immemorial antiquity; and for all the quiet night their rest would be in the home they loved.

'Crump folk going home!' she observed irrelevantly, her wistful eyes following their faint flight. 'The villagers call them that—did you know? They say it every night, when they watch them for the weather. ' "Crump folk going home!" '

She repeated the words under her breath, as the last bird dropped behind the hill; and he took both her hands in his, for the night was coming, and they must go. He spoke again, but she did not hear him, nor the golden singer still swaying on the young pine. All she knew was that Crump folk had gone home, leaving Deborah Lyndesay behind them, and that never in all her life would she find her way thither. At her father's death she would have to go south, and that would be the end of things for her. If she married Christian, rightly or wrongly, she would still belong to

Crump. It was the only way left; yet she fought hard, for she knew she was wronging him—and always the land cried to her in answer. The power stronger than herself drove her as she looked him in the face at last.

'I'm not brave enough to refuse,' she said wistfully. 'Surely we care enough to make it right? But oh, Christian, I doubt you're patting me on the head!'

CHAPTER XVI

VERITY put a hand round the curtain and waved wildly, and Larruppin' Lyndesay, who had been at the beck of those fingers too long not to recognise them in any circumstances, stopped trying to sell programmes to people who had them already, and shouldered his way on to the stage, where a crowd of piqué nightmares, rather terrible in their exaggerated make-up, were busy settling themselves upon insecure pedestals.

The gas smelt vilely, and already the whole place was hot and airless. Larry tugged uneasily at his stiff collar, and wriggled uncomfortably in his evening clothes. He was frightfully sleepy, too, having been out on the moor all day, and he wondered how on earth he should ever pull through the sing-song without a snore. He met Verity's agitation rather unsympathetically, looking gloomily at the dainty little figure in its short skirt and coquettish hat, and wished she were out in the rain with him in a Burberry, and only the painting of Nature on her face. Billy-boy Blackburn, it seemed, had not yet put in an appearance, and Verity was beginning to be alarmed.

'Oh, of course I can start out an' hunt for him, if you like,' Larry said morosely. 'I shan't have to go scoutin' very far. The Red Lion is his favourite restin'-place. If not, there's the Brown Cow,— just as soothin'. Never say die. But if he doesn't turn up without bein' booted, I should say leave him where he's roostin, an' plank along without him.'

'We can't! He's the making of the whole thing. Everybody depends on him.' Verity looked worried and rather helpless; a totally fresh attitude to which the young man's heart warmed. 'Do have a look for him, Larry! We ought to start, in a minute.'

'All right. I'll see where the bounder's hidin',' —Larry turned, obedient though disapproving,— 'but I warn you I shall make a point of usin' my own discretion. If I find him goin' strong, I shall detain him on licensed premises, an' you can send old Grange runnin' at ten o'clock to shove us both under the pump!'

Verity's heart smote her for a moment. Perhaps it was scarcely fair to send young Lionel Lyndesay scouring after a doubtful blacksmith through a series of equally-doubtful pubs; and moreover she was rather afraid of her black donkey, to-night. He looked older, and, being tired, much less sunny and complaisant. Indeed, there was something almost grim about his bullet head and big shoulders and his grumbling bass. For the first time she felt him tug at his leading-strings.

She laid her hand rather timidly on his arm, and he wanted to kiss her on the one bit of eye-brow which had escaped the pencil, but the whole effect was distasteful to him, and again he thought longingly of Burberries and a certain bog on the moor that had played him desperately false.

'You'll do no more of this sort of thing, do you hear?' he added, almost roughly. 'It's not fittin'! This isn't the time for jawin', but I've been meanin' to say somethin' for weeks, an' the Lord only knows what it's been like, holdin' it in. This is goin' to be the wind-up of your private Hippodrome, so you can just be makin' the most of it, an' gettin' ready for shuttin' down!'

He stumped off again, and fell almost into the arms of Grant, sitting in the middle of the front row. He greeted him moodily.

'Goin' to start an opposition meetin', old man? Verity's agitatin' somethin' alarmin' because that prize squawker of hers hasn't turned up yet.'

'Do you mean Blackburn?' Grant got up, paling slightly, and Larry nodded.

'He's found missin', an' I'm off Sherlock-Holmesin' round the village pubs, an' if he's not in drawin'-room form I'll have an amusin' evenin' entertainin' him on my own. You can trust me for that.'

'I'll come with you,' Grant said impulsively, but Larry would have none of him.

'Thanks. I can stand up to Billy all right without any parsons holdin' my hat,' he returned unkindly. (Larry, as well as Christian, had figured in the ring, but had been pronounced unsafe.) 'If you're hankerin' after bein' useful, you can start in sellin' the programmes,' he added, thrusting the pink papers into Grant's hands, 'an' be sure you're on the spot an' throwin' flowers if any of the squawkers gets a really bad drop.'

He disappeared beyond the fast-filling seats; and, as he went out at the main entrance, Billy-boy slipped in by the stage-door. A minute earlier, Larrupper would have discovered him, as he had prophesied, fortifying the artistic temperament in the Red Lion; but he was still sufficiently sober to read a clock, and an ironic Providence steered him safely past Verity with a respectful salute to his place beside the piano. The curve of the grand formed a comfortable prop, and his trainer, beholding him decorously seated, breathed a sigh of relief and took a final glance at the audience before ringing up the curtain.

The room was full, now, the whole district being well represented, from the dear old things who had known her from childhood and thought her amazingly clever, to the dear young ones who were being brought up in the same belief and the fear of Cantacute. They had come prepared to enjoy themselves, confidently looking for a good programme. Verity knew the standard they expected, and thought uncomfortably of one or two doubtful items; then recollected Billy-boy's magnetic genius for keeping stragglers together, and took heart.

Christian and Mrs. Stanley were sitting in the second row, with Rishwald within 'collecting' distance just behind, and Callander, looking uneasily for fire-exits and ventilators. The Bracewell girls, inspired by the atmosphere, were trying to persuade the doctor to join a choral society. Perhaps they remembered Garrick's advice to his tongue-tied acquaintance,—'If you c-c-c-c-can't s-*speak*, why d-d-don't you *sing*?'

Deb had come with the Savaurys. Roger

Lyndesay had a horror of stuffy rooms and noisy
entertainments. He liked best his own fireside,
with a pipe and some queer old book of Westmorland history that had long 's's' spiking up and
down the page. Savaury purchased three programmes from the somewhat abashed parson,
and asked if the living required supplementing;
then buried his nose in the pink sheet, snorting
contemptuously as he recited the items aloud.

"'I know a lovely garden'—h'm—that's the
chemist, isn't it? Verbena hairwash, I suppose,
and camomile tea. "I see you on every side"—the
policeman's wife with the squint. Mrs. Andrews
—"Come where my love lies dreaming"—as if one
could, when he's been in the churchyard these
last ten years, and a very good thing, too! Here's
another garden—"Beautiful Garden of Roses"—
(so *tiresome* never to get away from Nature!) and
—dear, dear! This is really *too* much—"Leaving
yet Loving"—duet by the schoolmaster and the
assistant teacher who has just given notice. I
shall complain to the County Council!'

Christian leaned back to ask Deborah some
question about the performance, and she answered casually, without lifting her eyes from the
programme. She had been stopping at Heron,
helping Verity with her preparations, so had only
seen him once since that mystic hour in the gloam-
ing which had entrapped them both. The 'once'
had been but a lightning interview snatched in
the street while Verity threw skirts at various
squawkers' doors, and they had had little chance
of improving the situation, either way. She had
impressed silence upon him rather fiercely, and
had stayed awake half the night, recalling his hurt

and puzzled face. It was all wrong,—she felt it in every nerve—and wondered how long the situation would last. She had started at least half a dozen letters that would have brought it to an end, but always some little thing had stopped her,—some chance word or thought that sent all the springs of longing flowing back in the same direction. How easily things might have been so graciously otherwise, had those fatal words never been spoken on the old bridge! They cared enough,—she almost believed,—understood enough, to have been happy together, with the promise of something greater to come; but Slinker stood between, and across the dawn of the new hope the old doubt lingered in Christian's eyes. She was taking him as she would have taken Stanley—for Crump. His mother's words—'You would have married Christian on the same terms!' —haunted him, sleeping and waking, torturing him past endurance. The affinity born of the long day in the open and the quiet evening at dusk had vanished, leaving only a sense of upheaval and strain and helpless bewilderment. Things *could* not be right, as they were; yet how to mend them? They groped for each other in the dark, and, touching hands, found each a stranger where had been a friend.

Going wearily over the same ground, her eyes resting miserably on the back of Christian's head, she became suddenly conscious that Callander was watching her, and wrenched her attention back to Savaury and the programme.

Callander had called, the day after the meet, to apologise for his desertion.

'I thought you were coming, too,' he said

bluntly, 'or they'd never have got me inside! I was just backing out when Lyndesay told Miss Bracewell he was on his way to tea with you, so I knew you were all right. He said something about a fender-stool and a brown tea-pot, and made off after you. I suppose he caught you up?'

'Yes,—in the next field. What did he say about the tea-pot?'

'I didn't quite grasp it. Something about you having one at Kilne. Miss What's-her-name said—'Oh, I *quite* understand! How sweet of you to admire your poor relations' tea-pots!' and Christian looked at her for a whole minute. Then he said—'Miss Lyndesay and I have an ancestor who made tea for his Queen in a brown tea-pot. Since then, it has been the fashion in our family,' —and went away very politely; and Miss What-d'you-call-her snapped at me for forgetting to shut the gate. She must have put his back up, for Lyndesay never shoves his ancestors down your throat. When we got inside, Miss Braces sent the silver tea-pot back to the kitchen, and ordered an enamel thing with a cracked spout that poured all over the place. Were you long in getting home?'

She forgot how she had answered that. Perhaps not at all. She knew by now that Callander didn't always need an answer.

'Everybody's here from everywhere,' Savaury was saying, waving his eyeglasses and turning to stare, as only he could stare, at the people behind. 'It's astonishing how we all turn up at these tiresome old things,—almost as if we couldn't help it. I suppose we get into the habit, like standing up for the National Anthem, and ordering the usual

Christmas dinner even if everybody in the house has dyspepsia. Of course, Verity is quite clever and all that kind of thing, but she's not very good at taking suggestions. It's so *tiresome* when people won't follow really valuable advice. I often send her heaps of music, but she's never used a note of it yet. I see Mrs. Gardner is here in her cinematograph dress,—sequins, you say?—oh, possibly, but just as upsetting to the optic nerve. And really, somebody ought to tell Mrs. Broughton that green velvet is unlucky, and you can't be too *careful* when you're just out of the Divorce Court, —well, Petronilla, I suppose Deborah has *heard* of such a thing in this enlightened age, and you've broken that fan over me once already!'

The curtain went up, then, and he settled himself blissfully to fresh criticism.

'Now, did you ever—! I ask you—*did* you? Is it paint or mortar, I should like to know? And why white powder on a chin receding at least 45 degrees,—not to speak of ruddy rouge on a nose that certainly shouldn't be encouraged? Oh, of course Verity is quite charming, but I'm not altogether sure that it's quite the *thing* to look as stage-finished as all that. Too suggestive of our new peerage, don't you think? The singing? Oh, fair; yes, *fair*. A little unsteady, perhaps, and a shade of difference in opinion as to——Surely there must be something wrong?'

There was certainly something wrong, and everybody in the room was beginning to realise what it was. Verity had grasped it from the start of the opening chorus, for Billy-boy had roused suddenly from his state of somnolence and dashed spiritedly into his part. She could feel him lurch-

M

ing against the piano as he put on pace with each verse. At first there was merely an added swing to the usually rather tame opening, but, as the speed grew, and Verity's fingers began to race along the keys, the choir took fright. The last verse found everybody in a different bar, and Billy finished in a triumphant bellow, topping a crashing discord that made Savaury jump clean out of his seat.

Verity hurriedly dragged out the next song, trying to look as if nothing had happened, and beckoned to Harry Lauder to begin, praying that her fallen star might recover during the next item; but the soloist had barely got to his feet before the black-haired giant was in front of him, pushing him aside.

'Now don't you get shoving where you're not wanted, Tom m'lad!' he reproved him genially, barring his progress with a piqué arm. 'My song this—"Honish"—you know "Honish," Tom m' lad? Men not shinging all to sit down!'

He waved his arm pleasantly, and Harry-Lauder-Tom-m'lad sat down instantly, not on his pedestal, unfortunately, but very sharply and suddenly on the floor; while Verity, afraid to interfere, yet still more afraid to let him continue, tried to order the rebel back to his place.

'Your turn next after this, Billy!' she observed, with as good an imitation of Pélissier as she could command. 'It's "Queen amang the Heather" now, you know. Give Mr. Bell a chance!'

But alas! Billy was beyond even her influence. He staggered to the front of the stage and treated the scandalised audience to a confidential wink.

'Goin' to shing "Honish"!' he announced sweetly. 'Honish my girl, as everybody knowsh.

Everybody got a honish, like me,—everybody in thish room!' Here he fixed a pleasant and meaning gaze on Savaury, who went pink all over and waved his glasses, and would have stood up and argued the point had not Deb on one side, and Petronilla on the other, held him firmly in his seat.

Billy-boy set his feet squarely apart, and contrived to look over his shoulder at the piano without actually taking a header into the nearest singer's lap.

'Now, then, come on, Honish, my dear!' he addressed his petrified leader, with a particular brand of smile that had never yet come within her experience. 'Give us the twiddley-bitsh at the start, an' we'll show 'em all whatsh what,—see if we don't! Good little Honish—come along!'

He filled his big chest without waiting for her, and let out one long, pure, golden note, just as Verity, wringing the hands of her soul for Larrupper scouring beer-shops, beheld Grant's thin fingers snatch the curtain-ropes from the paralysed attendant, and snap it down before Billy-boy's open mouth and astonished eyes. Christian and Callander had risen to follow him when he made for the steps in a single bound, but he frowned them back as he slid behind. Billy could give him half a dozen inches and as many stone, but he had him off the stage and into the greenroom before the audible gasp of horror had died away. 'Go straight on!' he threw at Verity as they disappeared; and, as the audience broke into kindly applause which was none the less hopelessly ironic, the curtain went up again on a bruised but heroic Harry Lauder.

He was trembling in every limb, and Verity's hands shook as they struck the keys, her eyes filling with tears of relief; but between them they sang 'Queen amang the Heather' into the very heart of the crowd, so that the sixpennies, even at this early stage, caught the infection and plunged into the chorus. This time, the applause covered no awkward situation, and Verity smiled gratefully at the shaking station-master as he trembled back to his seat, before she beckoned to a shy bunch of curls to carry on the programme. In spite of Harry Lauder's gallantry, she had little hope of averting failure. The star's magnetism and the star's songs were alike lost to them, and with them the glory of the concert; and Curls, whose memory was as circuitous as her hair, was scarcely likely to fill his place.

Her recitation was inaudible to any but the first four rows, and Savaury so far forgot himself as to prompt at one of her many sticking-points, to Petronilla's utter confusion and shame; while the last verses had an accompaniment of yawns and ribald remarks from the sixpennies, who found this dull fare after the Highland lover. She was not much more than a child, and she finished in a series of gulps; her father and mother holding hands in the background and looking as though they would cry, themselves, on the slightest encouragement, in spite of their paint and giddy Pierrot hats; and though Christian tried to save the situation by throwing her a large azalea which his housekeeper had forced upon him at the last moment, a deadly panic fell upon the unfortunate troupe. Indeed, the next 'item' flatly refused to come forward at all, and Verity, beseeching him in an imploring undertone, was making up her mind to provide half the concert on her own account, when a miracle occurred. Grant, in full Pierrot costume and armed with a banjo, got Heaven knows where, marched gracefully on to the stage.

The first long moment of intense and unbelieving surprise was followed by a thunderous burst of appreciation, in which the unhappy performers joined with one accord; and, having acknowledged it with a smiling bow, the newcomer utilised the tail of it as cover for a few quick words with the stupefied lady at the piano. Then, stepping to the footlights, and accompanying himself on the banjo, he sang the promised 'Honey'.

Nobody but Savaury noticed that Billy-boy's large clothes hung painfully loosely upon the thin young parson. Nobody but Savaury had a shock when they saw the clerical collar bravely announcing its profession above the frivolous Pierrot frill. And even Savaury forgot to gasp at the wicked little cap cocked above the ascetic face, in the extreme excellence of the performance.

Such was the spectacle that greeted Larry, returning tired and cross from his fruitless search, —fruitless, indeed, since Billy was slumbering happily in the green-room, while Grant, in his astounding costume, held the audience in close and sympathetic attention, backed bravely enough, now, by the chorus, strung to action once more. Only Verity sat silent by the piano, with her hands in her lap, and her eyes on the floor, and in her heart a fighting mixture of thankfulness, admiration, relief, and shame.

'So the minutes slip away—' Grant sang sweetly, twanging the banjo mechanically in the terrible nightmare which had suddenly caught him in its grip; then missed Verity's pretty voice behind him, and threw all the soul of him into the refrain.

> 'Nother night we'll both be dead:
> 'Nother couple dance instead:
> Honey! Lift your pretty head—
> Honey, there'll be dancin' in the sky!

He not only sang, he danced, danced like a leaf, like a feather, an indiarubber ball,—danced as even Billy-boy had never danced! And from that moment his clerical reputation was gone for ever.

Larrupper dropped into a chair beside Callander, and let out a volley of demand, ejaculation, and applause.

'Wish I'd been on the spot!' he muttered worriedly, when the other had briefly put him in possession of the facts. 'I'd have taught Mr. Billy-boy an interestin' sing-song with a dog-whip! But I was busy crawlin' behind settles an' peerin' into parlours, an' gettin' myself disliked somethin' amazin', lookin' for the drunken squawker. I'll have some charmin' moments alone with him, by an' by! But can't old Grant just sing an' twiddle that banjo! Who'd have thought he'd got it in him? You don't look a bit like shoutin', old man. One might think you were used to it!'

'So I am,' Callander answered calmly. 'I knew Grant intimately before he was ordained. He was the crack entertainer of our particular neighbourhood,—always figuring on somebody's charitable platform. I've heard him sing "Honey" scores of times,—seen him as Pavlova, too, in frills. He can play anything and sing anything that he's once heard. Mean to say you folks didn't know? You're mighty slow at picking up facts! He's as clever as they're made, though he's a little bit out of practice—for him. Been starving himself for his thankless village, I expect, poor little chap! I wonder what the Bishop will say when this gets round to him?'

But Grant had left the Bishop in the green-room with Billy-boy and his parson's clothes, and had sunk every other consideration before the success of Verity's concert. And a success he made of it, indeed! Never deliberately asserting himself, he was yet definitely behind each performance, blending, guiding, smoothing over awkward places; and once, when an accompaniment disappeared, he sat down at the piano and played it by ear. At the end, dropping his banjo, he sang his mother's cradle-song, and when he had persistently refused demands for an encore, some enterprising soul requested a speech. The cry was taken up at once, and, after a moment's hesitation, he got up and came back to the foot-lights.

'I hope to Heaven he's not goin' to say anythin' about Billy!' Larrupper agitated, nearly pushing Callander off his chair. 'So upsettin' for Verity, don't you know? Hadn't I better stop him jawin' by callin' three cheers?'

'Don't you worry!' Callander said tranquilly, levering him gently back into his own seat. 'Grant knows the right thing to do as well as any-body. He wasn't *born* a parson. And your Miss

Verity may be jolly thankful she had him at her back!'

Grant spoke in a rather low tone, looking pale against the painted faces round him, and also rather exhausted. He was out of practice, as Callander had said, and a young, unmarried parson has the poor very much always with him, as well as (most often) a more or less inadequate housekeeper.

'I want to thank you very much for your kindness,' he began, hugging his banjo rather nervously. 'We've all done our best,—I'm sure you know that,—and your kind encouragement has helped some of us to do better than our best. I expect some of you are a little surprised to see me here to-night in this position,—perhaps even a little shocked—so I should just like to tell you how much I've enjoyed it. Some people think a parson doesn't enjoy making a fool of himself anywhere but in his own pulpit, but it isn't true. "'Nother night we'll all be dead," and perhaps even a parson will be glad then that he had a last dance. In any case, this parson is proud and happy to have had a chance of serving Miss Verity Cantacute. You none of you need telling what Miss Verity does for Cantacute; it's before you every day, speaking for itself. A gentleman of my acquaintance—and of hers—said to me the other night just this—gave me this very pithy and definite summing-up. "Miss Verity," he told me, "is top-dog here in Cantacute!" That was his tribute to her—"Miss Verity is top-dog in Cantacute." Ladies and gentlemen, I wish to subscribe to that tribute. In kindness, in charm, in sweetness and sympathy, in our affection, our admira-

tion and our respect, Miss Verity is indeed top-dog
in Cantacute!'

He stepped back, and Larry grinned delight-
edly, stumbling to his feet at the call of the
National Anthem.

'If that doesn't send my little girl scootin'
Arevar way,' he told himself gleefully, 'all the
Larry Lyndesays in the world will never do it!'

CHAPTER XVII

THEY were left alone on the empty stage—Verity
and her champion at need, shut in by the thick
curtain from the ebbing crowd beyond. She had
closed the piano, but she still sat beside it, looking
at the polished lid, while he stared tensely at
the heavy drapery, afraid to stay and yet unable
to leave her. When she began to speak, he turned
quickly and took a step towards her. She was
still looking at the lid, running a finger along the
bevelled edge.

'Will you tell me why you did it?' she asked in a
low and unemotional tone; but he did not answer
—only stood in the middle of the stage, looking at
her very intently and very tenderly. If she had
raised her eyes, at that moment, she would not
have needed to repeat her question.

'You won,' she went on, in the same curiously
flat voice. 'You were right and I was wrong. I
should have thought you would be glad to see my
concert spoilt—to hear me blamed on Billy's account. You need not have saved me. Why did
you do it?'

'You can't *really* think that I should have been
glad to hear you blamed,' he answered gently.

'You don't know much about me, but you know a little. You can't think that!'

'It would have been natural. It is true that I have set myself against you ever since you came to Cantacute. I was afraid of your influence. I was afraid that the people would learn to think more of you than they did of me. I meant to keep them at all costs; and the cost was——'

'Billy-boy Blackburn's soul!' he finished for her, and there was silence. Then—'You didn't understand,' he added presently, searching pityingly for excuse.

'Oh, yes, I did!' Verity answered proudly, raising her head at last, quickly. 'I knew that you were doing Billy good—that you were keeping him straight in a way absolutely beyond my power. I knew that he hadn't been drinking for months, and I couldn't bear that he should owe it to you. I never meant to lead him back into temptation, but I *did* mean to show you that he would follow me if I chose to call. I thought I could hold him—I felt certain of it. In my vanity I believed that he might fail anybody else, but never Verity Cantacute. I was wrong and you were right. You've won!'

'Ah, don't speak of it like that!' he remonstrated in a pained voice. 'We might be enemies, you and I—and surely—*surely* that isn't the case! It's all been a wretched misunderstanding, and now we must make it our business to put Billy back on the right road between us. I don't want you to feel that I owe you a grudge, or that you are under an obligation to me. Either would be intolerable! Just be friends with me, won't you, and let us forget the sadness of to-night?'

She did not answer, and he went on earnestly, leaning a hand on the piano.

'I should just like to tell you, Miss Cantacute, what was the "job" I was so loth for Billy to shirk. I had got him to sing to the old folk at the Workhouse, two or three times a week, and you should have seen how they loved it, and how he enjoyed doing it! He went regularly, and he was always sober. Generally he sang hymns, but not invariably, and the old people used to join in with their shaky old voices. It's difficult to think of Billy as an angel, isn't it, Miss Verity, but I can assure you he looked like one, then! He was so happy in his "job", and because he was happy he took peace and happiness with him, and left them behind him. And then *you* called him, and the "job" went to the wall. The old folk sit and wait for him, night after night, and he does not come. There is one old woman he used to call his mother, who puts up her wrinkled hands and cries as the hours go by——' He took a quick step to her side, his voice breaking into passionate contrition. 'Oh, forgive me, forgive me! I never meant to hurt you like that!'—for Verity had given way at last, and was weeping her heart out on the piano lid.

Tentatively he put out a reverent hand, and laid it gently on the bright hair peeping from under the foolish little cap, his voice shaking with love and tenderness and pity.

'I didn't tell you to hurt you! I only wanted to show you a little how things looked on the other side. You mustn't be unhappy. I can't bear to see you fret. We'll have Billy back at the Workhouse to-morrow, and between us we'll put things right again, God willing! Don't cry. It's dreadful to see you cry. *Oh, Honey, lift your pretty head!*'

He had never meant to say it, but it had been cradled in his mind so long, it came to his lips before he knew, and with it all the incense of his love. It brought her to her feet instantly, and as she stood staring at him with wet, startled eyes, the man behind the parson drove him forward and caught her hands. So Larrupper found them, dashing into the wings after seeing the Savaurys to their carriage—the pale Pierrot and the painted Pierrette, standing together on the darkened stage.

'Parson or Pierrot, I love you, Verity!' Grant was pleading, but Verity stopped him with a quick movement.

'Don't say any more, Mr. Grant!' she said clearly, looking straight at him with the courage born of her pity and shame. 'I am engaged to Lionel Lyndesay.'

CHAPTER XVIII

'I'M comin' home with you,' Larrupper announced, stepping after her into the Heron brougham. His face was quite colourless, and he did not look at her. 'Old Grange is follyin' behind with the car, but there's somethin' I want to say to you, an' it won't improve with keepin'. Then I'm goin' back for a chin-chin with Blackburn.'

'You're not to say anything to Billy!' Verity exclaimed angrily. 'Leave him to Mr. Grant. You'll only make things worse.'

'That's just what I want to make 'em!' Larry responded grimly. 'I mean to make 'em so bad that there'll be no dancin' except on crutches for the next six months. It's no use arguin', my dear girl. This is a man's job, so you may as well stop worryin'.'

'Oh, but don't you understand——?' Verity began piteously, and stopped, for she had seen his face by a passing lamp, and she was afraid. They drove back to Heron in silence.

Mrs. Cantacute was already upstairs when they got in, and they went up together to tell her how things had gone. She worshipped every hair of Larry's head, and he spent many an hour with her, cheering her after his own peculiar fashion.

Oh, it had been a complete success! they informed her, carefully leaving the awkward details to be broken later. A crowded house and a most appreciative audience. Everything, in fact, that could be desired.

'And how did my favourite song go?' gentle Mrs. Cantacute inquired eagerly. 'You know the one I mean, don't you?—the song with the pretty refrain—"Honey".'

Verity coloured to the roots of her hair under her paint, for Larrupper was looking at her mercilessly across the bed.

'Oh, it was the song of the evenin'!' he answered easily and with effusion. 'Went like steam an' took like influenza. Everybody in the place goin' away hummin' it, even carpin' old Savaury an' his pampered darlin' of a coachman. I mustn't stop, though, dear old sweetheart. Grange is outside, waitin', an' he'll be hungry after all that yowlin'.'

'Send him in for something,' Mrs. Cantacute begged, as he stooped to kiss her. 'And mind you get what you want yourself, Lionel. You know you are at home here, don't you?'

'Thank you, old dear!' Larry answered gently, without looking at her; but when he was downstairs again, he refused Verity's hospitality brusquely.

'I don't want anythin' in that line,' he said rather roughly, 'and old Grange can go on starvin' a bit longer, for a change! I told you I'd somethin' to say to you, but I don't fancy talkin' to a painted marionette, so suppose you go away an' wash your face!'

'I'm not in a mood for being "talked to",' she replied, flushing indignantly under his disapproving gaze. 'And if you can't be even moderately polite, you had better go away and let me get off to bed, for I'm simply dead tired.'

'You'll have to keep awake, anyhow, till I'm through,' he said doggedly. 'But I want to talk to the girl I'm used to seein', an' not to a music-hall turn. You'd better do what I say, or there'll be all the more time goin' beggin' for Billy.'

When she had gone, he remained beside the dying fire, alternately staring moodily at the flickering coal and addressing himself gloomily in the overmantel. Deborah had been right, he told himself, miserably. The crisis in their light love-making had come at last, and neither he nor Verity knew how to meet it. Would the bond between them really bear the strain? Or would to-morrow see the beginning of a new and empty life, separated from the old, happy, laughing one for ever?

She came back, presently, without her cap, her little face faintly flushed, her shining hair brushed in smooth waves from its Madonna-like parting.

'Now, what is it?' she asked peremptorily, anything but Madonna-like in demeanour. 'You seem in a shockingly bad temper, and I can't think why. After all, Billy-boy is no concern of yours in any way, and you've got to promise me before you go that you'll leave him alone.'

'It's every decent man's concern when a low cad's insultin' a lady,' Larrupper answered stubbornly. 'I ought never to have allowed you to have anythin' to do with him, but you're always so set on havin' your own way, there's no movin' you. Well, you can have any way you find pleasin' when I'm through with Billy.'

'No, no, Larrupper—*please*!' she begged, growing alarmed before his steady grimness. 'It's true I ought never to have asked him, but I thought he would keep straight for me—indeed I did! He's never failed me before. There seems to have been a sort of fate in it. Oh, I know I did wrong in not leaving him alone, but you won't improve matters by going for him or—or hammering him. He'll only turn nasty, and never look at any of us again. That's the way to send him to the dogs for life.'

'An' the best place for him!' Larry added heartily. 'It's no use bullyin' me. This is man's work, as I told you before. An' I'm not starvin' old Grange for the pleasure of talkin' about Blackburn. There's somethin' else. That parson was makin' love to you!'

Verity crimsoned for the third time, slowly

and painfully. She had never before known a moment's embarrassment with Larrupper, but to-night he seemed like a stranger, with his black brows drawn together, and his gloomy eyes searching hers. There was something menacing about the set of his heavy shoulders and the droop of his bullet head.

'Yes,' she admitted in a low tone. 'He—asked me to marry him. It doesn't seem fair to tell you, but I think you know, without it. You needn't be jealous,' she finished quickly, following an hysterical impulse to say the most hopelessly wrong thing possible.

'Jealous?' Larry's dark face flushed violently. 'Jealous of old Grant? Did you think I came bargin' in at this time of night just to tell you I was jealous? Then you're wrong. I came to ask you a straight question, an' if you can give me a straight answer without any shilly-shallyin'—and the right one, mind you!—I'll make a night of it with old Grange over the '84 port. But if you can't—if you *can't*——!' A dog-like anticipation of trouble came into his dark eyes as he looked at her, and his hand shook on the mantelpiece, for everything hung on that question, and he was afraid both of the answer and of himself.

'It's just this!' he said heavily. 'A man doesn't go askin' girls to marry him without thinkin' about it a bit beforehand, especially when he's tuckered out like an Aunt Sally an' a bit of Barnum mixed. Old Grant isn't the sort, either, to be plungin' into proposals without so much as a twinge of warnin'. He must have been goin' that way for weeks, poor old chap, an' gettin' worked up for the jumpin'-off. Now I'm askin' you—

did you know he was fallin' in love with you, or did you not?'

'Yes, I knew,' Verity answered, quietly but without hesitation, as he paused for breath. 'It isn't difficult to know a thing like that, Larry, whether one wants to or not.'

'No, I suppose it's generally shoutin',' he agreed moodily. 'I'd have seen it myself if I'd gone to the trouble of lookin'. But there's somethin' more. A girl can't help a man carin' for her, but she can play fair, all the same. Did you do right by old Grant, my dear—or did you lend him a hand to makin' a fool of himself, leadin' him on with your smiles an' your pretty little ways? Did you play fair by the parson, old girl—that's what I'm wantin' to know?'

She said nothing, this time, only turned her head away from him, and slid a hand over her eyes, while he stood beside her, breathing heavily, doggedly demanding the truth he hated but had already guessed.

'Oh, darlin', can't you lie to me!' she heard him say under his breath, passionately beseeching, and she shook her head without turning, knowing there was no need of words. He uttered a curious sound, half-sob, half-exclamation, and after that there was a long pause. Then she felt him leave her and move across to the door.

'I must be gettin' off,' he said easily and cheerfully. 'Old Grange will be freezin', I'm afraid, an' he'll not get the '84, after all, dear old thing! Hope you won't be too dog-tired in the mornin'.'

She straightened herself, then, and swung round, looking at him with miserable eyes.

'I always knew this was bound to happen,' she

said. 'I knew a day would come when you would see me as I am, and not just as you chose to see me. You've always made an idol of me, though I've tried hard enough, in all conscience, to undeceive you! I'm not a goddess to be worshipped or a baby to be petted and soothed. I'm simply a woman chock-full of faults, and if you'd shown me you knew it and didn't mind, you could have had me long since. Now—I'll never be your idol again. It's true that I knew Mr. Grant cared—true that I encouraged him. I won't lie to you. I was jealous of his influence in the village, and I knew that if he fell in love with me he'd have to lay down his arms. So I led him on. Do you hear, Larry? Take that home, and get it deep down into your soul. *I led him on!*'

Larrupper winced sharply and unmistakably, but he smiled quite pleasantly.

'What's the use of worryin'?' he replied, falling back upon his usual formula. 'We'll all be feelin' better, to-morrow, an' we'll swim along somehow without smashin' one another, you'll see! You'll not think me rude to be goin', will you? I'm sure I can hear old Grange weepin' outside.'

He opened the door; then paused again.

'There's just one other thing, if you don't mind my mentionin' it? You told old Grant that you were goin' to marry Lionel Lyndesay. Well, it isn't true about Lionel, whatever it may once have been about Larry. Larry's wantin' you with every little bit of him, but Lionel isn't goin' to take the risk!'

CHAPTER XIX

A THREATENING sky was scudding before a fast-rising gale, and an ominous dread lay over the marsh, but Roger Lyndesay walked in a sheltered corner at Kilne between borders of yellow crocus. The hill behind stood like a giant screen between him and the rough weather coming straight from the sea. There was a stone seat let into the side of the fell, where he rested, every now and again, looking through the swaying veil of budding branches to the creepered house where he and his forefathers had lived so long, and from its windows had watched ceaselessly over Crump. Even now, though the years were passing, the prestige of the agency still remained with old Roger. Any old tenant, questioned in a hurry, would still have given his name. Rent-day found most of them still besieging his door. Even Callander had a curious feeling that he himself was no more than pupil or assistant to the fine old man.

Pacing slowly in his shelter, Roger found himself wishing, with the ache of an old hurt apparently long healed, that Deborah had been a boy. With his own death, and her possible marriage to a stranger, their particular branch would be cut from the old root for ever. It hurt him to think that Kilne would pass into other hands; that others, not of his blood, would sit in his window and look across the river with different eyes. They would never know the myriad faces of the land as he knew them; nor watch as he for the continual miracle of the sun springing red over Cappelside, or dropping yellow behind the Hall, or

flinging long shafts of gold down the shadowed
aisles of beech. In how many years would they
learn the perfect moment when the avenue was
at its best; the time of year when the rooks held
parliament on the hill; and just what trick of wind
brought the clearest music from the kennels?
In how many generations would they come to
pass the deer without seeing a single head raised
in fear, or stretch an empty hand for the gentle
nibbling of the collared King of the Herd? Would
they heed the kingfisher at his evening drink,
or the corncrake calling the scythe all night
long, or the sleek head of the otter rising from
the deep pool under the old bridge? And would
they sit in the dark, alone and perfectly content,
watching the lights of Crump across the black
water as men watch shrine-candles in the dim
church of their worship? These things, that made
the life of his soul, were the natural heritage of
a son of Kilne, who needed scant initiation into
their mysteries. But there was no son at Kilne;
only a daughter, into whose hands the birthright
of love and service could never fall.

He was roused from his brooding by the sound
of hoofs stamping at the gate, and with some
curiosity he trod slowly round to find Slinker's
wife on the point of slipping from the saddle. His
mind had been so much in the past that his fast-
fading memory failed to put a name to her, and
as she stooped with a smile to hand him a letter,
mourning-edged, his courtly old heart warmed to
her grace and spirit.

'For Deb,' she told him, as he took the envelope,
and was on the point of asking to see her when her
horse, which had been plunging and backing,

swung her across the road and almost on to the
iron railing.

'He's girthed too tight, I think,' she explained,
when she had brought him back and slid to the
ground. 'He's a perfect mount, as a rule, but he's
been behaving badly all the way, so I think there
must be something wrong.'

She pulled off her gauntlets and lifted the flap,
but Roger Lyndesay interposed with a courteous
movement.

'Allow me!' he said gently, and she stood aside
while he loosened the girths; the horse standing
quietly enough, even turning his head to push
softly at Roger's shoulder. And she knew, as
she watched, why Deborah's hands were so like
Christian's.

When he had settled things to his satisfaction,
and dropped a last caress on the smooth neck, the
old man turned with a smile and gallantly offered
his palm to mount her; but she stepped back,
shaking her head, the embarrassed colour rising
to her eyes.

'Not that!' she said firmly, as he stared in surprise. 'I can't allow you to do that. That sort of
thing's for gentlefolk, Mr. Lyndesay, not for old
Steenie Stone's daughter!'

A faint flush swept over the ivory face, and the
proud old back made an effort after its ancient
dignity.

'You are Stanley's widow—Mrs. Lyndesay?' he
asked coldly and with a touch of resentment, as
if she had entrapped him, helpless, into an impossible situation.

'That's what they call me, here.' Mrs. Slinker
nodded, with her hand on the stirrup. 'I don't

call myself that, you may be sure, least of all to *you*, Mr. Lyndesay! You think I'm an interloper, I know, and you're quite right. I've no business at Crump—I know my place well enough for that. There are plenty of folks ready enough to cocker me and tell me I'm a fine lady, but for all that I don't forget who I am. And I remember you, Mr. Lyndesay, ever since I could walk. You used to come over to my father's, often, and you always had a look and a kind word for me—*then*. I can see you now, cantering into the yard on that grand chestnut of yours—they've always had chestnuts at Crump, haven't they?—and all the stable doors flung wide for you to have your pick. You did all the choosing for William Lyndesay, I've heard Father say, and he kept a fine stud up at the Hall in those days, didn't he?'

Old Roger was half-turned to the gate, looking down at the road, but she could tell that he was listening.

'Old days are best, after all, aren't they?' she went on, with a wistful drop of her voice. 'I used to stop up at Dockerneuk when I was a girl— many a happy time I've had there; I've had nothing like it since. Now I'm stopping at the Hall—it's queer, isn't it? My father made a lot of money, you know, and he had me well educated —when he could get me to leave him and his horses! And when he died, I went abroad for a bit; my sister had married in Canada, and it was pretty lonely for Nettie Stone. I'd known Stanley as a boy, and I came across him again at Taormina—well, we needn't talk about that, need we? But I'd like you to know that I haven't forgotten my place. My father thought the world of you

and your judgment, and he taught his daughter
to do the same. I'll always have that picture of
you, riding into Dowgill, straight as an arrow,
on Crump Clever Lass, with all the doors flying
open, and my father on the step, smiling and
touching his hat. I may seem a rank outsider,
Mr. Lyndesay, an impertinent upstart to an aristocrat like you, but I'm touching my hat to you
all the time in my heart!'

Roger turned slowly and looked at her as she
stood fumbling with the stirrup, her pleading eyes
fixed on him, and the deferential sentences hurrying each other from her lips. Then he swept his
hat very low, and offered his hand a second time
for her foot. She accepted it, now, with a tremu-
lous smile; and, as he put it up, the next moment,
to straighten her habit, she caught it between her
own, palm upward, looking at it. 'Only a little
dust,' she said, very tenderly and reverently.
'Nothing to hurt even a Lyndesay! And I didn't
weigh much heavier, myself, did I? I shall always
remember that you paid me the greatest honour
of my life!'

She turned her horse and rode away quickly,
for the tears were in her eyes, and Roger Lyndesay went slowly into the house with the note.

He found Deb in the pantry, polishing the silver
candlesticks which had been William Lyndesay's
last gift to him; and again, as he looked at her
bright youth and alert grace, the longing came to
him that she had been a boy. He passed his hand
lovingly over the shining metal, and along the
inscription with its sincere words of recognition.

'They are yours, Deb, remember,' he said, laying down the letter, as she put the leather back in

its place. 'If I had a son, they would be his, of course, but, as it is, they are yours. Keep them always. Don't let any of the Morton people have them.'

'Just let them try!' Deb answered defiantly, hugging her treasure jealously in her arms. 'Don't be afraid, Dad. I'll never let anybody else put a finger on them. And I'll stick to them if I'm starving in the street, with the pair of them tucked safely under my shawl!'

'You should have been a boy!' he sighed, giving vent to his insistent thought at last. 'As it is, you will have to leave Kilne when I am gone. If you had been a boy, you would have had the agency, and stayed on here for life. You would have taken on the work as a matter of course.'

'Should I?' she asked, with her eyes on the candlesticks.

'Why, certainly—if you had been a boy. You would have belonged to the old place like the rest of us. As things are, you cannot be expected to feel the call.'

'Can't a girl feel it, then?' Deb inquired, without lifting her eyes. 'Does a girl never hanker after her father's profession, and feel that the rest of life is nothing beside it?'

He smiled faintly with a touch of amusement, shaking his head.

'How should a girl hear a call of that kind? It's the men that count in that, not the women— never the women. If I had had a son, *he* would have heard it. You have been a good daughter to me, Deborah, but it takes a man to understand these things.'

He went back into the garden, after that, forgetting that he had said nothing of Mrs. Stanley, and for a long time Deb stood rigid, gazing into vacancy, the candlesticks clasped in her arms. All the hidden longing of her childhood, all the repressed passion of her later years, rose and swept over her in a flood, and sobbed and tore at her heart. Not even her father, living in such close communion with her, had guessed at the motive of her whole being. If only she had been a boy—ah, if only she had been a boy! But she was nothing but a helpless, useless girl, and soon, very soon, perhaps, she would be in exile, as the boy need never have been. She was a girl, and she would have to go. She gripped the candlesticks tighter. In that moment she swore to marry Christian, no matter what the rash act might bring—pain, shame, or lifelong remorse; and the ironic gods, who await our flashes of complete decision to hound on their instant refutation, loosed their leash.

She had avoided him since the concert, disappearing along side-roads and sending down messages of excuse when he called; but all that was over. She would avoid him no more. This one means of restitution was left to the girl who ought to have been a boy.

At last she drew a long, sobbing breath and stirred, setting down the candlesticks and reaching for the forgotten note. Its contents came as a sharp surprise, for they requested her attendance upon Mrs. Lyndesay at her earliest possible convenience.

Her first impulse was to let the command—for it was nothing less—pass unnoticed, but she reflected that, in the circumstances, such flagrant independence would scarcely be wise. She could marry Christian, of course, in the face of his mother's opposition, but the situation was more than likely to be sufficiently unpleasant, in any case, and only folly would deliberately add to it. She dressed slowly, knowing she would go, but debating the point impatiently, nevertheless, and turning even at the gate on a sharp impulse of resentment and defiance. An old hawker, passing, lifted his ragged whip and shook it at her with a toothless smile.

'Never turn back, lady!' the old voice creaked across the wall. 'It's bad luck to turn when you've once started. You'll not prosper, lady! You'll rue it before morning!'

She laughed, waving her hand after the rattling cart, and forgot the superstition on the spot; but later—that very night—the warning came back to her, knife-edged.

Still, the incident had shaken her out of her morbid self-introspection, and she walked rapidly to Crump, refusing stoutly to fear what lay before her. It was foolish to cross bridges until you came to them, and the unexpected might prove pleasant, after all. Perhaps an apology for the slight on her father—but even her sudden change of mood could not show her Mrs. Lyndesay apologising to anybody about anything.

Nettie appeared from the stable-yard as she approached, and came to meet her. She wondered whether Deborah knew of her recent interview, but, as the girl said nothing, she guessed that the old man had not told, and she held her peace. Not until years after he was dead, did she tell

Roger Lyndesay's daughter of the little scene she had held sacred so long.

'I don't know why you were asked,' she observed, as they went up the approach together. 'She never mentions you to me, you know, and I can't exactly make a point of discussing you. I was just asked to deliver the note, that was all. It's ripping of you to come, *I* think. Wild horses wouldn't have dragged me if she'd treated me as she's treated you.'

'I was born at the beck of Crump,' Deb answered, looking up at the old house. 'It's in the blood, and I can't help it. *You* can afford to snap your fingers at it, but Kilne must come running if it lifts a hand.'

'I wish to goodness I *had* snapped my fingers at it!' Mrs. Slinker said sadly, as they went in. (She had not seen Dixon for a month.) 'Rishwald dines here to-night,' she added, in a lighter tone. 'I'm getting rather worried about him, to tell the truth. I fancy he thinks I'd make a nice match for his Tobies and Queen Annes. No—not there' —as Deb turned instinctively towards the library. 'Upstairs, in Stanley's own room—horrid little smoke-pot! You know it, of course, so I'll let you go alone; but if she gets really rampant, just let out a yell, and I'll come up at a gallop.'

She let go the girl's hand rather reluctantly, for Deb had unconsciously gone white; and then, on a sudden impulse, she stooped and kissed her.

'I'm older than you,' she said, almost apologetically, 'older and harder, and I've got used to the atmosphere of this mouldy old place. I won't let it suck the soul out of me. It gets you by the throat, doesn't it, when you come in? It's—it's the old lady!'—she nodded upstairs, a look half-mischievous, half-frightened, on her face—'Mrs. Lyndesay and that vampire of a tree out on the lawn. When they're gone, please God, there'll be a clean wind blowing through Crump!'

She disappeared, and Deb, ascending past an open window facing west, was caught in a great blast of air, shaking the pictures on the walls, and shrieking eerily round the eaves, as the tide rose and the gale grew steadily from the sea. She drew in a deep breath of it before she climbed the last stair and knocked at Slinker's door.

Personality clings to a room long after the occupant is dead, especially if it be left untouched, and as she entered, meeting the portrait's meaning smile, it seemed to her that Slinker himself was there indeed. She had forgotten the picture, and the shock of it held her captive for a moment, until, dropping her eyes, she met the same disconcerting smile on the cold lips of his mother. Her first words made her start, translating as they did the thought in her mind.

'Oh, yes, he's here!' Mrs. Lyndesay said coolly. 'You felt him when you opened the door—don't deny it. He is here, all the time, listening when we speak.' She looked round at one of the big chairs by the fire, and Deborah felt a sudden fear thrill the morbid atmosphere already invoked. Yet the eyes that turned back to her were sane enough, and hard as gems are hard, as the light on a new-drawn sword, and the line of Lake hills before rain.

'People never die,' said Mrs. Lyndesay. 'You think you've got rid of them, but they come back —they always come back. Yet Stanley is dead in the eyes of the world, and Christian follows him. That is sufficient for you. You would have married Stanley; and now you mean to marry— his heir!'

Deborah drew back, the blood surging to her face, for she had never thought of this. Christian had passed his word to say nothing, and she had given no soul on earth a clue to their secret.

'You wonder how I know?' Mrs. Lyndesay asked smoothly. 'It is simple—these things are always simple.' She indicated the window looking towards the stables. 'One of the boys was talking of you, to-day. He had followed hounds, it seemed, the day of the Crump meet. He informed an assembly of open-mouthed employées that he had seen Christian holding your hand. Does it please you to be meat for gossip in the mart of the stable-yard?'

Deb, beaten to the wall, looked helplessly round the room, only to be conscious of enmity everywhere, from the polite-sneering portrait to her late picture-postcard rivals. She wondered vaguely what had happened to her own photograph, and concluded that Slinker's mother had destroyed it. Meanwhile, the passionless voice went on relentlessly.

'It is a fortnight since the meet, and you have not as yet seen fit to give me any information on this point. I must conclude, therefore, that you intend to be married secretly, so that you can snap your fingers in the face of disapproval, mine and that of every right-thinking individual. For I know that you *do* mean to marry my son. I have known it—subconsciously, I suppose—ever since the day of Stanley's death. You mean to marry

Christian as you would have married his brother
—for Crump!'

There was a pause, and then Deb said—'It is
true!' as she had said once before on a similar
night of storm, in the library downstairs.

The other looked at her with a certain cold
wonder.

'Lyndesays are all ambitious,' she said, 'all
ambitious and all proud. I myself am a Lyndesay
born, as you know. But you are more ambitious,
prouder, surer of yourself than any of us. You
would seize Crump in the teeth of all right feeling, decency and respect, grasping an honour
snatched from the very hand of the dead. Was
there not enough of the scandal laid to your credit,
that you must force another upon the family.'

'The scandal was not of my making!' Deb replied, and the elder woman gave a curious laugh.

'Stanley is listening, remember! Perhaps *he*
could tell us how you tempted him, how the force
of your passion to be mistress of Crump carried
him off his feet and made him false to his vows—
for a while. He would have gone back to his
wife—I, his mother, tell you that. Do not flatter
yourself that you would have had him, in any
case, had he lived. He would have gone back to
his wife! You came at a time when he was lonely
and unhappy, and you drew him to you by the
same spell that you have thrown over Christian.
But the one escaped you, and so shall the other
—ay, if he has to follow the same road!'

'Stanley came to me of his own accord!' Deb
began hotly, and stopped, for the insidious atmosphere crept upon her, filling her with doubt.
Perhaps, after all, she had drawn Stanley without

knowing it. He had ignored her, at first, but, later, when she had turned on him on the subject of some ill-used servant, he had laughed at her and made friends with her; and after that he had seemed unable to keep away. His eyes had followed her hungrily and almost helplessly, and in her presence he had been generally good-humoured and even kind. Had she indeed a spell that drew these men to her whether she would or not? The thought struck her sharply that even Christian had never said he loved her. He did not love her, she felt that, but she had thought him near it. Was it just the charm working, and no more—the attraction of her longing, the magnetism of her passionate desire?

'Christian pities you!' the voice went on cruelly. 'He realises all that you lost when you lost Stanley. He thinks he owes you his brother's debt. He does not love you—surely you cannot imagine that? Christian does not care for women. He is as cold as Galahad. But he can give you as much as Stanley could have given you—his place and his prestige, his house and his money, his carriages and horses, his hothouses, hounds and men! He thinks you are breaking your heart for these—all the things after which a poor relation naturally hankers—and he is generous enough to wish that you should have them. Christian would always have given his last coin to a beggar—and this is yours. A delicate position, isn't it?' she sneered. 'Will you still take Crump at the price?'

Deb said 'Yes!' faintly enough, but clinging to her determination and nebulous hopes in spite of the crushing opposition closing about her. She had had a vision of things come right, up on the hill alone with Christian, and its fragrant promise clung to her dimly, even yet. Moreover, she would never crawl to this woman.

Mrs. Lyndesay seemed puzzled. She had been so sure of her instrument, and she wondered where her touch had failed.

'I thought not even you could have sunk to that!' she said, at last. 'Will you marry a second man who cares no more for you than for a pet horse or hound?'

Deb winced and looked away, and this time the other followed her glance as it went back to the place where her photograph had hung. 'Christian took your picture,' she said casually. 'I missed it, one day, just after he had been in. It was last year—months since—when he hardly knew and was scarcely interested in you, so you will not be able to flatter yourself that he was in love with you *then*! I suppose he took it because he was sorry for you—that is Christian all over. He always hated this room, and you were obviously out of place among these birds of a feather!'

She waved her hand scornfully at the cheap faces she hated, yet which she permitted no one else to handle, and sat back, satisfied, awaiting results. And she had every reason to be satisfied, for her last speech had clinched her argument in full, though after a fashion of which she did not dream.

Deb stood staring at the empty space, unconscious for the moment of the evil presences lying in wait, seeing only the kindness in Christian's face as his hand went out to her, and the delicate chivalry that had hastened to shield a girl he scarcely knew and could hardly respect. He filled the room in spite of his brother—at that instant, Slinker was certainly and praisefully dead—and the dream on the hill caught her again in its rosy fingers. The inner meaning of her heart-searchings came home to her in a flash of revelation, and she understood why she had hesitated to wrong him and herself, as she had never hesitated with Stanley—why she must give him up now when he had grown to fill her whole world. For she knew at last that she loved him.

The room ceased to have any hold on her. The portrait's eyes claimed her no longer. She turned back to Mrs. Lyndesay, bewildering her with a sudden smile.

'I will give him up!' she said definitely, in a tone that held neither resignation nor defeat, but something brighter and braver than had ever purified the atmosphere of Slinker's lair. 'I will give him back his promise—not because you have badgered me into submission, nor because I am afraid of gossip or the idle chatter of a few stable-boys, but because I know something now that I did not know before. I could hold him in spite of you, but I will not try.

'I will not try!' she said a second time, and laid her sword at her enemy's feet.

There was a moment's silence, while the mistress of Crump leaned across the table, staring into the girl's face; then pushed back her chair with an abrupt movement.

'Why, I believe you love him!' she exclaimed incredulously, and, as Deb looked at her, saying nothing—'You poor fool!' she added harshly; and at that moment Christian knocked and entered.

'Am I interrupting?' he asked pleasantly, looking from one to the other. 'Nettie told me Deborah was here.' He held out his hand, and she put hers into it mechanically. 'When you've finished, will you lend her to me for a little while? Callander and I have been hammering away at that boundary dispute, and Deb is sure to know the rights of the case.'

'Deborah is here to show you the rights of some other question,' his mother replied curtly, rising. 'I will leave you to discuss it.' She moved to the door, but Christian put out his arm.

'Please explain!' he said gently. 'What have you been saying to Deborah? Anything that concerns her concerns me—now.'

'She is here to undeceive you on that point. I am aware that you have foolishly allowed yourself to be entrapped into an engagement, much as your brother was caught before you, but that, too, is at an end. You have me to thank for your liberty. Deborah has given me her word to set you free.'

Christian, his mind in a whirl, looked across at Deb, standing motionless by the window, gazing down into the yard. Something had happened, though he could not even begin to guess what it was, except that in some mysterious way his mother had come to know of the contract on the hill. But at least she should not interfere. She had taken something from him once already in this very room, but she should never take from him the man's right to choose his own mate. His colour rose as he still barred her exit.

'I don't understand how you know anything about it,' he said quickly. 'Not that it matters.

Of course we should have told you very soon. I should have liked you to have been glad, but I want Deborah for my wife, in any case, and, if she is willing to come to me, I will not let anything else stand in the way.'

'You will find more than enough in the way,' Mrs. Lyndesay answered strangely. 'You will find—Deborah herself!' And at her imperious gesture he lowered his arm and watched her pass from the room. Deb's heart followed her in a faint thrill of feeling towards a personality she had always hated. At least she had not betrayed her, even by a hint. For the first and last time in her life, she was grateful to her.

She stood by the window, thinking hard. It was plain that Christian was not ready to let her go. His liberty would have to be forced upon him, for she had passed her word and she meant to keep it. She might have risked her soul for Crump, but she would not throw her new-born love into the scale.

He came to her quickly, demanding—'What does it mean?' puzzled and impatient. 'Who can have said anything to my mother? Not you, of course. But who can possibly have told?'

'That imitation Sherlock—a stable boy!' she answered lightly, looking at the wide quadrangle of buildings below. 'One of your small fry saw us, up on Linacre, and Mrs. Lyndesay overheard the result of his observations.'

'Then that settles it!' he said definitely. 'You must give me permission to announce our engagement at once.'

But Deb shook her head.

'Your mother told you that I had thought

better of it. It's the truth, so you may as well accept it without argument. I expect you'll be rather relieved, as a matter of fact. You're too nice to be married for your property, Christian, and I think I'm too nice to be married for pity.'

'Pity!' He took her hands and turned her towards him, keenly searching her face. 'Why, Debbie dear, you can't really think anything as silly as that! We're such good friends, you and I—don't let my mother's bitterness wrench us apart.'

'We can still be good friends,' she answered steadily. 'It isn't as if there had ever been any—anything that mattered—between us. These last two weeks don't count—not as they would have counted if we'd—cared. You were feeling chivalrous, up at Linacre, and I was lonely, thinking of the day when I should have to leave Kilne. That's not sufficient foundation for a lifetime together, and we knew it well enough, even then. Let's go back to what we were. After all, no—no harm—has been done.'

'No harm?' Christian echoed. 'It depends what you mean by that. How can we go back? And of course these two weeks count! Do you think a man ever feels the same towards a woman after he has once thought of her definitely as his wife, even for a day? It's absurd to talk like that. You're mine, and I mean to keep you. Have I done anything unconsciously to make you change your mind?—or is it just my mother's influence and no more? You don't like me less than you did, do you?' he went on earnestly. 'I'll cut my throat if you don't go on liking me, Debbie dear!'

She laughed, though the tears were behind.

'You're as nice as ever you can be! I've told you that, once, already—too nice to be handed over to anybody you don't want so frightfully that you'd climb the stars for her. And that isn't how you feel towards a "friend", Squire Lakin' Lyndesay!'

'But I do!' he protested hotly. 'I don't only think of you as a comrade, though you're the best a man could want. I think of you as the woman I love——'

'Ah, don't say it!' She stopped him, her voice full of pain, and they stood silent, staring out of the window.

Which of them was right at that moment he could not have told. He was only conscious that she was necessary to him, that she filled an empty place in his heart, strengthening his hand by the touch of hers. He saw her as a kindred spirit upon whom he could rely, a fountain of that sympathy of which he had been so stubbornly deprived, the dearest part of the new life he had been called upon to lead; and he could not let her go. He tightened his clasp on her hands and drew her nearer.

'You've been thinking things, all sorts of absurd and unkind things, and my mother's been thinking other things for you; but now you've got to think with *me* and listen to *me*! I want you for my wife, Deb, and it doesn't matter a jot *why* you marry me as long as you *do* marry me, so tell me I still have your promise, and trust me to bring my mother round, after a while.'

'It doesn't matter?' Deb looked at him intently, sadly, yet with a touch of mischief in spite of her aching heart. 'It doesn't *really* matter if I marry you for a daily drive behind liveries, rather than for the sake of belonging to you and being your wife?—not because I want to be with you always, and because of the way you smile and speak, and bring the sunshine with you wherever I happen to be, but because it is a fine thing to be mistress of Crump, and to have the first place at dinner parties, and all the county kow-towing to me, hat in hand? It doesn't *really* matter?'

His face fell boyishly, and she drew a sharp breath of mixed relief and pain, for if he had loved her he would have known how hopelessly she had betrayed herself in that last speech. He would have caught her in his arms and crushed her foolish argument into silence; not have stood looking down at her doubtfully, as Christian was doing, half-smiling and half-abashed.

'But you *do* like to be with me, don't you?' he asked anxiously; and she just answered, 'Oh, Christian!' rather hysterically, trying to free her hands, and, after a moment's struggle, he let them go.

'I don't believe that you only care for the flesh-pots,' he said, his face very troubled. 'You always make out that you do, but anybody who knows you as well as I do can see that you're not really like that. It's only natural, of course, that the place should appeal to you. You're not a Lynde-say for nothing. But you're too fine a nature to marry a man for whom you had no feeling whatever. If you care for me only a little, Deb, we'll get along all right and make life a success. Others have done it who didn't start with half as good a friendship as ours. Tell me it's not just the place and nothing else, and I'll keep you in spite of everybody, in spite of my mother, in spite of yourself. Tell me you care a little!'

'As I cared for Stanley!' she answered steadily, making a last effort; and, as the portrait flashed back upon their consciousness, it seemed to both of them that Slinker himself was in very truth standing there between them.

CHAPTER XX

CALLANDER was in the hall when they went down, and he took Deborah home. He wondered a little at the ceremoniousness with which Christian took leave of them at the door, but he was often puzzled by the mixture of boyishness and dignity in the young man, and thought no more of it. As for Deb, she was too busy holding to her hat in the teeth of the now flying gale to yield any satisfactory psychological impression. He had long since realised the affinity between the two, but exactly where they stood he could not guess.

As they left the park by the lower lodge, the Whyterigg car turned in at the gates, and roared past them in the fading light.

'There's Rishwald,' Callander remarked, looking after it. 'Mr. Lyndesay will be late. Mrs. Stanley was ready for dinner long since, and kept coming out of her room and signalling me with hair-brushes to know whether you were still in the house.'

'It was good of you to wait,' Deb replied mechanically. Her brain was still numb after the late strain, and she felt dazed by the rushing tumult around her.

'I wanted to walk home with you,' he said simply. 'I knew Christian was engaged, and it isn't a night for a lady to be out alone;' and put his arm before her as he spoke, for a torn branch came whirling heavily to the ground at their very feet.

She could hear the big tide filling the river, and wondered if the sheep were safe on the mosses, and whether the low-lying farms were trembling for the sea-wall. She could not help remembering that on such a night Slinker had gone to his account. On such a night Christian had come into her life; and, on this, its counterpart, he was going out of it. A thought struck her, and she half-stopped, looking back to Crump.

'What is it?' Callander asked. 'Have you forgotten something? I will go back for it.' But she turned again, shaking her head.

'It was only an old superstition that came into my mind,' she explained, when they came under the lee of the Kilne wall, and she could get her breath. 'They say Lyndesays of Crump always die in a gale. I suppose it's absurd, but it's a fact that Stanley died on a night like this, and William Lyndesay, too. Of course there is many a storm which brings no disaster, and it can't be anything but a curious coincidence, but Crump has many a frowning fate against it, as you must have found, by now.'

'Yes, the estate seems to reek with ill-luck,' Callander said thoughtfully. 'I'm always running up against samples. And how firmly everybody believes in it, too! This field must not be ploughed—nothing would spring in it. Sheep can't be heafed on that fell—they would die in a week. In a certain shippon the dobbie milks first; and so on. It has a certain charm for an outsider, but it is awkward from a business point of view, and must be decidedly trying if you take it all to heart.

'There's a big wrestling-match on at the Academy, to-night,' he added, presently, 'and Christian has promised to look in. I'm going up for him, so can keep an eye open to see that the gale does him no harm!' he ended laughingly, as they reached the gate.

'Thanks!' Deb returned, smiling. 'It's all non-sense, I suppose, and you must think me very silly, but I'm just as governed by the old traditions as all the rest.

'I'm glad you came here,' she added, on a sudden impulse. 'I'm glad you'll have Kilne when we're gone. It knows you already—don't you feel it when you come in? I couldn't have gone away, leaving the house to a stranger.'

'There is no need for you ever to go away,' he answered quietly. 'This isn't the time for speaking, but you may as well know it. Think it over, my Lady of the Land!'

He went away without waiting for an answer, and she stood in the porch, looking across to the lights of Crump starred steadfast on the frantic night, and her heart reached piteously across the cleaving water. Then, conscious of a great unwillingness to leave the wildness without, she went wearily into the house.

.   .   .   .

Even the most perfect of servants has his moments of temporary aberration, and, when Mrs. Slinker came lightly down the stairs in clinging, gleaming, ivory satin, with pearls twisted round her head and pearls shining from her throat, it was scarcely surprising that the first footman should drop the steel poker and stare like a very kitchen-maid.

'She's a bloomin' bride!' he informed the underworld, when he had got himself (furtively staring to the furthest limit) safely out of reach. 'A bloomin' bride—that's what she looked, and no mistake about it! Satin and ropes of pearls, and twinkly things on her shoes, and a colour like the light shining through that there ruby sugar-bowl! You take my word for it, she's making up her mind to get married again—*soon*!'

'Then it's Whyterigg,' announced the second, who had just reached the blissful stage at which he was permitted to make observations without being unduly snubbed. 'I hung up his coat when he came, and there was a hard thing with corners in his pocket that couldn't have been anything else but chocolates. *He* has a kind of white satin and ruby look about him, too. Bet you what you like it's Whyterigg!'

'Rishwald's running her hard,' the cook agreed. 'My young man says his car's always in the village, and Rishwald peering into shops and looking lost, and then rushing inside to buy things he can't want anyhow if he thinks folks is looking at him. And last time he came he never touched that vol-o-vong I sent up extra-special. There's bound to be something at the back of *that*. My aunt! she's doing well for herself—first Crump and then Whyterigg! None so dusty for a horse-dealer's daughter, is it?'

'I don't believe she'll take Whyterigg,' a quiet,

refined-looking girl spoke up from beside the fire.
'She's only cared for one man all her life, and we
all know who that is! I used to see a lot of Nettie
Stone before she was sent away to finish her
education, and she was in love with Anthony
Dixon, even then.'

'Go on—you and your Anthony Dixon!' the
cook sniffed contemptuously. 'As if anybody with
a chance of Whyterigg would be cracked enough
to give Dockerneuk a second thought! She's
travelled far enough from her Dockerneuk days,
I'll be bound. Satin for Anthony Dixon! Pearls!
Twinkly things on her toes! A fat lot *you* know
about it, to be sure. Rishwald it'll be, you'll see,
and another slap in the eye for their precious
county!'

Rishwald was distinctly of the same opinion,
judging from the atmosphere of tender possession
with which he instantly surrounded the bridal
vision. He even forgot certain tea-spoons of quite
historic importance, and was content to whisper
illiterate nothings into a charming ear, while the
footmen eyed him through the open dining-room
door, and laid bets as to his probable chances.

Christian was late, as Callander had prophesied, and when he entered at last it was with a
double apology.

'You'll think me frightfully rude, of course, and
I'm wretchedly ashamed, but I was unexpectedly
detained; and, to make matters worse, I'm afraid
I shall have to go down into the village, later on.
I suppose you wouldn't care to come along?—a
wrestling-match, you know—some of your men
are down,—yes, yes, you'd rather stop here, of
course—I quite understand! I seem to have

made a muddle of things, somehow—I've rather
a knack, that way,' he added, with a sudden little
laugh, at which Nettie looked up quickly.

Something had happened, she knew, upstairs
in that detestable little room which had never
harboured anything but trouble; something that
had sent Deborah away without a word to herself, and set that hurt, puzzled look in Christian's
kind eyes. To-morrow, she would find out, and
by hook or crook things should be put right; but
to-night was *her* night, and she could spare no
thought for any one else. The gale had set her
blood racing in her veins—wild blood that came
through a questionable pedigree from lawless
Border thieves of the North; and the interview
with Roger Lyndesay had carried her back with
a rush to the happy days of her early girlhood,
when she and Dixon were stepping on the border-
land of love, and the shadow of Crump was far
enough from their young glamour. The old man's
courtly action had given her back her self-respect
as nothing else could have done, setting her free,
it seemed, for the future. For the second time she
shook off her dead husband's clasp, and deliberately took her life in both hands, calling on the
gods of field and fold.

Dinner was a rapid meal, and, when the ladies
rose, the men followed very shortly. Rishwald
drew Nettie to the piano, but, though she played
when he asked her, she would not sing, for in her
ears was a rioting song of hope and fear, so tem-
pestuous that she marvelled others could not hear
it. His head swam as he bent over her flushed
cheek and shining gown, hungering for some
response to his passion, and nearer complete

abstraction from self than he had ever been in his life, or would be again.

Christian sat by the fire, sunk in a deep chair, his face hidden in a cloud of smoke. Near him, his mother bent closely over a fine square of lace, her thin, powerful fingers moving lightly among the threads. They never looked at each other—these two. The veil of bitterness between them was stretched to-night as far as the stars.

'If you would give us a week at Whyterigg,' Rishwald was saying quite humbly, 'I should be honoured to arrange an old-time concert in the musician's gallery. A harpsichord—viola da gamba, and so on—the musicians in costume, of course. Does the idea please you?'

He bent nearer, and at that moment a bell rang, far at the back of the house. Nettie started violently, her hands dropping from the keys, and she half-rose, looking at the stairs; but, before she could move, one of the men entered with the message that Anthony Dixon wished to see Mrs. Stanley.

Slinker's wife came out from behind the piano.

'Bring him here, please,' she said quickly. 'I will see him here. That is, if you will excuse me!' she added, turning apologetically to her hosts.

'My dear Nettie!' Mrs. Lyndesay's eyebrows went up in cold disapproval. 'If you must see the man—and surely it cannot be necessary, at this hour?—the hall is scarcely the place for an interview. The steward's room, Matthew, or the east parlour.'

The servant bowed and was turning away when Mrs. Slinker checked him. She stood in the middle of the hall, a radiant, gleaming figure, scattering the gloom of Crump like a high-held lamp, showing beside the rigid blackness of her mother-in-law like a shining lily beside a bough of yew.

'No—wait!' she said clearly, putting out her hand, and Christian, through the smoke, saw that her wedding-ring had disappeared. 'I prefer to have him brought here—if you will forgive me. Do as I say, please!' and the startled footman threw a frightened glance at the elder woman, and fled. For the first and last time in her life, Nettie Stone was absolute mistress of Crump, and she never forgot it.

Anthony came into the hall shyly, but with his beautiful dignity unimpaired. His hat was off, and his hand went up in salute as his tranquil eyes travelled deferentially round the circle. Christian nodded cordially through his screen of smoke, and Rishwald, though deeply annoyed by the interruption, acknowledged his greeting with a stiff bend of the head; but Mrs. Lyndesay merely stared at him in cold surprise, and the quick blood rushed to his tanned face as he realised her resentment at his presence.

'I'm sorry if I'm intruding, ma'am,' he said quietly. 'I'm here by order. Mrs. Stanley sent me word she had something to ask me.' And Slinker's wife, her face all laughter and tears, walked up to him and said—'That's so, Anthony! Will you marry me?' and laid her hands on his breast.

In the mighty pause that followed they were still as stone, spectators as well as actors in the swift little scene; and then came a soft, final sound

—the closing of the library door. Even Rishwald saw clear at that moment, and he knew that he had lost. There was one thing at least Whyterigg would never take from Crump.

Mrs. Lyndesay stood up and reached for the bell, but Christian slid his fingers over the ivory knob before she could press it.

'Leave that, Mother!' he said with gentle force. 'This matter is for ourselves only. I'll not have Anthony turned like a dog from Crump.' He dropped his hand and stood up beside her, staring at the still, concentrated figures, conscious only of themselves.

'Turn them out!' Mrs. Lyndesay said in a low, harsh voice, and suddenly she began to shake like a leaf in the wind of her wounded pride. 'Turn them both out—the woman, as well—the low-born thing that in my folly I raised to our level! She shows her breeding at last, insulting us under our very roof. Turn them out! If William Lyndesay were alive, he would have them whipped from the door!'

The fierce words reached the culprit, and Slinker's wife dropped her hands and turned towards the furious voice, paling a little, though her eyes were full of soft light.

'I'm sorry,' she said gently, 'but I had to do it— it was the only way to make Anthony believe I cared. Yes, turn me out—*please* turn me out— quick!—and then—he'll take me in!'

She stretched out her hands, half-laughing, half-crying, and Christian went across to her and caught them in his own.

'Oh, Nettie, how mad you are!' he exclaimed, divided, himself, between laughter and tears.

'You foolish, ridiculous, utterly adorable thing! As if you'd ever be turned from here while Crump is Christian's roof!'

But Anthony stepped forward with a certain dogged resentment, his quiet face working painfully.

'All the same, it's done, sir, asking your pardon! It's not true that William Lyndesay would have turned me out. He never gave me a wrong word. But neither Anthony Dixon nor aught that belongs to him needs telling to go more than once. Nettie comes home with me to-night to my mother, and while I live she never crosses the door again!'

'Come, Anthony—take time to think——!' Christian expostulated, hurt yet conciliatory, but Dixon waved him aside.

'Where's your cloak, lass?' he said to Slinker's wife, and with a low laugh of pure happiness she caught up a rug that Christian had given her at Christmas, and threw it round her, following Dixon to the door. As he opened it, she turned abruptly, and took a last look at the rigid figure by the fire, its scornful eyes following her with open hatred, and for a long moment the two women stood staring at each other across the hall. Then Slinker's wife uttered a passionate little sound, part sorrow and part justified relief.

'You never really loved me,' she said, 'never, never—except as Stanley's chattel! I'm sorry, I think, but it makes things easier.' Then she stepped back to Christian, caught his hand and kissed it. 'Good-bye, Youngest One! Don't forget me. I'd stay with you if I could, but I'm called home, and you won't grudge me that. Oh

Laker dear, at least there's one lost dog no more a-seeking!'

At the foot of the steps he saw Anthony throw his arm around her, and Nettie lay her face on his breast; and his eyes were wet when he stepped inside and shut them out.

CHAPTER XXI

HIS mother had disappeared when he came back into the hall, but Rishwald, emerging from the library, was struggling into his coat. He asked for his car, checking Christian's apologies with a certain amount of dignity, and, in spite of his disastrous evening, shaking hands warmly with his somewhat forlorn-looking host, who smiled dismally when he had gone. No doubt he would find adequate consolation in his Tobies and Queen Annes.

Racing upstairs, Christian changed rapidly into morning clothes, for he expected Callander at any moment, and, when he came down again, he noticed that the door into the garden was open. On a sudden impulse, he went out, to find his mother standing under the old cedar, looking up at its swaying canopy.

The gale was at its height, now. The wind ran and roared through the wood like a horde of yelling satyrs, and beat at the old house as if it would rive the stones asunder. The cedar groaned as it wrestled in the arms of its mighty antagonist, straightening its old limbs and lifting its tossed head, only to be bowed to the earth anew. Sometimes, as it bent, Mrs. Lyndesay was lost to sight beneath the straining boughs, and Christian fought his way out to her, and laid a hand on her sleeve.

'You'd better come in!' he shouted, his mouth close to her ear. 'It isn't safe, out of doors—especially here. The wind's taking the trees all over the garden, and the old cedar's rotten all through.'

She obeyed reluctantly, and, as the full force of the wind met them round the house, she staggered and caught him by the arm, afterwards allowing him to support her across the lawn. It came to him, as he did so, that this was the first time in his life that she had turned to him for help: the first occasion since he had grown to manhood on which she had touched him of her own accord.

Once inside, she sank panting on the window seat, while he put his shoulder to the door and shut out the shrieking void.

'A Lyndesay's Night!' she exclaimed, as he came back to her where she sat, her white face framed by the oak of the wall and the wild night without. 'A Lyndesay's Night! The tree is calling for one of us, Christian. Is it for you or me?'

'Neither, I hope!' he answered as cheerfully as he could, lifting his coat from a peg near, and slipping it on. 'Certainly not you. And, for me, I am not ready to go yet. I want much more of life before I follow the Tree.'

'But I should be glad to go!' she broke out passionately. 'I want nothing more with anybody. Judases—Judases—the rotten world reeks with them! I've only loved three people in the whole of my life, and each of them played me false. Oh, God! is there no end to it? Judases—Judases—every one!'

She wrung her hands together, rocking to and fro until her widow's cap touched the leaded pane. The ice was broken at last, and the torrents of hidden anguish came racing into view, carrying all before them. Christian shrank a little, appalled by the force of her unwonted distress.

'All false!' she cried again. 'That woman, to-night—she lied when she said that I did not love her. I had grown fond of her. She understood me better than anybody; better than my own mother or my own children. There was something frank and brave about her that got at my heart, something that seemed mountains high above the mud of treachery. I believed in her, in spite of the secret marriage; and all the time she stayed with me for her own ends, not for my comfort—not because I cared for her, but merely to gain a man who did not trust her—and with cause! That was Nettie Stone. Let her go!'

She finished with her hands locked on her knees, her figure bent forward, her staring gaze on the floor.

'She loved him,' Christian said gently. 'She played a big stake, and she took a big risk. And he trusts her, now.'

'Then there was Stanley,' she went on, apparently without hearing him, 'Stanley, who was the light of my eyes and my very soul. He was born at a time when I had begun to think I could not go on living, and his babyhood was the one bit of heaven I shall ever know. But, as he grew up, day after day I saw where he was going. I watched him grow from a careless boy into a despicable, dissolute man. When once love sees, it has the terrible lightning-clearness of the gods.

I watched him backing slowly into hell—the hell where I myself was already, with all mothers in like case. When the Tree took him, I was glad, for I thought everything was ended, and the long strain of deceit over. Then came the last scandal. I knew most of the others, and he knew that I knew. But this, the greatest thing in his life, the worst and yet perhaps the best thing he had ever done, he kept from me. He was false to me as to everybody else.'

'He is dead, Mother. Try to forget,' Christian put in, moved to a sudden passion of pity. 'We are left, you and I. Let us help each other, if we can!'

She lifted wide, strange eyes to his pitying gaze.

'You help me? *You?* I would not owe you a paltry kindness, or a single kindly word!' She stood up abruptly, throwing back her head, and for a brief moment he looked, shuddering, behind the Lyndesay mask. 'I have always hated you— you don't need to be told that; but you need to be told why. There was another I loved—your father. And you are William Lyndesay's son— William Lyndesay who was false to me almost from our wedding-day, and with whom I lived twenty years, holding my peace! Ay, there is more than one curse on Crump. No wonder we are a byword in the countryside for all that spells sorrow and hate and death! We are cursed down to the very soil we tread, and up to the roof of the shambles where we die. Judases! Judases all!' She sank back, putting her hands to her face. 'Take your pity and your help elsewhere—you who look at me with William Lyndesay's eyes!'

The hall bell rang, and Christian stepped

quickly between her and the approaching servant.

'Mother!' he pleaded earnestly, very low, bending over her. 'I am myself as well as my father's son. I am your child—no treachery in the world can alter that. Forget, if you can. In time you will forgive. We are so alone, Mother, you and I!'

His voice shook as he put out a hand and laid it on hers, a passionate need of sympathy strong upon him, and his heart drew to her when she showed no outward resentment at his touch. She turned her head to the window, where by the wild light from the hurrying sky they could see the tree lashing to and fro.

'The Tree calls,' she said quietly, as Callander came in behind them on the wind. 'The Tree is hungry and calls. Now may the Tree take me before I either forget or forgive!'

. . . .

During their breathless fight across the park, the two men had no words to spend on each other, and Christian's restless brain raced like driven quarry through the twisted tangle of the day. His interview with Deborah seemed already blurred and far off; his mother's fierce monologue a nightmare to be shaken clear. Only one picture stood out brightly on the crowded canvas, sweet and gracious against the troubled bewilderment of the rest. He saw Anthony's arm go round the woman he loved, and Nettie's head sink to its place at last.

That was love, then—the thing of which Deborah had said he knew nothing; the going into a place apart of two souls, for whom even the dark avenue of death could hold no fear. Nettie had been his comrade, his strong stay, but for Anthony she would be only a woman, weak for the glory of his strength. Not in comradeship alone lay the secret, not even in mutual reliance and support, unless crowned and welded by the unpurchasable magic, lacking which the highest must stay sealed. Deb had been right; he had not understood—but he understood, now. Farmer and horse-dealer's daughter were priest and priestess of his vision.

'We're late,' Callander observed, when at last they struggled into the village. 'But most of the men would be late, too, I expect, so it doesn't really matter. The Whyteriggers must have had a tough fight for it across the mosses.'

It was with a sense of relief that they stumbled out of the merciless night into the warmth and brightness of the hall, packed from platform to gallery, for it was a special night, and the Crump Silver Belt was up for competition. Moreover, this was the first time that Christian had appeared at a meeting since his brother's death, and all his admirers were there to greet him. They got to their feet as he came in, and a shower of caps darkened the air on a mighty cheer for Lakin' Lyndesay. The older men, who had known him from childhood, crowded round him, grasping his hand, while the lads in the background eyed him with reverent awe, for he held a record that could not be beaten by any in the room.

He passed the gauntlet of outstretched hands by gradual degrees, and came laughing to the platform, where a chair had been kept for him, and a morose Larrupper greeted him with a dismal nod. The cheering was still raising the roof as he took his seat in the centre, and the Crump men came out *en masse* to give them a final yell. Still the familiar faces pressed upon him, and still the welcoming hands went out. Even Larrupper thawed at last in the general enthusiasm, and clapped him cheerily on the shoulder as the oldest Crump tenant worried his way through for a word with the squire.

'Eh, Laker lad, but I be main glad to see thee back!' he quavered, holding to the young man's hand as much for support in his agitation as for greeting; and Christian laughed and pushed him gently into his own chair, while a dozen eager sportsmen fought and scrambled after another.

The umpires restored order, at last, and the ring was cleared. The crowd subsided, and presently the men began to come out in wrestling-kit, white, yellow, or even purple; richly embroidered, in many cases, for there was a prize to be won by the best costume. At the edge of the ring, the ponderous but still light-footed umpires, themselves old wrestling champions, grunted curt orders at competitor and partisan alike.

Christian leaned forward after the first clean fall, his breath coming fast as the glamour of the game gripped him afresh. He had the names of all the great wrestlers by heart, from the Cork Lad o' Kentmere, who won his Troutbeck home in a tussle before Edward VI, to Jemmy Fawcett, Jackson of Kinneyside, and the best men of his own day. Jemmy Fawcett was one of his favourites in history, a little ten-stone man of five foot seven, who had been known to fell seventeen stone, even with a handkerchief to lengthen his reach. Then there was Belted Will; and Bone-setter Dennison, who dislocated his opponent's shoulder in a fall, and put it right again before leaving the ring; others, too, whose names rose slowly to the surface of his mind as he watched.

This was not one of the weekly matches, but a competition open to the district and to all weights, though the fact that the men were mainly drawn from Crump and Whyterigg caused the party feeling between the two villages to run high. The Crump men did well, at first. Long John Carradus had little trouble with young Harry Newby, a lightweight, whose favourite chip was the somewhat dangerous 'hank'—dangerous, because it has the knack of felling the aggressor instead of the defendant. Lowther disposed of his man with a swift back-heel; and the inside click finished a Whyterigg favourite whose chances had been highly assessed. The brawny Arevar cowman had done himself proud by drawing the pick of the room, and was greeted with uproarious, derisive cheers as his knotted arms went heavily round Gaskarth's slender waist, his coarse blue shirt and clumsy fustians in striking contrast with the white elegance of the other. He made a great parade of finding his hold, ramming his rough head against his opponent's cheek, and breathing heavily, while Gaskarth padded lightly round him, taking his time, and smiling gently at the cowman's mighty lumberings and strenuous efforts to force him to close. He got his hands together at last, swiftly and unobtrusively, and allowed his enthusiastic foe to swing him about the ring for a few moments, for the amusement of the spectators, smiling blissfully all the while; then, suddenly striking inside and lifting at the same time, held the astonished Samson helpless in his grasp before laying him gently and almost affectionately on the mat. Christian uttered a sharp word of applause, and Gaskarth, hearing it through the general laughter, acknowledged it with a lifted finger. He had learned his quiet science from Lakin' Lyndesay himself.

The following half-dozen pairs gave little sport, and Christian, running his eye over the men, had already come to the conclusion that Gaskarth had no need to fear anybody present, when the last couple of the first round took the mat.

One of the two he knew, but the other, whom he took to be a Whyterigger, was a stranger to him, a big, fair man scaling fourteen stone, with a splendid pair of shoulders slightly overweighting the rest of him, and a long reach. He had a sullen expression, and a temper not thoroughly under control, Christian judged, noticing his restless hands as the Whyteriggers went down before Crump. He strode on to the mat aggressively and rather contemptuously, and made short work of the young groom who fell to his lot; barely stopping to shake hands before marching off again.

After that, Christian watched him intently as he lived through the next few rounds, foreseeing that he and Gaskarth would meet in the finals, and hoping to see him downed—not because he was an outsider, but because the man's attitude annoyed him, lacking as it did the frank heartiness of the genuine sportsman. His science was creditable—he knew more than a little—did not rely entirely, by any means, upon his strength

and lightness of foot; but it was evident that he
was not popular, though his favourite trick was
the showy swinging hipe which takes so tremen-
dously with the crowd. And once, when he felled
Lanty Strickland, a beginner who had fought his
way gallantly to the last round, finishing him off
with needless force, after a fashion of which Gaskarth would never have been guilty, an ominous
murmur ran through the room, checked instantly
and gruffly by the umpires. Christian pricked
his ears, looking more intently than ever at the
stranger. During the last eighteen months he
had got out of touch with wrestling-gossip, but
he knew that behind that murmur was something of older standing than to-night; a grudge
born, not of the moment, but of settled prejudice.
He tapped one of the committee on the shoulder,
and learned the man's name to be Harker; and
when, as he had anticipated, he came out with
Gaskarth for the finals, he settled himself keenly
to enjoy the contest.

Gaskarth was not smiling, now. He knew he
had big work before him, to be approached
seriously; yet that hardly accounted for the fact
that he offered his hand with less than his usual
open good-will, or that the crowd, while urging
him to 'Git on to him, Bob! Good lad, Bob! Mind
what thoo's at!'—had scarcely a word or even a
name for the other.

They fell to;—Gaskarth, quiet in all his move-
ments, from the settling of his chin to his easy,
circling step and the swing of his sinewy reach;
but Harker closed and unloosed rather fiercely,
in a manner more suggestive of real combat than
of scientific play. Gaskarth got hold soon, too—

it was only his cowman friend whom he played for the fun of the crowd—but Harker dallied beyond all reason, irritating the spectators and drawing reproof from the umpires, at the same time wearing his opponent in a manner scarcely worthy of his superior strength and weight. He got hold, at last, though—a greedy hold, Christian noticed, that made Gaskarth bite his lip with annoyance, and a brilliant struggle followed, during which the stout umpires were harried from pillar to post by the indignant sportsmen whose view they blocked. The hold was too much for Gaskarth, however, backed by Harker's greater power, and he went down at last before the swinging hipe which had sent the others to the mat. He got back on him, though, in the next round, taking very good care that holds should be fair, this time, and with his usual neat inside stroke flooring his man in a few seconds. Harker got up, frowning, as the other pulled him to his feet, and in the pause before the last round stood breathing hard, his thick, fair brows drawn sharply together.

But it was not until the third round was well advanced that Christian discovered the real cause of his unpopularity. Not only was he maddeningly slow to 'close for fair', but, when once at grips, he deliberately forced Gaskarth's arms upward above his shoulders, until their heads were set crown to crown, the deadlock ending in a futile slipping of holds. Time after time this happened, earning the disapprobation of the umpires and the open condemnation of the crowd. Gaskarth, not a man of particularly powerful physique, depending more upon his knowledge of the game than on sheer strength, began to show signs of exhaustion as this senseless waste of energy continued.

Dripping with perspiration in the crowded, airless room, he looked across to Christian, lifting his eyebrows meaningly, to be answered by an understanding nod, and Gaskarth was comforted, though he knew he was done. His fine temper broke a little when he took hold for the last time, and he endeavoured to force himself over his adversary in a final spurt; but the edge had been worn off his delicate dexterity, and, instead, he went hurtling over his opponent's head, and lay panting, looking up into Harker's sullen eyes.

There was a pause for realisation, and then, as he dragged himself up, grinning humorously and reaching out an ungrudging hand, a storm of disapproval broke from the room. Shaking his head rebukingly at the demonstration, he walked cheerfully back to his corner, but Harker stayed doggedly on the mat, waiting for the winner's ticket, and staring defiantly around him when the paper was in his hand. The discontent was so marked that the big referees looked appealingly at Christian, who responded by rising to his feet and holding up his hand for silence.

'Did you give the fall?' he asked quietly, when the last murmur had died down, and, as the umpires reluctantly signified their assent, he beckoned Harker forward, lifting the belt from the table beside him. From the platform he looked down into the square, dogged face, and in spite of his forced impartiality, his voice was cold as he spoke the usual formula of presentation; but, when he would have handed him the trophy, Harker shook his head brusquely, and stepped back.

'I haven't won it yet, sir,' he said, rather insolently, 'though I mean to have it in the end, all right! There's one Crump man that hasn't come out against me, and that's yourself!'

The colour flamed into Christian's face as he stood with the belt in his hands, lifting his head rather haughtily; and instantly from the disappointed assembly a chorus of demand was flung towards him, the more insistent pressing to the very steps.

'Take him on, sir! Give him a taste of the old stuff. Topple him over! Lakin' Lyndesay! Lakin' Lyndesay! Give him Crump——!' and it seemed to Christian that he himself was borne bodily upon the wind of tumult as his name ran from mouth to mouth.

The men on the platform gathered round him urgently; the oldest tenant clung to his arm, quavering and imploring, eager to see him justified; and even Larrupper added his pithy persuasion.

'Get along down, Laker, an' break the beggar's neck!' he growled. 'Or, if it's not dainty enough handlin' for Lyndesay of Crump, I'll sail in an' do it myself!'

'No, no, Larry! I can't have you landing in the police-court,' Christian laughed, torn between his hunger for the game and the memory of an extorted promise. Perhaps, too, as Larrupper had so delicately hinted, Lyndesay of Crump was loth to meet the upstart challenger, but the primitive man at least was all agog to prove his mettle. He looked hesitatingly round the urgent faces, the sea of entreaty surging in his ears. The events of the long day had swung him far from his normal temperate attitude, and at that moment he did not care greatly what he did or by what influence he was led. More than one tie had been definitely broken during the last few hours, and the promise might as well break with the rest.

Only Callander hesitated, driven by his undertaking to Deborah, and, curiously enough, his very protest clinched consent. Callander had never seen him wrestle, Christian remembered suddenly, and his boyish vanity rose to back his natural desire. Fate had used him none too kindly, that day, leaving him with a sense of having been found wanting, of having missed by an ace a gift he was not strong enough to hold. He felt humiliated, sunk in his own eyes, and he longed to set himself right at least on this, his own peculiar ground. Moreover, Callander had never seen him wrestle! Afterwards, he remembered how that touch of innocent folly had swung the balance on the fatal side.

He caught Harker's eye and nodded, and instantly the hard-used caps soared up once more; and, as he shook himself free from the exultant press, he saw old Parker beckoning him anxiously from a door behind.

'You'll excuse me taking the liberty, sir,' the butler apologised, trembling in every limb with excitement, 'but I ventured to slip down, just to see what was going on, and at the same time I brought the old rig down with me! You see, Mr. Christian, I thought they'd like as not want you to turn out, and I didn't fancy the things not

being on the spot, so I hope you'll excuse me
having brought them along. Oh, sir! It's like
old times, isn't it?—and mind you give him a bit
of Crump's best!'

That was sufficient, if any extra pressure were
needed; and they disappeared behind the stage,
while the umpires growled the meeting into a
semblance of order, and Harker flung himself
down to rest, his heart beating fast in spite of his
outward indifference.

It is always the dependants of an old house who
nurse and keep alive any feud that may be going
—the family servants, the old keepers, the workmen on the estate. Theirs it is to see that the bad
blood should be kept running; no matter how
sweetly, on the part of the masters, righteousness
and peace may have kissed each other. Crump
and Whyterigg had shaken hands and buried the
knife, but Christian's old nurse would not sit at
meat with Rishwald's chauffeur, nor the head
gardener so much as exchange a cutting with
Whyterigg's horticultural head. Harker was well
come for this sort of thing, being a son of the now-
pensioned Whyterigg coachman and a lady's
maid also bred on the spot, who had handed on
to him their lusty hate of Crump almost as a
sacred duty. 'Whyterigg thieves' and 'Crump
liars' had constituted the common interchange
of courtesies between the boys of the two villages,
and though education and sport had done much
to root out the old feudal folly, the opprobrious
term still rankled in Harker's mind. He now held
a Whyterigg farm, but until the present year he
had been with an uncle in Cumberland, so that
he knew nothing of Christian beyond his sporting

reputation, seeing him through the smoked glass of inherited hostility more as a symbol than as a man. In his mind had always been a half-formed determination to meet Lakin' Lyndesay on this one possible ground of equality, and now his opportunity had arrived. He meant to make the most of it. The old coachman and the lady's maid would surely weep tears of joy if he could carry home a victory over Crump.

There was a stir on the platform, heads turning to the inner door framing the illuminated countenance of the old butler; and then Christian ran down into the ring, his nerves thrilling to the affectionate recognition flung him from all sides. He wore the pale orange they all knew, his fair head shining against the black Crump cedar embroidered on the chest; and, as he stood, waiting, the full light falling upon his bright, frank expression and clean-limbed grace, Harker, approaching, was conscious of unwilling and deeply heretical admiration. And Callander's heart warmed to his young employer, for all that he guessed him to be the unconscious barrier to his dearest desire.

They shook hands quickly and got to work, and were barely into holds before Harker realised that he was overmatched. He had placed his opponent at Gaskarth's valuation, or little higher, and for a few moments he was conscious of a deadly helplessness under the other's superior skill. Christian seemed to read his purpose at the instant it was framed, and his foot was changed or his weight thrown on the opposite side in what appeared an impossible fraction of time. He was cool, too; patient, and most terribly certain,—

moreover, he was unexpectedly strong. Try as he might, Harker could not raise his hold as he had raised Gaskarth's. Christian was always ready for him, and any attempt to force things brought him perilously near his own destruction. Once, indeed, he did go down, but with a powerful effort he brought his man alongside, and the umpires gave it a dog-fall. He got up trembling and breathing hard, but now he, too, was cool. He set his teeth, doggedly weighing his chances. Christian scaled no more than eleven stone, if he touched that, and he was out of training, while the Whyterigger was in the pink of condition; having, too, the slight advantage in years which tells so enormously at a certain age. But he was nowhere near him in knowledge and lightning judgment, and he saw that he must depend on his endurance and his magnificent lifting powers if he were to come off victor. A few seconds later he was lying on the mat, laid there as lightly as a child, sent down by a simple back-heel accomplished in the one fateful second in which he had advanced his left foot an inch too far.

In the next round he held the advantage for some time, having managed to secure his favourite monopolising hold, and after a hard struggle he succeeded in forcing Christian over; but with beautiful dexterity the younger man twisted from beneath before striking ground, and reversed the positions. Harker saved himself likewise, by a marvellous exhibition of strength which brought him a grudging cheer, but he had lost his first supremacy completely, and, when he put in the hank desperately, the initiated knew he was at the end of his resources. A dogged clinging together for several minutes almost without movement ended in a sharp release and the dropping of both men, Harker under.

Three out of five had been the test arranged, but already the spectators looked upon the match as won; and Harker, after a long rest, stood up to what was probably the last round, filled with bitter resentment and hot humiliation.

Yet he started carefully enough, schooling himself to patience, strung to his highest point of wariness and ingenuity; and presently he became conscious of a faint wonderment, for something was evidently the matter with Christian. During one of the pauses when they drew apart before clinching, he saw that his opponent's eyes had a dazed and distant look, as if his mind had ceased to concentrate on the game; and though, when they closed again, he seemed still in full command of his science, Harker's hopes rose.

It was eleven o'clock. From the church hard by, the strokes reached them in spite of the wind, and the white-faced timepiece in the room replied punctually to its greater brother. Christian knew that, at Crump, the clock in the stable-yard would be equally faithful, for, only that afternoon, crossing the park, he had heard the chimes mingle and clash. His eye stayed mechanically on the white surface as he circled round the watchful Harker, his hold already joined; and, as the last vibration died, a swaying blackness came over him, veiling his eyes. He was back again under the ancient cedar, the big wind roaring in his ears, the staggering giant threatening him with its monstrous, thrashing arms. He felt them crashing upon him, so seemingly alive in the murderous intensity of their purpose that he stepped back, desperately striving to elude their reach; and in that instant Harker took hold. He closed so fiercely, tautening his muscles and lifting in the same movement, that Christian winced sharply, and the shock snatched him back to the work at hand. Struggling to collect his scattered senses, he resisted Harker's repeated attempts to put in the hipe, and, anxious to finish the round, tried both the outside stroke and the inside in quick succession, but with no result. A demon seemed to have entered into Harker, roused by the realisation of his opponent's sudden weakness, and he saved himself time and again, often without knowing how, as they swung from end to end of the ring, twisting, lifting, wrenching, straining, with hard-coming breath and scarlet faces, until even the hardened watchers wondered that any men could last so long at such a pitch. As in a dream, Christian heard the impatient—'Stir about, umpire!' snapping like pistol-shots from every side.

There were pillars at the end by the door, stout, carved shafts, supporting the heavy gallery; and, as the combatants panted down the mat for the last time, the close-pressing crowd parted a little before their violent approach. Christian's clouded eyes went back to the clock, as if magically drawn, and at that moment Harker put in the cross-buttock with a mighty heave, sending him flying through the air clean off the mat and against the unguarded pillar. He struck the deep carving with his head, and lay still. It was five minutes past eleven.

. . . .

Roger Lyndesay fell asleep when the wind dropped, but Deb, cruelly wide awake, could not persuade herself to follow him upstairs. Instead, she flung a scarf over her head, and went out to the gate. It was close upon midnight, but to her surprise Crump lights were still burning; and, as she stood, resting in the quiet after the storm, she heard horses galloping down the park. They turned out by the lower lodge and were lost for a moment; then came on again, the hoofs beating nearer and louder; and something fateful in their frantic speed sent her out into the road to await their approach. The black night hid the horsemen until they were close upon her, but one had a lantern at his saddle, dancing like a will o' the wisp, and by its light she saw that he was Dixon of Dockerneuk. She cried after him, then, and he checked violently, swinging his horse completely round, while the other raced on into the night.

'Is anything wrong?' she asked anxiously, coming quickly to his stirrup, and he nodded, panting, as he bent towards her from his labouring mount.

'It's Mrs. Lyndesay!' he told her, when he could get his breath. 'The old cedar's taken her, at last, and it's gone itself along with her—just as eleven o'clock struck, they say. The servants heard the crash and ran out, and they found her underneath. They were nigh scared to death with that and the storm, and they sent for me. Even Parker was down at the wrestling, and there was nobody else to see to things. Yon's a groom gone on ahead for the doctor, and I'm seeking Mr. Christian to tell him, poor lad! You'd best keep it from your father till morning, Miss Deborah.'

She agreed quickly.

'I won't delay you, Anthony,' she added; and then, struck by a sudden thought, stopped him a second time. 'But where is Mrs. Stanley?' she went on, puzzled, and got no answer, for Dixon, his ear bent towards the road, was listening to the slow tread of many feet.

They came from the direction of the village, growing steadily louder, and presently, after a questioning, anxious look at the girl, he turned and rode slowly to the foot of the bridge, Deb clinging to his leather. There they waited in a tense silence, straining their eyes through the dark.

When at last the dim figures were limned on the night, it seemed to them that the whole village was coming to Crump. Here and there a lantern swung in the dense, hushed crowd, and, in the midst, borne by his own wrestlers, Gaskarth at his head, the master of Crump came home, covered and very still——

Deb moved under the lantern, and a man in advance hurried towards her; and, when he saw her eyes, any hope that he had cherished for himself fell shrivelled to the earth for ever. She looked up at him dumbly, terribly.

'Hurt—not dead!' Callander answered with merciful directness. 'He was thrown, wrestling. We got the doctor at once. He has hopes——' He stopped, for the doctor was at his side, and Dixon speaking hurried fearful news from his saddle. Suddenly Deb began to laugh very low, making him shiver.

'It's a Lyndesay's Night!' she said. 'A Lynde-say's Night! They follow the Tree! Christian, too—all of them—they follow the Tree!' And she laughed again.

He put his arm round her and drew her into the blackness under the bridge, and together they watched the procession pass; Larruppin' Lynde-say walking with his hand on the stretcher. Anthony Dixon turned his horse close behind, and followed his silent master. The dim, voiceless crowd passed heavily into the park.

. . . .

All night long Nettie watched by Christian's bed, while messages went out to the nearest nurs-ing-homes in the district. Anthony's vow had been broken in a few hours—she was back at Crump already. Indeed, she had been waiting on the steps when the ghostly cortège had shuffled up the drive.

In a far room the dead mother lay unaware of her son as he of her; and out on the smooth lawn the uprooted cedar spread its huge branches like a monster octopus flung dead. It had had a dramatic end, Nettie thought, shuddering in re-membrance. One Lyndesay it had carried with it, and another seemed far on the road. It was certainly true that the Lyndesays went out vio-lently and not as other folk. Yet, if Christian lived, surely the spell would now be broken for all time? If Christian lived—! She looked at the still, fair head with earnest affection, the tears rising to her eyes, and a past conversation floated back into her mind. The gruesome link between the master and his forebears was gone for ever. If Christian lived, he would be left standing alone.

CHAPTER XXII

AUGUSTUS began the afternoon by a dastardly theft. Meeting a lady of similar age and costume (three years and a short serge frock), inordinately inflated by the possession of a small Union Jack, he took it from her by silent force, and without the slightest change of expression on his deadly serious countenance. When she had been reduced to dismal shrieks on somebody's doorstep, he marched into the Bank and demanded a copper from the manager, who, finding him intimidating to the last degree, hastily handed him the required sum from his own pocket.

Larruppin' Lyndesay's car was standing empty in front of the Bunch of Acorns, at the mercy of any marauder, and Augustus did not hesitate a moment. Even at that age he had a cultivated taste in cars. He did not require telling that the long, shining monster was of the best of its kind, and therefore worthy in all respects of his attention. Leaving the Bank with the air of a man who had paid in fully a quarter of a million, he crossed the road, flag in hand, and climbed with some difficulty into the front seat.

The manager came to his door to watch developments. A ribald crowd of small boys gathered round the car, pointing out the awful penalties certain to befall the offender when discovered; but Augustus, unmoved as the soft spring sky above him, sat serenely on the padded seat, swinging his small, bare legs, and clasping his pirated Jack tightly to his bosom.

Larrupper came out, presently, followed by an obsequious landlord. His air of reckless cheerful-

ness seemed to have vanished completely; he
looked older and thinner, and his eyes were
tired, like those of a man who has kept anxious
vigils.

'Well, good-day, Mr. Lionel!' the landlord was
saying. 'It's fine news that Mr. Christian's going
on all right. We've all been terribly anxious. I'll
see about those siphons you ordered, sir, and—
oh, great snakes!'

He had caught sight of Augustus.

'If it isn't that there limb of Satan, making free
as usual with other folks' property! Excuse me,
sir, I'll soon get him out of this. He's the worst
boy in the place!'

'Boy?' Larrupper queried, looking at the petti-
coat and the silken hair.

'Boy, sir; and worse than fifty boys together,
for all he looks so blessed saint-like. Now, Augustus, this ain't *your* car! You've got to quit. Come
along, now, like a good lad. Your ma's wantin'
you.'

Augustus awaited his approach with complete
indifference; only, when the landlord's nervous
fingers closed round him, he opened his mouth to
such an appalling extent and with such alarming
suggestiveness, that the enemy dropped him like
a live coal.

'He do yell that powerful, sir!' he explained
apologetically. 'You've no idea! I'm feared to
start him. Seems as if he would bust hisself, at
times.'

He made way for various other acquaintances
of the interloper, including the policeman, who
tried both blandishment and coercion by turn,
only to be similarly baffled; watched by Lar-

rupper, leaning against the doorpost, with list-
less amusement.

'Wantin' a ride, perhaps,' he observed at last.
'Well, I've plenty of time for loiterin'. I'll take
him out a mile or two, as he seems to think the
old 'bus worth patronisin'. Somebody tell his
mother I'll look after him.'

From the tonneau he unearthed a fur rug
and a muffler which he wound round his small
passenger; then, scattering the crowd, started
the engine, and climbed past Augustus into his
seat.

'Happen he'll want to get out when he feels
hisself moving!' the landlord remarked hope-
fully, but he did not know his man. Augustus sat
like a rock. If his face changed at all, it was
merely to allow a faint expression of pleasure to
find place upon it. So he was carried away, his
curls fluttering in the wind of the car, his solemn
eyes fixed steadily in front of him.

Larrupper stopped after a short run and suggested return, but found himself met by strong
opposition. He went on again, pausing every
mile to say—'Shall we be goin' back, now?
Aren't you gettin' fed up, old man? Mother will
be missin' you,——' only to have his remarks
contemptuously ignored, while the least attempt
to turn the car was met by the silent opening of
the dreaded mouth.

Even touching insinuations to the effect that
he was tired, that the car was tired, that Augustus
himself was tired, proved useless, and presently
he gave up the struggle. He drove on, immersed
in his own thoughts, his cap pulled gloomily to
his eyes.

The long weeks in a house of sickness had left him weary both mentally and physically, but he stayed doggedly at Crump, like a hound refusing to leave its master's door. His affection for Christian had struck deeper roots during this terrible crisis, and, though he could do nothing for him, he insisted on stopping near him, worrying the nurses with endless questions, and distracting both Nettie and Parker by declining to eat. Occasionally he drifted up to Dockerneuk, and every day he took bulletins to Kilne, but he could not fathom Deb's attitude. If he was late, she met him on the road, questioning him with a fierceness that almost frightened him; but, when his news was once told, even at its worst, she had seemed curiously indifferent.

To-day, however, things were changed. To-day, Christian had taken a big stride, and Larrupper had seen him for the first time. The unwonted tears still came to his eyes when he reviewed the greatness of his relief, paired with the shock of meeting the faint shadow that was his cousin. He had been very quiet in the sick-room, a perfect marvel of restraint, the nurses had agreed, much as they would have agreed if a Newfoundland's tail had tactfully missed the china; but, when he had got himself somehow to Kilne, the restraint had vanished, and he had let himself go. How was a chap to do otherwise when at last he saw the old look in Deb's eyes, and heard Roger Lyndesay, standing at his window, say 'Thank God!' as a man before a High Altar? Deb had put her hand on his head and soothed him in the quaint, motherly way she kept for Larry only, and for the first time he found himself able to tell her of his other trouble that had taken the brightness out of the sun. He had been too much chilled by her strange aloofness to mention Verity before, but now he gave her as much of the story as he loyally could, and Deborah's intuition told her the rest.

'You couldn't expect to go on smoothly for ever, Larry,' she said gently. 'Life isn't just full tide and a ripple before the wind. But I think you're treating this too seriously—I do indeed! Verity *is* straight, whatever nonsense she may talk about herself; and, in any case, eleven o'clock at night isn't a particularly clear-headed hour for discussing a question of ethics. Verity's very highly strung, you know, and she's always a bundle of nerves after handling a village team. Billy-boy would have sent most girls into shrieking hysterics! You should have gone home and slept on it before saying anything. You would both have been saner in the morning.'

'Even the mornin' couldn't alter facts!' Larrupper stuck to his point. 'She went out of her way to hurt a well-meanin' chap like Grant, playin' him gently till he was gaspin', an' then pullin' him neatly up the bank. You can't say that's bein' well brought up. An' it's no use your tellin' me that she didn't mean it, because she assured me honest injun that she *did*, an' besides, I heard old Grant askin' her, myself.'

'My dear boy, Grant would have fallen in love with her, in any case!' Deb said cheerfully. 'How could he help it—seeing her every day? *Any* man would—especially with a housekeeper with a squint. Verity doesn't need to lay herself out to attract. She's one of the most fascinating people that walk. Grant's fate was sealed from the moment he accepted Cantacute.'

'Of course I'm not sayin' he should have had the rotten cheek not to like her,' Larry returned, 'but I do think he'd never have got as far as proposin' if she hadn't started in assistin'. Old Grant's so almighty honourable, an' so amazin' humble in his own eyes.'

'Pooh!' Deb shrugged her shoulders lightly. 'I dare say he's got his share of vanity, like every other man—let's hope so, anyhow. Of course, I'm dreadfully sorry for the nice little thing, and he was a perfect brick over that concert, but he'll recover all right when once you've got Verity safely at Arevar. After all, he's only known her a very short time, and he was certain to fall in love with *somebody*. People who don't get enough to eat are always star-gazing after something. Privation destroys their sense of proportion. Anyhow, it's perfectly absurd to talk as though Verity had committed a crime. Look at all she's done for Cantacute! It was only likely she should rebel when he tried to take the lead. A woman has only one natural weapon, Larry—you can't expect her to fight on your particular lines. You may not like it, but for that you must blame the Power that made her. I wonder how far *your* superiority would get you without brute force to back you up in a hole! I think you're a pig to be hard on Verity. Who was it said he'd be waiting to console her when she discovered that life wasn't all beer and skittles? You've a short memory, my friend. I don't believe you love her one atom, so now you know my candid opinion and can go away home!'

'I *do*! But she led him on——' Larry repeated doggedly, whereupon she took him by the shoulders and put him out.

'I'd shake you, if such a thing were possible!' she said. 'You're an ungrateful, hidebound heathen! Now, see here. You can run over to Heron with these handkerchiefs, and if you dare to come back without making your peace with Verity, you needn't show your face at Kilne again. Oh, Larry, Larry!' her voice followed him to the gate, as he went obediently. 'Just be thankful she's alive and loves you—not lying crushed under a cruel tree or broken to bits by a clumsy brute! How much would you care *then* for a dozen misguided Pierrot parsons?'

But it was not until he was close at Crump once more that the true inwardness of this speech dawned upon him.

Well, he and the handkerchiefs were on their way to Heron, but Heaven alone knew what he would do when he got there. Not apologise, anyhow. He might be a stupid sort of chap, but at least he knew what was straight an' what wasn't, an' he couldn't say it was all my eye an' Betty Martin when he was still blushin' over what she'd done. It was a sickenin' business an' very tryin' —tiresome, old Savaury would say.

He was passing Tasser, at the time, and round the bend he came on Savaury himself, industriously sprinkling the March dust with a large watering-can. He was so much astonished that he pulled up dead, or Savaury would certainly not have recognised him, with his cap on his nose and a companion of such tender years at his side.

'Where on earth did you pick that up?' he exclaimed; in his amazement allowing the watering-can to expend itself upon his own boots. 'And where the dickens are you taking it, either?'

'I didn't pick it up,' Larry answered gloomily. 'It picked *me* up. And I'm not takin' it. It's takin' itself. I'm allowed in the car on sufferance, merely because I know a bit about drivin'. I say, hadn't you better be goin' in an' changin' your boots?'

Savaury passed the insinuation scornfully, though he moved the can, and put the question to which Larry had already grown so used. 'How is Christian?' he asked.

'Oh, gettin' a move on at last, thanks very much! I saw him this mornin' for a few minutes. A bit gone to seed, of course, but they tell me they'll soon have him bloomin'. Had a narrow shave of goin' out—poor old Laker!'

'I'm glad to hear it.' Savaury was obviously relieved. 'Very glad! It's so tiresome when one's friends are ill. One quivers every time the bell rings. And Petronilla's always coming in with false reports. She collects them in the village— like measles. I haven't had a meal in peace since the poor young thing was damaged. One was never sure when one might have to jump up and pull down the blinds.'

'I'll wring your neck, if you don't stop jawin', you callous little blighter!' Larry flung at him, leaning forward threateningly, and Savaury went pink and looked haughty; then came closer and put a hand on the car, his tone changing.

'That's all right, my dear boy. It's only my

tiresome way of putting things. I'm more glad than I can say that he's better. He's a good lad, and he'd be a loss to Crump.'

'If you'd seen him, this mornin', as white as washin' an' as thin as a window!' poor Larry got out with difficulty. 'I don't feel like jokin' about it yet.'

'I'm not joking, Lionel. If I talk nonsense, it's because I'm so exceedingly relieved. I've known Christian since he was a little blue-eyed morsel afraid to open his mouth before his mother. I used to be terribly sorry for him—he seemed so lonely. He was always glad to get away from Crump, and—I'll tell you something—one day I stole him! We had him at Tasser all day, Petronilla and I, and he played with all Petronilla's account-books, and had a steeple-chase over the drawing-room furniture, and an auction of the old prints and the china. We've a broken bit of Dresden in a glass case, that we still call "Christian's Catastrophe". Petronilla won't have it thrown away. I'm very glad for Petronilla's sake that the boy's improving. Perhaps now I shall be able to get her to sleep without having to count sheep for her all night.'

'Have you seen Verity lately?' he added, stepping back. 'She's been weighing on my mind, too—she looks so depressed and—to tell the truth —*cross*. I offered to send her a song, the other day, and she actually said she hated music, and never wanted to sing a note again. So tiresome when quite nice young people grow up ill-tempered and rude!'

'Perhaps she wasn't feelin' well,' Larrupper replied, his old loyalty driving him to her defence.

'I'm goin' over to see her, now. No message, I suppose?'

'Oh, my love, of course. My love!' Savaury responded loftily. 'At least she's never refused that, *yet*, though there's no knowing what she'll come to. And you can bring hers back—if you've any to spare!'

He smiled joyfully as Larry coloured to the eyes, convinced that with him lay the clue to Verity's 'tiresome' behaviour, and sprinkled a shower of blessing as the car moved forward. Then he went in to tell Petronilla about Christian.

Augustus had sat as still as the Sphinx through this interview, and indeed Larry had forgotten him completely, until a finely-modelled little hand crept presently into his line of vision, and planted firm little fingers on the steering-wheel. He found himself staring at it as if fascinated— it was so soft and round, so dimpled, and so— small. The arm peeping from the muffler was soft and round too; it seemed ridiculous that it should ever grow an iron bunch of muscle like his own, handle a heavy car, or send a man to destruction by a wrestler's chip. Yet Laker had been such another as this mite—Savaury remembered him, and had cherished an old pot for his sake; even he himself, even *he* had been a lovable little child, once. It was queer how the little beggars got round you, how out of proportion they made other things appear, the little stupid things which seemed so huge when you brooded about them in your silly head. It was good for a man to have to look after one of them—stopped him worrying about his own idiotic troubles. It would be jolly to have one always at hand, he thought. They were so attractive, too. That absurd arm—he was ashamed to find himself wanting to stoop his head and put his lips to it. The fierce ache in his heart lessened. Something tolerant and tender stirred in his breast. Perhaps he *had* been hard on Verity, after all. Savaury had said she was cross, and that was a sure sign she was unhappy. It was no use telling himself that she deserved to be—the fact that she was miserable hurt him none the less. What had the frantic tragedy been about, after all? Old Grant? Well, why in Hades shouldn't old Grant dree his weird like every other earth-bound brute? It was cruel to think that Verity might be acutely unhappy. Why, she might even be crying! His foot went to the accelerator. He had never seen her cry for herself. It didn't bear thinking of. Oh, why hadn't he spoken to her more gently! She was only a little thing, and so dear. There was nobody like her in the whole world.

Rattling up to Heron door, he saw Verity on the lawn, and checked by the big beech. When she recognised him she turned and walked quickly away; and then just as quickly turned and walked back again. Augustus' expression changed definitely; this time in the direction of annoyance.

'Mother is downstairs, if you would like to see her,' she said politely. 'Is that your latest thing in mascots? I hope the Cruelty man isn't on your track?'

'You're a bit insultin',' Larry observed distantly. 'This trustin' gentleman commandeered the car in Crump. He's not takin' any harm at present, though I dare say he'd like a piece of cake or somethin', wouldn't you, old man? I've brought you a note from Debbie an' a rather squabby thing in parcels.'

'Oh, the handkerchiefs, I suppose? All right. I'll fetch the kiddie some cake. Don't trouble to get out unless you're going in. Just throw them over.'

'I'm not in the habit of throwin' things either to or at ladies,' Larry replied rather stiffly, climbing out. 'An', now I come to think of it, you haven't asked any charmin' questions about Christian.'

'I don't need to. I cycled to Crump, this morning, to inquire, and had quite a long talk with Mrs. Stanley. We've sent over, every day, of course. I'm so delighted he's on the right road, at last.'

'You came away without lettin' me know?' Larry asked incredulously. 'You were actually in Crump, talkin' to Nettie, without so much as askin' to see me? I must say you have a fetchin' friendly way of doin' things!'

'Well, but, Larry, one doesn't call at a house for bulletins, and ask to see a man who really ought to be living somewhere else altogether. Besides,' she went on, in a lower tone, 'I wasn't sure you would care to meet me. I knew—Lionel—wouldn't, anyhow.'

'Lionel wants shootin'!' Larrupper observed thickly, very red and embarrassed, kicking the front tyre nervously. 'It's all been Lionel's muddlin' from beginnin' to end—the grousin', interferin' blighter! He gets attacks of thinkin' he knows better than anybody else, an' starts makin' himself a blatant, rampin' nuisance. I've

brought him over by the scruff of his neck to lick
your boots; but, of course, as I keep tellin' him,
he can't expect to find you very forgivin'. Still,
there's just the chance you'll stretch the hand of
blessin' on Larry's account. Larry's an ass, but
he's very well-meanin', an' if you can see your
way to lookin' over things for his sake, I'll promise
you that skunk Lionel shan't ever get rampin'
round any more. I hope you'll think it over, an'
give us both a chance.'

There was a long pause; and then, just as she
made an effort to speak, Augustus, reaching too
far in a vain endeavour to persuade the steering-
wheel to continue his journey, fell heavily to the
floor. Larrupper spun round on the instant and
snatched him up, taking him in his arms and
soothing him with a skill very surprising in a
young man whose solicitude had hitherto been
mainly expended upon motors. Verity listened
in amazement to nursery endearments apparently quite at home on his lips, and a faint smile,
first amused and then tender, came to her own.
This was certainly Larry in a new light.

'I'll fetch the cake,' she remarked, turning
hastily to the house, and added, 'Poor little man!'
as Augustus resumed his seat, stooping to kiss his
tear-stained cheek. He looked so like a newly-
escaped cherub, with his solemn eyes and curling
hair.

But Augustus hated women. He liked men-
things with strong arms that could hold you without hurting you, and send shining monsters along
the road at a deliriously exciting speed. Glancing
at her stolidly, he lifted a chubby hand and
slapped her face. The next moment she was in

Larrupper's arms, with her injured cheek against his coat. Augustus stared solemnly at the gravel.

'Seems almost as if he'd been sent on purpose,' Larry observed presently, when at last they found time to attend to him again, 'though I'm not saying' he has a very elegant way of mendin' things. Still, it's not for Larry Lyndesay to be findin' fault with the gods. Run along in for the grub, darlin'. It's astonishin' how we keep forgettin' the poor little chap!'

'Old Savaury sent you his love,' he went on, when she came out again. 'The dear old fuss-bird was soothin' the dust with a sprinkler. He seemed hurt in his mind because you'd given up singin'. You might write, askin' for a song or two—he's worth cultivatin'. How's Billy-boy?' he added suddenly, stooping to start his engine.

'He came and apologised. He was—oh, Larry! —almost broken-hearted. I—what a heartless wretch I've been!'

'You're my sweet sweetin',' Larry answered tenderly, 'an' that's all you need get botherin' about at present. I must take this blusterin' pirate home to his mother, but I'm comin' back this evenin', so don't you go runnin' to church or any nonsense of that kind. An' when we've settled our own future moorin's, we'll see what we can do for Debbie an' old Laker.'

'I'm very much afraid we can't do anything,' Verity said sadly. 'There's something there I don't understand, and the only person who is in the least likely to know is most certainly not in the least likely to help. I mean Mr. Callander.'

'Why not, old dear?'

'Because he's in love with Deborah himself.'

Larry whistled with understanding as he scrambled to his seat.

'So there's another broken heart goin' beggin'?' he observed cheerfully. 'It's gettin' to be quite the fashion, isn't it, darlin'? I'm sure I hope it's consolin' to old Grant!'

'Oh, Larry!' Verity smiled reproachfully, and went round to bid Augustus good-bye.

'Shake hands, Mr. Cupid!' she coaxed. And Augustus shook hands.

．　．　．　．　．　．　．　．

The car whirred back through Crump to the pink-washed house, where the passenger actually allowed himself to be discharged without demur. His mother, murmuring embarrassed thanks, was at a loss to understand why Mr. Lionel should regard her erring son so tenderly. 'You'll be the death of me!' she remarked despairingly, as the car slid away. And, for the first time that afternoon, Augustus smiled.

CHAPTER XXIII

'THE land is positively hilarious!' Christian remarked, from the library window, looking out on the April afternoon. 'I've never seen Crump smile before, but to-day the dear old thing is frivolling like a child!'

Callander left his books at the table and came to his side.

'It's like the rest of us—throwing up its hat because you're about again. Thank Heaven you're on your feet at last!'

'I've been a horrid nuisance, I'm afraid,' Christian said remorsefully, 'but I'm not going to bother you any more. Even my head doesn't dither when I walk. You've all been frightfully good to me.'

'It's just possible that we liked it,' Callander answered drily. 'And you certainly did your best to escape our attentions.'

'Yes, I suppose I had a narrow squeak. I wish my grandfather's taste in pillars had been less elaborate. The last thing I remember seeing was the clock-face. I've been haunted by clocks all the time I was bad—great, staring, white-moon-things, always striking eleven! You'll think I'm a morbid ass——' he turned his shoulder rather nervously—'but I can't help feeling that if she—my mother—hadn't been under the Tree at that hour, I should have been the one to go. It meant to have one of us. I suppose, after a manner of speaking, she saved my life.'

'More than time she did something for you!' Callander growled, and apologised in the same breath, since she was dead and defenceless.

That Lyndesay mask, at least, he had never seen lifted.

'You'll be glad the tree is gone, surely?' he added. 'It ought to be a relief to feel that you have a decent chance of dying quietly of Anno Domini like the rest of us.'

Christian shrugged his shoulders.

'I feel—lonely!' he confessed rather shame-facedly. 'It's absurd to let a tree make any differ-ence, and most people would think I was talking off the top. But there's a hole in my life like the hole in the lawn. I can't explain. It's there, that's all. You'll have to prop me pretty hard, Callander, old man!'

'I'll send for another bottle of that tonic,' the other answered in his matter-of-fact way. 'You'll take hold all right when once you're thoroughly strong. As for being lonely—that's easily mended. Every man crosses a desert sometime in his life, and you've passed yours. You'll be marrying before long, of course.'

Christian flushed violently with the transparent colour of the convalescent.

'That's hardly likely. Crump has a way of destroying the balance of things. It either dwarfs or ennobles one. I want a woman to see me as I am—not through a series of magic mirrors.'

'You've got Crump on the brain—you Lyndesays!' Callander grunted impatiently. 'Why on earth shouldn't a girl be glad to marry you for your own sake, I'd like to know? I'm not in the habit of throwing flowers at people, but you must have a pretty good idea what I think of you, by now. Try some decent girl, and see if she doesn't think the same.'

'I did try,' Christian replied quietly, 'and the answer was as I told you. Crump!'

Callander stared at him for a moment in silence.

'Queer!' he muttered to himself at last, turning away. He had not guessed that things had gone as far as that, nor could he understand why Christian should be so blind. Deb's secret was plain enough to him. She must have deliberately placed Crump as a barrier between herself and the man she loved. But again why? Or did the matter lie at the door of the inscrutable Lyndesay whom the Tree had taken? He stayed by the window, puzzling, as Christian turned restlessly back into the room.

'She was quite frank with me. She told me that if she married me it would not be for myself but for what I could give her, and she wouldn't do it. She said it wasn't fair. I'm not blaming her—she was straight, all through—but it's not very encouraging to one's personal estimate, is it? You see, I've not exactly had a surfeit of love. Nobody wanted me as a child, and, if you're not loved as a child, you find it hard to believe that anybody can love you afterwards. But we were good friends, and we were in sympathy. I had begun to think she might care, in spite of my background, even though she had taken Stanley——' He pulled himself up sharply, and then went on again—'You know, of course, I suppose? It can't be a secret from you. There's only one woman ——' and poor Callander echoed the words under his breath, looking out at the calling spring day.

Why had she been at such definite pains to keep Christian in the dark? he wondered, his mind revolving ceaselessly round the same point. What held her back from all she needed most? Not fear of Mrs. Lyndesay or of tattling tongues, he was sure of that; nor, indeed, any shirking of the future. What *had* held her? And at that moment Christian quite unconsciously gave him his answer.

'She said I did not love her,' he continued from the leather arm-chair into which he had dropped rather wearily, in spite of his boasted strength. He might almost have been speaking to himself, and Callander kept his back turned, guessing that nothing but the dependence of recent illness would have led him to unveil his mind so frankly.

'Perhaps, if you're not loved, you don't learn to love—no, that's a rotten way of looking at it! It's a poor sort of creature that can't persuade a woman that he wants her. Yet I cared, and I couldn't do it. Or perhaps I didn't care enough —*then*.'

Callander made no answer, for he heard steps along the hall. He saw now what had happened; why Deb, who would have sold her soul for Crump, had yet flung it aside. The decision had evidently been final—Christian would not approach her again, nor would she ever attempt to bring him back. The way was clear for himself, if he chose to take it. He, at least, would have no difficulty in persuading a woman that he loved her! The older, harder, stronger man shrugged his shoulders mentally, and then reminded himself that Christian had scarcely had a chance, since Deb had wilfully misled him. Yet, in this, as in all similar cases, it was up to each man to look to himself. He had only to keep his mouth shut, and Christian would never know what he knew—what Deb's face had told him under the lantern on the old bridge. They were best apart, too, these fated Lyndesays, with their fanatical harbouring of terrible tradition and drear belief. It would be folly for them to marry, he told himself, and was instantly reproached by the memory of Christian's frank eyes and the bright freshness of Deb's presence. Well, well—granted, however grudgingly—should a man yet be forced to cut his own throat—to send another hot-footed to the woman he loved? Need a steward serve his

master beyond the limits of good business faith?
Only a fool would do it, or an idealist like Roger
Lyndesay, in whom feudal loyalty was little less
than monomania. *He* had no forebears urging
sacrifice, no passionate creed to draw his will;
nothing but his own ethical standard and the
tender filament of a woman's happiness.

His unseeing eyes rested on the clean world
outside, as he listened vaguely to the stammering
agitation of a voice behind him, and Christian's
quiet, encouraging replies.

After all, it was not a question either of
Christian or of himself, but of Deb. Curious that
he should have taken so long to compass that—
he who had sneered and shrugged at his master's
slackness in loving! He had looked at it from the
man's point of view; suddenly he saw it from the
woman's. At least both she and Christian must
have their chance. It was an ironic fate that had
thrust the bestowal of it into his hands—he had
a sudden wild impulse to laugh aloud and beat
at the heavy glass before him. It was too much to
ask—a thousand times too much; yet the very
passion that had created the situation clamoured
to him to comply. With characteristic abrupt-
ness and decision he yielded, accepting, and
turned his attention to the scene in progress.

Just inside the door Gaskarth stood, cap in
hand, sponsor, it seemed, for the dogged, miserable figure by the library table. Harker had had
a bad time since the wild March night that had
ended so disastrously for Crump. The still figure
of his adversary had sobered his intoxication of
hate, and in spite of the threatening faces round
him he had insisted upon stopping for the doctor's

verdict. The latter's shaken head had roused the crowd to a frenzy from which Harker had had a very narrow escape, but Gaskarth had got him safely out at last, shoved him on his own bicycle and sent him home.

'Not because I care a foot of lead piping what happens to you,' he informed him frankly, 'but because I don't want Crump Wrestling Academy figuring in the police-news. You couldn't see you were heaving him at that d—d pillar, and you felled him right enough, though more by good luck than good management, I'll swear. I don't like your game, and I mean to keep wide of you, but I'll not have you lynched on Crump ground. *He* wouldn't have liked it. Me and Lakin' Lyndesay—*we* fight fair!'

This was bad enough, but his reception at home was worse.

Harker had found himself up against a second feudal precept that seemed curiously opposed to the first, yet ran with it amicably enough. 'Hate Crump, but leave it alone!' was the second article of the family creed. The old coachman's inbred respect for 'quality' suffered a rude shock at the news that his son had laid violent hands upon a Lyndesay. Worldly diplomacy, too, had its say, and very much to the point. This might mean the stopping of the pension and other disasters. Everybody knew—everybody, that was, but a daft lumphead—that Rishwald had been much at Crump, of late, bent on friendly terms and even more, and he was hardly likely to look favourably on the affair. It might mean that the young man would have to leave the farm, and serve him right an' all, *that* it would! Nobody but a fool would have got himself into the mess—this to an accompaniment of lady's maid's tears and a lament like a soughing wind—'Poor Mr. Christian! Poor, dear lad!'

All this struck Harker as distinctly unfair, which was scarcely surprising, and when, after a public reproof from Rishwald, he found himself shunned not only in his own and the opposing village but also at Witham market, the bitterness in his heart strengthened like a fed flame. He hadn't been given the belt, either; though, to do him justice, that was not by any means his first grievance. Still, he had won it. Taken altogether, it was an unrewarding world.

With Christian's first move towards recovery, however, had come a curt groom riding to the door with a shortly-delivered note, equally shortly received. The address was in Callander's hand, but the faintly-pencilled words within were Christian's own. Harker stared at them sullenly, fiercely-drawn brows shading miserable eyes.

'Your match,' said the straggling letters—'not to blame—going strong,'—the painful effort of them carrying to his hard wretchedness a frank kindliness that was like the touch of a tender hand upon aching eyes. He said nothing about the letter; but, after that, he was found time and again at Crump for news, the signed 'C. de L.' in his pocket giving him courage to face each hostile reception. And to-day he had gone boldly to Gaskarth, and begged him to procure him an interview. Lakin' Lyndesay's star pupil, adamant at first, had at last eyed him with gradually relaxing hauteur.

'Of course, if you're wanting to do the right thing, it's not for *me* to stand in your way!' he observed kindly. 'I'm a sportsman, myself. And of course I can get you in to see Mr. Christian, if I choose. Mr. Christian, he says—"Bob," says he, "you're heartily welcome, night *or* day!" Happen you could creep in along behind. I hope this here mix-up will learn you not to go about getting yourself disliked in future.'

He had engineered the introduction quite successfully, and now Harker found himself stuttering unready, half-sullen apologies, desperately wishing himself out of it, and cursing Gaskarth for his well-meaning murmurs from the door.

'There's no need for apology,' Christian stopped him quickly. 'It was a fair enough fight, and I've no complaint to make. Of course you didn't mean to throw me off the mat! Who but an idiot would think you did?' He looked round sharply at Callander. 'Has anything been said to him? Has he been blamed?' and frowned at his agent's lifted eyebrows. 'If there is any show of feeling, you can tell the offenders I'll deal with them myself. I'm not dead or likely to be, and I'll have no more ill-will grow out of this affair, so please let that be generally understood!'

'He has the belt, of course?' he added suddenly, and stared coldly as Callander shrugged his shoulders, and Gaskarth, red to the roots of his hair, glared at the carpet. 'No? I'll have something to say to the committee about this! If it was forgotten on the night, it should have been sent to him later. He won it, of course. Our match was merely an exhibition. You must have known what my wishes would be; you should have seen they were carried out. Where *is* the belt, by the way?'

'Here, I believe,' Callander answered gruffly, opening a cupboard and showing the prize within. The eternal Lyndesay revulsion had left him staggered, as usual. This was not by any means the doubting boy he had so casually despised. 'Some of the committee turned up with it, next day. Might have been a snake by the way they handled it! They wouldn't hear of anything being done until you could deal with the matter yourself.'

'The apology is undoubtedly owed to *you*.' Christian addressed the wrestler, standing up; but, when he would have handed him the belt, Harker shook his head again as he had shaken it before.

'I want naught with it!' he said ungraciously, yet with an undertone that was almost pleading, and his sponsor in the background went crimson a second time and drew circles with his boot-toe.

'You've got to take it whether you want it or not!' Christian said decidedly. 'It's your property, and I'll be hanged if I'll have it on the premises! And see here, my man, there's something else that's been weighing on my mind all the time I was ill. We didn't finish that round in the orthodox manner. Let's put it right, now!'

He held out his hand, and Harker, after a moment's hesitation, sent his own to meet it, his brain in a whirl. There must be something hopelessly wrong with the universe if he could feel himself deliriously honoured by a handshake from Lyndesay of Crump!

'I like that hold better than another of yours

I've tried!' Christian added cheerfully but with meaning, and Harker dropped his head as Gaskarth dragged him out.

'An' serve you darned well right!' he observed pleasantly, drawing a breath of relief as they left the house. 'Nearly wore me to chewed string, that you did, sliding down me like a bloomin' water-chute! It's a rotten game to be always slipping holds—water-chutin' the other chap into a wax! I don't approve of your style no more than I like your pretty way of taking prizes, but I'll tell you what I'll do. You come down now and again of an evening for a bit of a friendly tussle, an' happen I'll learn you better ways!'

Callander shut the door after the men and strode back into the room.

'I'm sorry about the belt!' he said abruptly. 'Of course the fellow ought to have had it, but at the time we felt more like using it to him than handing it over with a smile. Still, as you say, I should have known your wishes. I am here to know them.' Christian gave him a friendly nod of understanding, and he shut his teeth hard, setting his will at the last fence with a desperate lift. Then—'You must go to her!' he almost shot at him.

Christian stared for a moment, his mind travelling backward; then shook his head.

'I have no right.'

'You have the best right of all. She loves you.'

'She loves—Crump.'

'Of course she loves Crump!' Callander burst out angrily. 'Heavens, man! You talk as though it were a crime! She loves Crump in a way that you can't even begin to imitate, for all it's your own property. Don't you know *yet* why she would have married your brother? Have you spent hours at Kilne, watching her while the old man talked, and not guessed? Or can't you discriminate between mere vanity and greed and the pure flower of devotion? If you think it's money that draws her, you're wrong. If you think it's even pride of race, you're wrong! And it certainly isn't the trappings of riches, your servants and your forty bedrooms and your oak staircases and all the rest of it. It's every blade of grass springing upon Crump land; it's every furrow turned in Crump soil; every tree that draws life from it, and every sunset painted on its woods. She's not the last of the branch for nothing; and, above all, it's certainly not for nothing that she's Roger Lyndesay's child. You'll wonder how I know. Well, she didn't tell me—not consciously; but I *do* know, just as I know she loves you, though it's needless to say she never told me *that*. She knows best why she denied it to you—that's no business of mine. Anyhow, it's true, and you can take my word for it. Anybody but a morbid, star-gazing Lyndesay would have guessed it for himself!'

He stopped as abruptly as he had begun, picking up a bottle from the mantelpiece, and turning to the door. 'I'll drop this as I pass,' he went on, in his normal tone, and, when Christian protested that a servant could take it, putting out a hand to the bell, he checked him brusquely.

'*I* am your servant!' the elder man answered, with a kind of grim affection, and went out, slipping the bottle into his pocket.

Roger Lyndesay was sitting in the porch,

serenely content in the tranquil spring evening, which was yet full of crying life, from the lambs calling behind the house to the birds in the new green wonder of the trees. Deb came behind him, and had to put her hand on his shoulder before he turned his eyes from the fresh spring garment of the park.

'We did our best, didn't we, Deb?' he asked, looking up at her with a kind of mystic exaltation. 'We gave it all we could. It hasn't suffered in our charge, has it?'

He was following out some silent train of thought, but she did not need to ask what he meant. The pronoun set her heart beating. For once she was included; for once he saw her definitely linked to the long Kilne chain.

'Oh, yes, we've done our best!' she answered, with a thrill in her voice. 'We've put it first, always. We have given it—ourselves. And it will never really forget, whoever may come after us!'

She stepped outside, and for a moment stood looking at the splendid old man, framed like a delicate pastel by the clematis-covered porch. Of those dearest to us we have always one picture readiest to our hearts, and this was to be her memory of him, returning all her life in times of stress, with its atmosphere of fine achievement come to its evening peace.

Turning, at last, a sudden yearning took her towards the park. She began to walk quickly, without knowing why, climbing the shoulder of the hill; and, when Nettie hailed her unexpectedly across the turf, she had a curious feeling of having been checked on a definite errand. But Nettie evidently had need of her, and she allowed herself to be drawn across to the avenue and up towards Dockerneuk.

'I know you're in one of your "back to the land" moods,' Mrs. Slinker said apologetically. 'I could tell that by the way you were walking. But do spare yourself to me just for half an hour. There is something I must do, and I'm not brave enough to do it alone.'

In spite of her new happiness there was still about Slinker's wife a touch of the fear that had surprised Christian on Christmas Eve. The late tragedy had left a sinister shadow upon her well-balanced mind and splendidly sane outlook. The Lyndesay atmosphere had caught even Nettie Stone in the mesh of its creeping dread. The old horror was upon her, and she could not fight it. Not yet—not even *yet* had she eluded Crump.

'It holds me!' she said passionately, as they went up. 'Twice I've escaped from it, and twice it has brought me back. It can't bring me a third time, can it? Can it, Deb? But I'm afraid! Just because I'm happy, I'm afraid. I remember scoffing at Christian's morbid fancies, but now I'm a hundred times worse, myself. They're his inheritance, though,—and yours. You're entitled to your imaginings, but a horse-dealer's daughter has no business to be jabbering about the clutch of ghosts. They're dead—I know they're dead!— and yet I feel that both Stanley and his mother would get between me and my happiness, if they could!'

They were folding the sheep at Dockerneuk, and the air was thrilling with the deep call of the mothers and the tremolo answer of the lambs.

Dixon was by the farmyard wall, watching his flock come in, but he turned at Nettie's voice, and came to meet them, his slim little sheep-dog pressing himself delicately against Deb for notice. The old farm had the worn grayness of fine age set in the transcendently fresh youth of earth and atmosphere. The same quality of patient dignity breathed alike from Dixon and his background, making them one.

Deborah took the opportunity to wish him happiness, and the reserved northerner thanked her shyly, sending his quiet eyes back to his fields, with the far-off gaze of those who look abroad from dawn till eve.

'It's grand to have Mr. Christian about again!' he observed, presently, changing the subject as soon as courtesy allowed. 'He's a bit over-white and slender, yet, but he'll mend of that. You've seen him, of course, Miss Deborah?'—and all his native politeness could not completely conceal his surprise when Deb shook her head.

'His own people haven't had much chance of seeing him,' Nettie put in quickly, coming to the rescue. 'Half the county has been sitting on the doorstep for weeks, and of course the people who knew him least were the ones who came oftenest. Parker and I have had a fearful time chasing the old worries off the premises. Lots of them brought things to eat—Heaven alone knows why! Parker was simply raving, but the under-servants enjoyed them frightfully. Other people left tracts, and the Bracewells brought everything you could think of, from primroses to puzzles—horrid little brain-stretchers that made Christian's head wiggle, the moment he saw them. The Whyterigg car has been over, every day——' She caught Anthony's smiling, gently-chiding gaze, and dropped her own, but went on firmly. 'Mr. Rishwald's dreadfully upset about the whole affair—wrote Christian yards on the matter. He sent him an old silver porringer for his beef-tea, and—do you know?'—she looked laughingly at Deb—'it turned out to have the Crump crest on it!'

She drew the girl out of the yard with a gay nod to her lover, but in the lane she was silent until they stopped at the gate of the old Norman church.

'Do you mind coming in?' she asked. 'This is where I was making for. I'll tell you why, inside.

'Anthony is having the banns put up, on Sunday,' she announced abruptly, when they stood in the dimness of the ancient church, looking up, past the stone pillars and the gloom of the screen, to the Dutch lamps swinging before carved mullion and mellow glass. 'I can't stay on at Crump, now that Christian is all right again, and Heaven knows I'm glad enough to go, but for him! But there's a step to be crossed before I get to Dockerneuk, and oh, Deb, I'm afraid to put out my foot!'

She drew her up the aisle and stopped, pointing down; and under her finger Stanley's name rose to them from the stone slab before the chancel-steps. Over the family vault where Slinkin' Lyndesay lay buried, Nettie his widow would have to pass to her joy.

'I wanted to be married in a registry-office,' she went on—'another church—anywhere—but Anthony's mother has set her heart on being present, and she's too infirm to go far. How can I refuse anything to his mother? But I'm frightened—fool that I am!—frightened that Slinker will rise up and come between us, even at the last! Oh, Deb, if I should never get to Anthony, after all!'

She sank into a seat, covering her face with her hands, but Deb stayed in her place, looking down quietly at the freshly-lettered stone. Here, in the stillness of the sanctuary, she found again the Stanley whom she, and she alone, had known, and for whose sake she had been justified in her own eyes, and on account of whose memory she had never spoken a single bitter word against the man who had so basely deceived her. Only in his own sinister little room did the evil side of him, somehow kept fiendishly alive by his tortured mother, show her to herself as something for ever degraded and unclean. But, standing beside his grave, the balance of things swung true again; she saw her act as dangerous indeed, but not ignoble; misjudged, perhaps, but never sordid; and she took back her self-respect as a gift from the Altar.

Through her abstraction she heard Nettie's voice, tense and low, like that of one upon whom light has flashed, white and blinding.

'Perhaps it is because I wronged him that I am afraid! I never realised it before, or perhaps I never cared. I married him rashly, I left him heedlessly, and the vows I made are clamouring for their unpaid toll. Looking back, it seems as if all this trouble and tragedy should be laid at my door. If I had taken up my burden, you, at least, would have been saved your share. I might have saved his mother—she had some curious feeling for me; and—who knows?—I might have saved Stanley, too!'

But Deb, in that moment of readjustment, without jealousy and without resentment, knew that Stanley would never have touched the highest for any one but herself.

'I can't atone—it isn't possible. Anthony said there was never any going back in this world, and I thought I had proved him wrong, but every day I see more clearly what he meant. There's no getting away from the past. All my life Slinker will stand between me and the man I love!'

She rose and slipped her arm through Deborah's.

'It's just a year since he died—had you remembered? I came here to ask him to forgive me, to see if he would let me off, but he still hates me—he'll never let me go. If we could lift the stone, we should see him smiling, so sure of himself and of his power—smiling—smiling—— Deb, I'm not mad, am I? Come home, now, will you, dear? It isn't any use.'

They turned slowly up through the Crump chapel to the side door, and Deb laid her fingers in passing on the hacked armour of a couple of warriors clasped in each other's arms. Nettie looked at her inquiringly, and they paused beside the mutilated figures clinging so closely in the hour of death.

'They were Lyndesay brothers,' Deb explained, 'and one slew the other for a cup of water when they were lying wounded on some field of battle. But, when he saw what he had done, his madness left him, and he would not touch the drink. Instead, he placed the cup on the dead man's breast, and lay looking at it through long hours until he died. And, for many a year after, if any one had wronged a Lyndesay, he placed a cup of water, all unknown, upon his grave, and so the dead was appeased. Of course, the custom vanished centuries ago. I read about it in one of Father's old books.'

She stopped, puzzled, for Nettie was gazing at her with a curiously-arrested look, as men stare when the hand of a redeeming angel is stretched to them from the skies. Yet she said nothing; only, after a pause, smiled, and went out into the sun.

But, before night fell, the verger, wondering, found an ancient symbol on the worn slab at the chancel-steps; and for many a year afterwards a cup of cold water cried on Slinkin' Lyndesay's mercy. And Anthony Dixon's wife found peace.

Released by the top lodge, Deb left the road and sped quickly across the turf to the top of the park, like a light-footed thing of the woods homeward bound for its lair. She did not ask herself why or where she was going, only hurried, hurried, hearing her heart beating and the birds calling, and the thin, quickening cry of the lambs on every side. Below, to her left, the stately phalanx of the trees descended to the Hall, where the soft, gray smoke lifted its delicate pillars in the still, drawing evening, like folded cobwebs against the towering woods behind. In front, over the dropping parkland and the wide sands, the tranquil opal sky melted into the gauze-blue hills. To the right and far beneath, the heavily-shaded river ringed Cappelside in its shallow bed;

and in the hollow by the buckhouse the deer lay close.

Crossing the ridge she dived into the plantation, clinging to the steep face of the slope, and there, leaning against a tree, she found Christian —on Cappelside.

He was looking towards her as she came down, standing with his back against the tree and his head lifted, almost as if he expected her, and she went straight to him without any pause of hesitation and surprise, like one walking in a dream.

'Did you want me?' she asked simply, and Christian answered 'Yes!' just as simply, like children crying to and answering each other, and a change he did not understand came over her face, as if some hidden glory had set its lamp to her eyes and caught her whole soul in a quiver of light. She turned from him swiftly and dropped on the ground, hiding her face on her knees.

Puzzled and slightly alarmed, he stepped to her side and bent over her with an anxious question, and she shook her head without raising it; then threw out her arms and looked up at him with the same brilliant eyes.

'I'll tell you presently—presently!' she said. 'Oh, Christian, you've freed me—given me my right to my dream. All my life I thought I was stealing, and it was mine, all the time! It's mine now as long as I live.'

She gave a low laugh of pure ecstasy, and then, meeting his bewildered glance, came back to the reality of things and to the memory of all that had occurred since they had last met. The climb up the park had wearied him and set violet shadows beneath his eyes, tired lines in his thin face. His hands were thin, too, she noticed, pallid with the whiteness of hands that have lain helpless on a counterpane, and in his eyes was still the patient, inward look that comes with dangerous illness. And beyond all that there was an air of desolation strange in so young a man—almost the look of one bowing a beaten head to Fate. Her victorious gladness struck against it, wondering, and, with a heart charged to the brim with pity, she stretched out both her hands.

'Oh, how ill you look!' she exclaimed. 'How terribly ill and miserable and lonely! What can I do to help you, my dear, my poor dear?'

And Christian, with her face blurred to his eyes, conscious only of his desperate need of her and of her strength, clung to her tender hands and dropped beside her, hiding his face on her lap.

'Debbie, why did you send me away?' he asked, from his shelter. 'Couldn't you feel that I was yours, even if I didn't know it myself? You're all I've got in the world, and all I want. You mustn't send me away again!'

'I'll keep you till the stars fall!' she answered almost fiercely, closing her arms round him. 'I sent you away because I was afraid—afraid for your happiness. I lied to you, but I loved you all the time. I lied to you because I loved you, oh, blind and dearest heart!'

She stooped and laid her lips to his hair, and out of the spring magic every voice cried to her that she had ever loved; the chattering water-voice that has the note of rung silver in it; the liquid gold of the thrush, the diamond-clear whistle of the blackbird; and always the lamb's appeal and the mother's anxious answer. The

mighty dignity of the ancient trees, foiled by the
eternal freshness of springing grass, the smell of
the earth, the press of the turf—all that stood for
the heritage of Crump reaching forward and so
far behind, fused for the moment in the young,
pathetic figure at her feet, summoned her soul
from the hidden covert where it had crouched so
long, afraid; and Christian, looking at her at last
with clear eyes, knew that he saw her for the first
time.

'Tell me what it all means,' he said, 'why you
came to-night—your real self behind the mask—
Stanley—everything!'

'It reaches back to the beginning of things,' she
answered, smiling. 'Won't it tire you?'—but
when he shook his head and sat up, drawing
her against his shoulder, she opened her heart
with the passionate relief that only those know
who have carried locked lips through hungering
years.

'Do you remember what a queer little child I
was, Christian? Lots of people disapproved of
me, and some kind souls thought I was what
Brathay would call "nickt i' the head". I was
allowed to do pretty much what I liked after my
mother died, and I spent most of my time wandering about the estate, until I knew every corner of
it as well as Kilne itself. I wouldn't take any
notice of the "quality"—shut my mouth tight
when they spoke to me, and looked as though
they were trying to steal me; but anybody that
worked on the land I took to my heart on the spot.
All the ploughmen were my friends, the hedgers
and ditchers, the beaters and beckwatchers, down
to the poachers! Even the fearsomeness of keepers

I tamed, and they let me go where I chose—they made me as free of the woods as any other wild fledgling. And old Brathay—ask him some time what we were to each other in those days—the queer little child and the big huntsman! There was Bowness, too, a wild youngster kicked out of Whyterigg, whom my father shaped into the finest keeper on Crump. And Moorhouse and Fleming—oh, and heaps more—*they* were my education! Do you wonder that I lived and breathed Crump, with such surroundings, Father talking of nothing else, and all the old books to my hand? I was bred to it, too.' She gave the same ecstatic laugh. 'I'm not afraid to say it, now. You've given me the right!

'It didn't mean anything special to me, at first. It was just part of me, that was all. And then, one day, as all the Lyndesays do, I found my dream. I had been reading the list of Crump stewards, saying the names aloud until I reached my father's, and it came to me suddenly that this splendid inheritance of service was mine—the birthright of me, Deborah Lyndesay; and I ran out into the park and flung myself on the grass, kissing it, and saying over and over again—"I, too, will serve Crump! I, too! I, too!" sobbing for sheer joy. And then two workmen passed up the path to the Hall.'

She paused a moment, and by the restraint in her tone when she went on he guessed that the childish tragedy was as new and terrible to her to-day.

'My father was riding below them on the road, and they touched their hats as he went by. One of them stopped to look after him. "The last of the Kilne Lyndesays!" I heard him say. "The best and the finest—and the last. It's a sad pity!"

"'There's a lass, though, isn't there?" said the other, and the first man laughed as though he had made a joke.

"'Ay, and what use of that?" he said scathingly. "What can a lass do for Crump? As far as that goes, Roger Lyndesay might as well have neither chick nor child. Nay, he's the last, worse luck! The lass doesn't count."

'Oh, Christian, it's a long fall from Heaven! I'm broken and wounded to this day. My dream shattered in my hands. I was my ancestors' child, but I could not follow in their steps. I had all the love, all the courage, even the knowledge, but—I was a girl. I could not put my hand to the plough and drive a single foot in the Kilne furrow, though the heritage of desire was born in me as fiercely alive as in any son. Do people never think that a girl may feel these things, too—suffer and burn to follow in her fathers' steps and make herself one with them in her quota of good work? I never spoke of it. Nobody has ever known—not even my father; but the longing of it drove back upon me, eating the soul out of me. Even when I was away, the thought of Crump was a more vivid thing to me than the world around me; and when I came back it was like a resurrection—the pain of resurrection, too! Oh, Christian—that first year—— Each day I lived as a man before execution, knowing that one of them would bring my real life to an end.

'Then at last came—the way out. Stanley. It was the woman's only way out. You'll try to understand, Christian, won't you—won't you?

I knew what he was—it was impossible to live under Crump's very shadow and not know—but beyond and above all that he was something to me that he couldn't possibly be to anybody else. To begin with, he was Lyndesay of Crump, and I, Roger Lyndesay's daughter. With us lay the right to give him anything we chose, our last coin to help him, our sword-hand to save him—even ourselves. It's a right that can only be bought by perfect service—that's why so few people know what it means. But *we* know. Then, Stanley—needed me. Through me he reached out to the dream, and I could feel him struggling. That is why I've never blamed him, even in my thoughts. Because I loved Crump so much, I filled a want in him that was sometimes hungry and cried; and after a while he could not let me go. He—needed me.'

'As I need you!' Christian's voice answered her, low and passionate. For the first time, a thrill of sympathy vitalised the bond between his brother and himself.

'The letter of your mother's accusation was true; never the spirit. I would have married Stanley for Crump—for the soil, the soul of Crump—for *this*!' She struck her hand passionately on the turf. 'Just as I would have married you, dear heart, if I had dared to risk you one single hour of remorse!'

He turned her face and looked into her eyes.

'Kilne does not lapse,' he said. 'It comes home, that is all. The chain ends at Crump where it began—you bring it there. Doesn't that make you "count"?'

'Oh, yes, I count, at last!' she answered, with

the same vivid content. 'Your way and my way,
I count in both. Didn't you know what I meant
when I found you? It is said of Crump stewards
that they can be drawn to their masters by a
thought. You wanted me, and I came at once.
Somebody stopped me on the way, and I chafed
and ached until they let me go. I didn't know
why I was coming or what drew me, but you
called me and I came. To-day I stand in my
fathers' place, and put my hands between yours,
and my homage with them. All those gone before
know me and own my claim. I, too, can serve. I,
too, belong to Crump at last!'

. . . .

Under the hill the Hall sheltered, no longer a
crouching thing of menace but a man's quiet
hearth-place, breathing peace. The rooks were
coming back, calling their way over park and
village, ploughing steadily through the pure air
to their nests in the dim woods. The two lonely
young figures followed them: Crump folk all—
going home.

WORLD'S CLASSICS

ES in constant progress, containing over
undred volumes, and offering in a size
the pocket, and at a low price, the most
cks in the English language, with more
translations. Many of the volumes con-
ctions by the best modern writers.

SIZE, $6 \times 3\frac{3}{4}$ inches (as this list). Large
in opaque paper, in superfine art cloth.

ER of the volumes are also obtainable in
ain Moroccoette and in Natural grain
These are specially recommended for
on.

LUMES are obtainable through any book-

FOLLOWING LIST the books are classi-
low:

ies	*Letters*
raphy	*Literary Criticism*
iy	*Philosophy and Science*
-Greek and Roman	*Poetry*
	Politics, Political Theory,
nd Belles Lettres	*and Political Economy*
(Short Stories are	*Religion*
ed separately)	*Short Stories*
	Travel and Topography

DEX OF AUTHORS is given at the end of

PRINTED IN
GREAT BRITAIN
AT THE
UNIVERSITY PRESS
OXFORD
BY
JOHN JOHNSON
PRINTER
TO THE
UNIVERSITY

A LIST OF

WORL

CLASS

Oxford University

THE

A SERI
four
adapted fo
famous wo
than a few
tain introc

POCKET
type, on t

A NUMI
Pebble g
Morocco.
presentati

THE VC
seller.

IN THE
fied as b

Antholo
Autobio
Biograf
Classic
Drama
Essays
Fiction
grou
Histor

AN IN
the list

THE
WORLD'S CLASSICS

PRINTED ON OXFORD INDIA PAPER

The following Works are obtainable in superfine
maroon cloth, gilt lettered on back,
gilt top, and marker.

TWO VOLUMES IN ONE

THREE VOLUMES IN ONE

COMPLETE LIST OF THE SERIES

¶ *Anthologies*

A BOOK OF AMERICAN VERSE. Selected and edited by *A. C. Ward* (428).

A BOOK OF NARRATIVE VERSE. Compiled by *V. H. Collins*. Introduction by *Edmund Blunden* (350).

A BOOK OF SCOTTISH VERSE. Compiled by *R. L. Mackie* (417).

AMERICAN CRITICISM. Representative Literary Essays. Chosen by *Norman Foerster* (354).

ENGLISH ESSAYS, chosen and arranged by *W. Peacock* (32).

ENGLISH ESSAYS, 1600–1900, chosen by *S. V. Makower* and *B. H. Blackwell* (172).

ENGLISH ESSAYS, MODERN. Two Series. Selected by *H. S. Milford* (280, 406).

ENGLISH PROSE from MANDEVILLE to RUSKIN, chosen and arranged by *W. Peacock* (45).

ENGLISH PROSE, chosen and arranged by *W. Peacock* in 5 volumes: I, WYCLIFFE to CLARENDON; II, MILTON to GRAY; III, WALPOLE to LAMB; IV, LANDOR to HOLMES; V, MRS. GASKELL to HENRY JAMES (219–23).

ENGLISH PROSE, Narrative, Descriptive, Dramatic (MALORY to STEVENSON), compiled by *H. A. Treble* (204).

ENGLISH SONGS AND BALLADS, compiled by *T. W. H. Crosland*. New edition, with the text revised, and additional poems (13).

ENGLISH SHORT STORIES (Nineteenth and Twentieth Centuries), selected by *H. S. Milford*. Three Series (193, 228, 315).

ENGLISH VERSE. Edited by *W. Peacock*. I, Early Lyrics to SHAKESPEARE (308); II, CAMPION to the Ballads (309); III, DRYDEN to WORDSWORTH (310); IV, SCOTT to ELIZABETH BROWNING (311); V, LONGFELLOW to RUPERT BROOKE (312).

LETTERS WRITTEN IN WAR-TIME (Fifteenth to Nineteenth Centuries), selected and arranged by *H. Wragg* (202).

A MISCELLANY OF TRACTS AND PAMPHLETS. Sixteenth to Nineteenth Centuries. Edited by *A. C. Ward* (304).

PALGRAVE'S GOLDEN TREASURY, with 188 pages of additional poems from LANDOR to BLUNDEN (133).

READING AT RANDOM. A 'World's Classics' Anthology. Edited by *Ben Ray Redman* (410).

¶ *Autobiography*

AKSAKOFF (SERGHEI). Trans. by *J. D. Duff*. A Russian Gentleman (241). Years of Childhood (242). A Russian Schoolboy (261).

CELLINI (BENVENUTO) (300).

DE QUINCEY (THOMAS). Confessions of an Opium-Eater (23).

FRANKLIN (BENJAMIN). The Autobiography, edited from his original manuscript by *John Bigelow* (250).

GIBBON (EDWARD). Autobiography. Introduction by *J. B. Bury* (139).

HAYDON (BENJAMIN ROBERT). The Autobiography. Introduction and Epilogue by *Edmund Blunden* (314).

HUNT (LEIGH). Autobiography. Intro. *Edmund Blunden* (329).

MILL (JOHN STUART). Autobiography. Introduction by *Harold J. Laski* (262).

TOLSTOY. A Confession, and What I believe. Translated by *Aylmer Maude* (229). Recollections and Essays. Translated with an Introduction by *Aylmer Maude* (459).

TROLLOPE (ANTHONY). Autobiography. Introduction by *Michael Sadleir* (239).

¶ *Biography*

CARLYLE. The Life of John Sterling. Introduction by *W. Hale White* ('*Mark Rutherford*') (144).

CRABBE, LIFE OF. By his Son. Introduction by *E. M. Forster* (404).

DOBSON (AUSTIN). Four Frenchwomen: Charlotte Corday, Madame Roland, Princess de Lamballe, Madame de Genlis (248).

EMERSON. Representative Men. (With *English Traits*) (30).

FRANCIS OF ASSISI (ST.). The Little Flowers; and The Life of Brother Giles. Translated into English verse by *James Rhoades* (265).

GASKELL (MRS.). The Life of Charlotte Brontë (214).

HOUGHTON (LORD). Life of Keats (364).

JOHNSON (SAMUEL). Lives of the Poets. 2 vols. (83, 84).

MAUDE (AYLMER). Life of Tolstoy. 2 vols. (383, 384).

SCOTT (SIR WALTER). Lives of the Novelists. Introduction by *Austin Dobson* (94).

TREVELYAN (SIR G. O.). Life of Macaulay. With a new Introduction by *G. M. Trevelyan*. 2 vols. (401, 402).

WALTON (IZAAK). Lives of Donne, Wotton, Hooker, Herbert, Sanderson. Introduction by *George Saintsbury* (303).

¶ *The* '*Classics*', *Greek and Roman*

AESCHYLUS. The Seven Plays. Translated into English Verse by *Lewis Campbell* (117).

ARISTOPHANES. The Acharnians, Knights, Birds, and Frogs. Translated by *J. Hookham Frere*. Intro. *W. W. Merry* (134).

HOMER. Translated by *Pope*. Iliad (18). Odyssey (36).

SOPHOCLES. The Seven Plays. Translated into English Verse by *Lewis Campbell* (116).

VIRGIL. The Aeneid, Georgics, and Eclogues. Translated by *John Dryden* (37).

—— The Aeneid, Georgics, and Eclogues. Translated by *James Rhoades* (227).

¶ Drama

BROWNING (ROBERT). Poems and Plays, 1833–42 (58).

CONGREVE (WILLIAM). Complete Works. 2 vols. Introduction by *Bonamy Dobrée*. I, The Comedies. II, The Mourning Bride, with Letters, Poems, and Miscellanies (276, 277).

EIGHTEENTH CENTURY COMEDY. FARQUHAR'S Beaux' Stratagem, STEELE'S Conscious Lovers, GAY'S Beggar's Opera, FIELDING'S Tom Thumb, GOLDSMITH'S She Stoops to Conquer (292).

EIGHTEENTH CENTURY, LESSER COMEDIES OF THE. Edited by *Allardyce Nicoll*. The five comedies are ARTHUR MURPHY'S The Way to keep him, GEORGE COLMAN'S The Jealous Wife, MRS. INCHBALD'S Everyone has his Fault, THOMAS MORTON'S Speed the Plough, and FREDERICK REYNOLDS'S The Dramatist (321).

FIVE ELIZABETHAN COMEDIES. Edited by *A. K. McIlwraith*. Contains GREENE'S Friar Bacon and Friar Bungay, PEELE'S The Old Wives' Tale, LYLY'S Campaspe, DEKKER'S Shoemaker's Holiday, and the anonymous Merry Devil of Edmonton (422).

FIVE PRE-SHAKESPEAREAN COMEDIES. Edited by *F. S. Boas*. Contains MEDWALL'S Fulgens and Lucrece, HEYWOOD'S The Four PP., UDALL'S Ralph Roister Doister, the anonymous Gammer Gurton's Needle, and GASCOIGNE'S Supposes (418).

GOETHE. Faust, Parts I and II. Translated by *Bayard Taylor*. Intro. by *Marshall Montgomery* and notes by *Douglas Yates* (380).

IBSEN, HENRIK. Peer Gynt. Trans. with an Introduction by *R. Ellis Roberts* (446).

MARLOWE'S Dr. Faustus (with GOETHE'S Faust, Part I, trans. *J. Anster*). Introduction by *Sir A. W. Ward* (135).

RESTORATION TRAGEDIES. DRYDEN'S All for Love, OTWAY'S Venice Preserved, SOUTHERNE'S Oronooko, ROWE'S Fair Penitent, and ADDISON'S Cato. Introduction by *Bonamy Dobrée* (313).

SHAKESPEARE. Plays and Poems. Preface by *A. C. Swinburne*. Introductions by *Edward Dowden*. 9 vols. Comedies. 3 vols. (100, 101, 102). Histories and Poems. 3 vols. (103, 104, 105). Tragedies. 3 vols. (106, 107, 108).

SHAKESPEARE, Six Plays by Contemporaries of. DEKKER, The Shoemaker's Holiday; WEBSTER, The White Devil; BEAUMONT and FLETCHER, The Knight of the Burning Pestle, and Philaster; WEBSTER, The Duchess of Malfi; MASSINGER, A New Way to pay Old Debts. Edited by *C. B. Wheeler* (199).

SHERIDAN. Plays. Introduction by *Joseph Knight* (79).

TOLSTOY. The Plays. Complete edition, including the posthumous plays. Translated by *Louise* and *Aylmer Maude* (243).

¶ Essays and Belles Lettres

BACON. The Essays, Civil and Moral (24).

CARLYLE. On Heroes and Hero-Worship (62). Past and Present. Introduction by *G. K. Chesterton* (153). Sartor Resartus (19).

DOBSON (AUSTIN). At Prior Park, &c. (259). Eighteenth-Century Vignettes. Three Series (245–7). Four Frenchwomen (248).

TRACTS AND PAMPHLETS, from JOHN KNOX to H. G. WELLS (304).
WALTON and COTTON. The Compleat Angler. Introduction by
John Buchan (430).
WHITE (GILBERT). The Natural History of Selborne. With 16
illustrations by *E. H. New* (22).
WHITMAN. Specimen Days in America (371).

¶ *Fiction* (For SHORT STORIES see separate heading)

AINSWORTH (W. HARRISON). The Tower of London (162).
AUSTEN (JANE). Emma (129). Pride and Prejudice (335). Mans-
field Park (345). Northanger Abbey (355). Persuasion (356).
Sense and Sensibility (389).
BLACKMORE (R. D.). Lorna Doone. Introduction by *Sir Herbert
Warren* (171).
BORROW (GEORGE). Lavengro (66). The Romany Rye (73).
BRONTË (ANNE). Agnes Grey (141). Tenant of Wildfell Hall
(67).
BRONTË (CHARLOTTE). Jane Eyre (1). Shirley (14). Villette (47).
The Professor, and the Poems of the Brontës (78).
BRONTË (EMILY). Wuthering Heights (10).
BUNYAN. The Pilgrim's Progress (12). Mr. Badman (338).
BUTLER (SAMUEL). The Way of all Flesh. With an Essay by
Bernard Shaw (438).
CERVANTES. Don Quixote. 2 volumes (130, 131).
COBBOLD (REV. RICHARD). Margaret Catchpole (119).
COLLINS (WILKIE). The Moonstone. Introduction by *T. S.
Eliot* (316). The Woman in White (226).
COOPER (J. FENIMORE). The Last of the Mohicans (163).
DEFOE. Captain Singleton (82). Robinson Crusoe. Part I (17).
DICKENS. Barnaby Rudge (286). Christmas Books (307). Edwin
Drood (263). Great Expectations (128). Hard Times (264).
Old Curiosity Shop (270). Oliver Twist (8). Pickwick Papers.
2 volumes (120, 121). Tale of Two Cities (38).
DISRAELI (BENJAMIN). Coningsby (381). Sybil (291).
ELIOT (GEORGE). Adam Bede (63). Felix Holt (179). The Mill
on the Floss (31). Romola (178). Scenes of Clerical Life (155).
Silas Marner, &c. (80).
FIELDING. Jonathan Wild (382). Joseph Andrews (334).
GALT (JOHN). The Entail. Introduction by *John Ayscough*
(177).
GASKELL (MRS.). Cousin Phillis, and Other Tales, &c. (168).
Cranford, The Cage at Cranford, and The Moorland Cottage
(110). Lizzie Leigh, The Grey Woman, and Other Tales, &c.
(175). Mary Barton (86). North and South (154). Right at
Last, and Other Tales, &c. (203). Round the Sofa (190).
Ruth (88). Sylvia's Lovers (156). Wives and Daughters (157).
GOLDSMITH. The Vicar of Wakefield (4).
HARRIS (JOEL CHANDLER). Uncle Remus (361).
HAWTHORNE. House of the Seven Gables (273). The Scarlet
Letter (26). Tales (319).

HOLME (CONSTANCE). Beautiful End (431). Crump Folk going Home (419). He-who-came? (440). The Lonely Plough (390). The Old Road from Spain (400). The Splendid Fairing (416). The Things which Belong—— (425). The Trumpet in the Dust (409). The Wisdom of the Simple (453).

KINGSLEY (HENRY). Geoffry Hamlyn (271). Ravenshoe (267). Austin Elliot (407).

LA MOTTE FOUQUÉ. Undine, Sintram, &c. (408).

LE FANU (J. S.). Uncle Silas. Intro. by *Montague R. James* (306).

LESAGE. Gil Blas. Edited *J. Fitzmaurice-Kelly*. 2 vols. (151, 152).

MARRYAT. Mr. Midshipman Easy (160). Jacob Faithful (439).

MELVILLE (HERMAN). Moby Dick (225). Typee (274). Omoo (275). White Jacket (253).

MORIER (J. J.). Hajji Baba (238). Hajji Baba in England (285).

PEACOCK (T. L.). Headlong Hall; and Nightmare Abbey (339.) Misfortunes of Elphin; and Crotchet Castle (244).

RABELAIS. Gargantua and Pantagruel. Translated by *Urquhart* and *Motteux*, with notes and map. 3 volumes (411–13).

SCOTT. Ivanhoe (29).

SMOLLETT. Roderick Random (353). Humphry Clinker (290).

STERNE. Sentimental Journey (333). Tristram Shandy (40).

STEVENSON (R. L.). Kidnapped; and Catriona (297). The Master of Ballantrae (441). Treasure Island (295).

STURGIS (HOWARD). Belchamber. Intro. by *Gerard Hopkins* (429).

SWIFT. Gulliver's Travels (20).

SWINNERTON (FRANK). Nocturne. With a new Introduction by the Author (460).

TAYLOR (MEADOWS). Confessions of a Thug (207).

THACKERAY. Henry Esmond (28).

TOLSTOY. Translated by *Louise* and *Aylmer Maude*. Anna Karenina. 2 volumes (210, 211). Childhood, Boyhood, and Youth (352). The Cossacks, &c. (208). Iván Ilých, and Hadji Murád (432). The Kreutzer Sonata, &c. (266). Resurrection, trans. by *L. Maude* (209). Twenty-three Tales (72). War and Peace. 3 volumes (233–5).

TROLLOPE. American Senator (391). Ayala's Angel (342). Barchester Towers (268). The Belton Estate (251). The Claverings (252). Cousin Henry (343). Doctor Thorne (298). Dr. Wortle's School (317). The Eustace Diamonds (357). Framley Parsonage (305). The Kellys and the O'Kellys (341). Lady Anna (443). Last Chronicle of Barset. 2 vols. (398, 399). Miss Mackenzie (278). Orley Farm. 2 vols. (423, 424). Phineas Finn. 2 vols. (447, 448). Phineas Redux. 2 vols. (450, 451). The Prime Minister (454–5). Rachel Ray (279). Sir Harry Hotspur (336). Tales of all Countries (397). The Three Clerks (140). The Warden (217). The Vicar of Bullhampton (272).

WATTS-DUNTON (THEODORE). Aylwin (52).

WHARTON (EDITH). The House of Mirth. With a new Introduction by the Author (437).

¶ History

BARROW (SIR JOHN). The Mutiny of the *Bounty* (195).

BUCKLE. The History of Civilization. 3 volumes (41, 48, 53).

CARLYLE. The French Revolution. Introduction by *C. R. L. Fletcher*. 2 volumes (125, 126).

FROUDE (J. A.). Short Studies on Great Subjects. Series I (269).

GIBBON. Decline and Fall of the Roman Empire. With Maps. 7 volumes (35, 44, 51, 55, 64, 69, 74).

IRVING (WASHINGTON). Conquest of Granada (150).

MACAULAY. History of England. 5 volumes (366–70).

MOTLEY. Rise of the Dutch Republic. 3 volumes (96, 97, 98).

PRESCOTT (W. H.). The Conquest of Mexico. 2 vols. (197, 198).

¶ Letters

BURKE. Letters. Selected, with Introduction, by *H. J. Laski* (237).

CHESTERFIELD. Letters. Selected, with an Introduction, by *Phyllis M. Jones* (347).

CONGREVE. Letters, in Volume II. See under *Drama* (277).

COWPER. Letters. Selected, with Intro., by *E. V. Lucas* (138).

DUFFERIN (LORD). Letters from High Latitudes. Illustrated (158).

GRAY (THOMAS). Letters. Selected by *John Beresford* (283).

JOHNSON (SAMUEL). Letters. Selected, with Introduction, by *R. W. Chapman* (282).

SOUTHEY. Selected Letters (169).

WHITE (GILBERT). The Natural History of Selborne. With 16 illustrations by *E. H. New* (22).

¶ Literary Criticism

AMERICAN CRITICISM. Representative Literary Essays. Chosen by *Norman Foerster* (354).

COLERIDGE (S.T.) Lectures on Shakespeare (363).

ENGLISH CRITICAL ESSAYS. Selected and edited by *Edmund D. Jones*. 2 volumes: I, Sixteenth to Eighteenth Centuries (240); II, Nineteenth Century (206).

HAZLITT (WILLIAM). Characters of Shakespeare's Plays. Introduction by *Sir A. T. Quiller-Couch* (205). Lectures on the English Comic Writers. Introduction by *R. Brimley Johnson* (124). Lectures on the English Poets (255). The Spirit of the Age. (Essays on his contemporaries) (57).

HORNE (R. H.). A New Spirit of the Age (127).

JOHNSON (SAMUEL). Lives of the Poets. 2 volumes (83, 84).

MORE (PAUL ELMER). Selected Shelburne Essays (434).

SAINTE-BEUVE. Causeries du Lundi. (In English.) Two Series (372–3).

SHAKESPEARE CRITICISM. (HEMINGE and CONDELL to CARLYLE.) Selected and introduced by *D. Nichol Smith* (212).

SHAKESPEARE CRITICISM (1919–1935). Selected and introduced by *Anne Bradby* (436).

¶ *Philosophy and Science*

(For POLITICAL THEORY and RELIGION see separate headings)

AURELIUS (MARCUS). Thoughts. Translated by *John Jackson*(60).
BACON. The Advancement of Learning, and the New Atlantis. Introduction by *Professor Case* (93). Essays (24).
CARLYLE. Sartor Resartus (19).
DARWIN. The Origin of Species. With a new preface by *Major Leonard Darwin* (11).
REYNOLDS (SIR JOSHUA). Discourses, &c. Introduction by *A. Dobson* (149).
TOLSTOY. What then must we do? Trans. by *A. Maude* (281).
WHITE (GILBERT). The Natural History of Selborne. With 16 illustrations by *E. H. New* (22).

¶ *Poetry*

ARNOLD (MATTHEW). Poems, 1849–67 (85).
BARHAM (RICHARD). The Ingoldsby Legends (9).
BLAKE (WILLIAM). Selected Poems (324).
BRONTË SISTERS, THE. The Professor, by CHARLOTTE BRONTË, and Poems by CHARLOTTE, EMILY, and ANNE BRONTË (78).
BROWNING (ELIZABETH BARRETT). Poems. A Selection (176).
BROWNING (ROBERT). Poems and Plays, 1833–42 (58). Poems, 1842–64 (137).
BURNS (ROBERT). Poems (34). Complete and in large type.
BYRON. Poems. A Selection (180).
CHAUCER, The Works of. 3 volumes: I (42); II (56); III, containing the whole of the Canterbury Tales (76).
COLERIDGE. Poems. Introduction by *Sir A. T. Quiller-Couch* (99).
CONGREVE (WILLIAM). Complete works in 2 volumes. Introductions by *Bonamy Dobrée*. I, The Comedies (276); II, The Mourning Bride, Poems, Miscellanies and Letters (277).
DANTE. Italian text and English verse-translation by *Melville B. Anderson*, on facing pages, with notes. 3 vols. (392–4). Translation only, with notes, in one volume (395).
DOBSON (AUSTIN). Selected Poems (249).
ENGLISH SONGS AND BALLADS. Compiled by *T. W. H. Crosland*. New edition, with revised text and additional poems, 1927 (13).
ENGLISH VERSE. Vols. I–V: Early Lyrics to SHAKESPEARE; CAMPION to the Ballads; DRYDEN to WORDSWORTH; SCOTT to E. B. BROWNING; LONGFELLOW to RUPERT BROOKE. Edited by *William Peacock* (308–312).
FRANCIS OF ASSISI (ST.). The Little Flowers of St. Francis. Translated into English Verse by *James Rhoades* (265).
GOETHE. Faust, Parts I and II. Translated by *Bayard Taylor*. Intro. by *Marshall Montgomery* and notes by *Douglas Yates* (380).
GOLDEN TREASURY, THE. With additional Poems (133).
GOLDSMITH. Poems. Introduction by *Austin Dobson* (123).
HERBERT (GEORGE). Poems. Introduction by *Arthur Waugh* (109).
HERRICK (ROBERT). Poems (16).

HOMER. Translated by *Pope*. Iliad (18). Odyssey (36).

HOOD. Poems. Introduction by *Walter Jerrold* (87).

IBSEN. Peer Gynt. Translated by *R. Ellis Roberts* (446).

KEATS. Poems (7).

KEBLE. The Christian Year (181).

LONGFELLOW. Hiawatha, Miles Standish, Tales of a Wayside Inn, &c. (174).

MACAULAY. Lays of Ancient Rome ; Ivry ; The Armada (27).

MARLOWE. Dr. Faustus (with GOETHE'S Faust, Part I, trans. *J. Anster*). Introduction by *Sir A. W. Ward* (135).

MILTON. The English Poems (182).

MORRIS (WILLIAM). The Defence of Guenevere, Life and Death of Jason, and other Poems (183).

NARRATIVE VERSE, A BOOK OF. Compiled by *V. H. Collins*. With an Introduction by *Edmund Blunden* (350).

NEKRASSOV. Trans. by *Juliet Soskice*. Who can be happy and free in Russia ? A Poem (213). Poems (340).

PALGRAVE. The Golden Treasury. With additional Poems (133).

ROSSETTI (CHRISTINA). Goblin Market, &c. (184).

SCOTT (SIR WALTER). Selected Poems (186).

SCOTTISH VERSE, A BOOK OF. Compiled by *R. L. Mackie* (417).

SHAKESPEARE. Plays and Poems. Preface by *A. C. Swinburne:* Introductions by *Edward Dowden*. 9 volumes. Comedies. 3 volumes (100, 101, 102). Histories and Poems. 3 volumes (103, 104, 105). Tragedies. 3 volumes (106, 107, 108).

SHELLEY. Poems. A Selection (187).

TENNYSON. Selected Poems. Intro. by *Sir Herbert Warren* (3).

VIRGIL. The Aeneid, Georgics, and Eclogues. Translated by *Dryden* (37). Translated by *James Rhoades* (227).

WELLS (CHARLES). Joseph and his Brethren. A Dramatic Poem. Intro. by *A. C. Swinburne*, and Note by *T. Watts-Dunton* (143).

WHITMAN. A Selection. Introduction by *E. de Sélincourt* (218).

WHITTIER. Poems : A Selection (188).

WORDSWORTH. Poems : A Selection (189).

¶ *Politics, Political Economy, Political Theory*

BAGEHOT (WALTER). The English Constitution. With an Introduction by the *Earl of Balfour* (330).

BUCKLE. The History of Civilization. 3 volumes (41, 48, 53).

BURKE (EDMUND). Letters. Selected, with an Introduction, by *Harold J. Laski* (237). Works. 6 volumes. I : A Vindication of Natural Society; The Sublime and Beautiful, &c. (71). II : The Present Discontents; and Speeches and Letters on America (81). III : Speeches on India, &c. (111). IV : Writings on France, 1790–1 (112). V : Writings on Ireland, &c. (113). VI : A Letter to a Noble Lord; and Letters on a Regicide Peace (114).

ENGLISH SPEECHES, from BURKE to GLADSTONE. Selected and edited by *E. R. Jones* (191).

MACAULAY. Speeches. Selected, with Introduction and footnotes, by *G. M. Young* (433).

MACHIAVELLI. The Prince (43).

MAINE (SIR HENRY). Ancient Law (362).

MILL (JOHN STUART). On Liberty, Representative Government, and the Subjection of Women (170).

MILTON (JOHN). Selected Prose. Intro. *Malcolm W. Wallace* (293).

RUSKIN. 'A Joy for Ever', and The Two Paths. Illustrated (147). Time and Tide, and The Crown of Wild Olive (146). Unto this Last, and Munera Pulveris (148).

SMITH (ADAM). The Wealth of Nations. 2 volumes (54, 59).

SPEECHES AND DOCUMENTS ON INTERNATIONAL AFFAIRS (1918–37). Ed. *A. B. Keith.* 2 volumes (457–8).

SPEECHES AND DOCUMENTS ON BRITISH COLONIAL POLICY (1763–1917). Ed. *A. B. Keith.* 2 volumes (215, 216).

SPEECHES AND DOCUMENTS ON THE BRITISH DOMINIONS, 1918–31. Selected, with Introduction, by *A. B. Keith* (403).

SPEECHES AND DOCUMENTS ON INDIAN POLICY (1756–1921). Edited, with Introduction, by *A. B. Keith* (231, 232).

SPEECHES ON BRITISH FOREIGN POLICY (1738–1914). Edited by *Edgar R. Jones, M.P.* (201).

TOLSTOY. What then must we do ? Translated, with an Introduction, by *Aylmer Maude* (281).

TRACTS AND PAMPHLETS, A Miscellany of. Sixteenth to Nineteenth Centuries. Edited by *A. C. Ward* (304).

¶ Religion

THE OLD TESTAMENT. Revised Version. 4 vols. (385–8).

APOCRYPHA, THE, in the Revised Version (294).

THE FOUR GOSPELS, AND THE ACTS OF THE APOSTLES. Authorized Version (244).

THE NEW TESTAMENT. Revised Version (346).

À KEMPIS (THOMAS). Of the Imitation of Christ (49).

AURELIUS (MARCUS). Translated by *John Jackson* (60).

BUNYAN. The Pilgrim's Progress (12). Mr. Badman (338).

CONFUCIUS. The Analects. Trans. by *W. E. Soothill.* Introduction by *Lady Hosie* (442).

KORAN, THE. Translated by *E. H. Palmer.* Introduction by *Reynold A. Nicholson* (328).

TOLSTOY. Translated by *Aylmer Maude.* A Confession, and What I believe (229). On Life, and Essays on Religion (426). The Kingdom of God, and Peace Essays (445).

¶ Short Stories

AFRICA, STORIES OF. Chosen by *E. C. Parnwell* (359).

AUSTRIAN SHORT STORIES. Selected and translated by *Marie Busch* (337).

CRIME AND DETECTION. Two Series (301, 351). Stories by H. C. BAILEY, ERNEST BRAMAH, G. K. CHESTERTON, SIR A. CONAN DOYLE, R. AUSTIN FREEMAN, W. W. JACOBS, EDEN PHILPOTTS, 'SAPPER', DOROTHY SAYERS, and others.

CZECH TALES, SELECTED. Translated by *Marie Busch* and *Otto Pick* (288). Nine stories, including two by the BROTHERS CAPEK.

DICKENS. Christmas Books (307).

ENGLISH SHORT STORIES. Three Series. Selected by *H. S. Milford*. Introduction by *Prof. Hugh Walker* in Vol. I (193, 228, 315).

FRENCH SHORT STORIES. Eighteenth to Twentieth Centuries. Selected and translated by *K. Rebillon Lambley* (396).

GASKELL (MRS.). Introductions by *Clement Shorter*. Cousin Phillis, and Other Tales (168). Lizzie Leigh, The Grey Woman, and Other Tales, &c. (175). Right at Last, and Other Tales, &c. (203). Round the Sofa (190).

GERMAN SHORT STORIES. Translated by *E. N. Bennett*, with an Introduction by *E. K. Bennett* (415).

GHOSTS AND MARVELS and MORE GHOSTS AND MARVELS. Two Selections of Uncanny Tales made by *V. H. Collins*. Introduction by *Montague R. James* in Series I (284, 323).

HARTE (BRET). Short Stories (318).

HAWTHORNE (NATHANIEL). Tales (319).

IRVING (WASHINGTON). Tales (320).

MODERN GERMAN SHORT STORIES. Trans. by *H. Steinhauer* and *Helen Jessiman*, with an Introduction by *H. Steinhauer* (456).

PERSIAN (FROM THE). The Three Dervishes, and Other Stories. Translated from MSS. in the Bodleian by *Reuben Levy* (254).

POE (EDGAR ALLAN). Tales of Mystery and Imagination (21).

POLISH TALES BY MODERN AUTHORS. Translated by *Else C. M. Benecke* and *Marie Busch* (230).

RUSSIAN SHORT STORIES. Chosen and translated by *A. E. Chamot* (287).

SCOTT. Short Stories. With an Introduction by *Lord David Cecil* (414).

SHORT STORIES OF THE SOUTH SEAS. Selected by *E. C. Parnwell* (332).

SPANISH SHORT STORIES. Sixteenth Century. In contemporary translations, revised, with an Introduction, by *J. B. Trend* (326).

TOLSTOY. Nine Stories (1855–63) (420). Twenty-three Tales. Translated by *Louise* and *Aylmer Maude* (72).

TROLLOPE. Tales of all Countries (397).

¶ Travel and Topography

BORROW (GEORGE). The Bible in Spain (75). Wild Wales (224). Lavengro (66). Romany Rye (73).

DUFFERIN (LORD). Letters from High Latitudes (158).

MELVILLE (HERMAN). Typee (294). Omoo (275).

MORIER (J. J.). Hajji Baba of Ispahan. Introduction by *C. W. Stewart*, and a Map (238).

SMOLLETT (TOBIAS). Travels through France and Italy in 1765. Introduction (lxii pages) by *Thomas Seccombe* (90).

STERNE (LAURENCE). A Sentimental Journey. With Introduction by *Virginia Woolf* (333).